PRAISE FOR STINA LINDENBLATT

"I just love this book!...add in some tense situations and five (YES FIVE!) hot, sexy, alpha, ex-navy SEALS and you got me!" —A Book Lover's Emporium Book Blog (*While You Were Spying*)

"While You Were Spying is a heart pumping sexy read! You've got action, intrigue and suspense and then on the other hand you have sexual tension, swoony romance, and sassy banter."— Julia Red Hatter Book Blog

"While You Were Spying is a fun, intriguing, full of mystery, friends-to-lovers read. It was like reading a fun romcom wrapped up in a James Bond movie with lots of extra steam."— Kay Daniels Romance

"A feel good, sensual, intoxicating and sexy love story; if you love contemporary romance you do not want to miss *Decidedly Off Limits*." —Slick, Guilty Pleasures

"Sweet, sexy and invigorating, *Decidedly off Limits* is a friends to lovers story that is truly a breath of fresh air!"—Read & Share Book Reviews

"There are steamy moments but you are just left with feel good melty moments more"—Books Are Love (*Decidedly With Baby*)

"Be warned dear reader, this book will have you giggling and blushing as you devour it"—The Subclub Books (*Decidedly With Love*)

"...a truly unique and utterly swoon-worthy romance." – Mary Dubé at Frolic/USA Today's HEA (*Decidedly by Chance*)

"Stina Lindenblatt writes an emotional, heartfelt story about single parenthood, friendship, and love. Add to that great chemistry and tons of feels and this is a great book for anyone who enjoys this trope." – Ari at Red Hatter Book Blog (*Decidedly by Chance*)

"I can't wait for more Daniels brothers."—Mary at USA Today HEA (*Cowboy Most Wanted*)

"Are you in the mood for a fun, hot, sweet, romantic read that will have you blushing, laughing and glued to the pages then look no further than *Cowboy Most Wanted*."—The Subclub Books

"Holy words, batman!...Stina NAILED this book."—Garden Of REden (*Fix Me Up, Cowboy*)

"...it's an opposites-attract romance that will evoke all the feels." —Mary at USA Today HEA/Frolic (*Fix Me Up, Cowboy*)

ALSO BY STINA LINDENBLATT

Contemporary Romances

Carson Brothers Series

One More Chance

One More Secret

One More Betrayal

One More Truth

Spicy Romantic Comedy Novels

By The Bay Series

Decidedly Off Limits

Decidedly with Baby

Decidedly with Love

Decidedly with Mistletoe

Decidedly by Chance

Decidedly with Luck

Decidedly with Wishes

Copper Creek Series

Cowboy Most Wanted

Once Upon a Cowboy

Fix Me Up Cowboy

Visit stinalindenblattauthor.com for more books

SPYING UNDER THE MISTLETOE

STINA LINDENBLATT

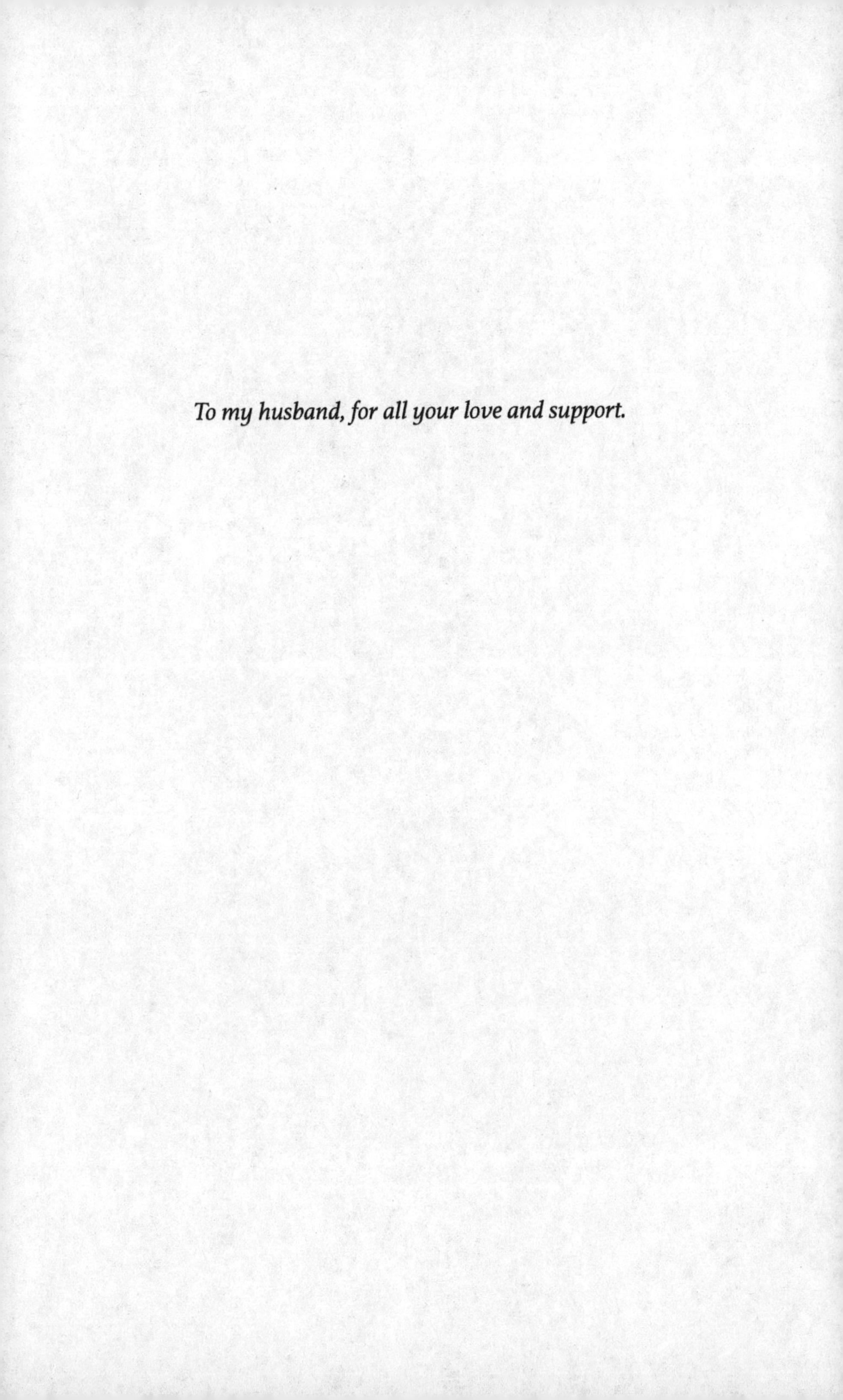

To my husband, for all your love and support.

SPYING UNDER THE MISTLETOE

1

LANDON

Life is sometimes nothing but a series of mistakes.

Mistakes that leave you wondering a few hours later what the hell you were thinking.

Mistakes that seem like a brilliant idea at the time.

"Ooh, coffee," my latest mistake says, walking into the kitchen, wearing nothing but a hockey jersey. *My* hockey jersey, which was hanging in my closet until a few minutes ago.

"I'm going to need that soon." I nod at the item of clothing.

The blonde, whose name I can't quite remember, sidles up to me. I met her at the bar Adam, Connor, and I went to last night. I hadn't gone there to get laid, but here I am, with a strange woman in my town house.

"I didn't know you play hockey," she says with a seductive purr. It was a turn-on last night. Now, not so much. "I loooove hockey."

Something about the way she says this hints that it's not entirely true. I recognize the look in her eyes from my days in junior hockey.

She's not a real fan of the game. Hooking up with hockey players is her sport of choice.

I'd dealt with a few of those in my past, back before I realized I'd never be good enough to play in the NHL.

I give her a single nod—because there isn't anything more to say on the subject. She's just reminding me why I don't typically bring one-night stands to my place.

Not that one-night stands are a habit of mine these days.

Blondie is one of those rare occasions.

She doesn't get the hint and leans against the granite kitchen counter. "Can I have some, please?" Her gaze drops to the mug in my hand, and I stiffen.

But while I'm not exactly happy she's still here, I'm not going to be an asshole and kick her out of my home.

Yet.

If she decides to overstay her welcome, I'll politely ask her to leave.

I remove a mug from the kitchen cabinet, fill it partway, and hand it to her.

"Thanks." She takes a sip and pouts at me. "You've already showered?" she says, stating the obvious. My hair's still damp.

My goal had been for her to wake up while I was in the shower and be the kind of woman who bails while the guy's preoccupied.

Instead, she slept the entire time and only woke up when the coffee had finished brewing.

"I was hoping we could shower...together." She flashes me a look that reminds me of Mojo—my colleague's Bernese mountain dog—whenever he sees his favorite treat.

Then she winks at me...which lasts an incredibly long time. Like her eye has frozen shut. "Oh, darn it. My false eyelashes are stuck together. Can you help me, Landon?"

Sorry, sweetheart, you're on your own.

Before I can voice that out loud, "Hit Me with Your Best Shot" plays from my phone on the kitchen table.

Saved by Pat Benatar.

"Sorry, I have to take this." *I don't suppose you'll be gone by the time I return....*

I pick up my phone and head upstairs to my office.

Inside, I close the door behind me. "What's up?" I ask Liam.

My boss.

The owner of Quade Security and Investigations.

My former brother in arms.

Liam doesn't call the team on a Sunday unless it's super important. He's a family man through and through—especially since his daughter was born over a year ago.

Cassie and his wife, Ava, are his world.

"I need you to come into the office this morning. I'm calling the entire team in."

"I'd ask what this is about, but now's not a good time for me to talk." I have no idea if Blondie's the curious type—if snooping gets her off. "As soon as I get some baggage out of my house, I'll be there."

Liam has been my friend for too long to miss the hidden meaning between the words. "You know, if you found a nice woman to settle down with, the overstaying-their-welcome baggage wouldn't be a problem."

"You sound like my mother."

"Your mom is a wise woman."

We end the call, and I head downstairs. Blondie is still in the kitchen, in my hockey jersey, coffee mug in hand, in no particular rush to leave. Her eyelashes are no longer stuck together.

"I have to go to work now," I tell her, hoping she gets the hint this time.

She frowns, her pout resembling that of a toddler denied a cookie more than it resembles the pout of a supermodel selling sexy lingerie. "Work? But it's Sunday."

I shrug because it is what it is.

"You never did tell me what you do for a living." She sips on her coffee.

"I'm a janitor. The usual weekend guy called in sick."

Rule #1 when it comes to hookups: Never tell them my real job.

Even if I don't mention the off-the-website part of the job—the part involving secret government contracts—telling women I work for a security and investigation company leaves them with all kinds of alpha-hero fantasies.

It makes me, in their eyes, more desirable, more exciting, than someone who cleans an office building for a living.

The frown between Blondie's eyebrows returns. "This is a really nice place for a janitor."

I don't dignify her comment with a reply.

Fortunately, she finally gets the hint, puts the mug on the counter, and heads upstairs to hopefully get changed. She returns a few minutes later in the dress she was wearing last night. Her hair is no longer messy.

"I had fun last night," she says, batting her eyelashes at me. They miraculously don't stick together this time. "I would love to see you again. Maybe we could catch a movie and dinner later this week?"

Her tone is not of someone hoping to be a booty call. It's more along the lines of wanting something I can't give—my heart.

Or what's left of it.

No, a woman didn't cheat on me or do me wrong. Just the opposite. My post-college girlfriend was the love of my life. I was positive she was it—the woman I would one day marry.

At least that had been my plan until she went out with friends. The next time I saw her, she was in a coma and on life support.

Her parents removed her from it a month later.

After that, I joined the military. And on more than one

occasion witnessed a brother die—and each time, like with my girlfriend, I was unable to do anything about it.

"Sorry," I tell Blondie, "but I told you last night it was a one-time-only deal. That hasn't changed."

She shrugs, the disappointment on her face nothing more than a flicker. A minute later, the front door clicks shut behind her.

I grab my jeep keys and head out the front door. The crisp November air is heavy with the promise of rain.

A faint whimper, almost a squeak, draws my attention to a bush on my property. I walk over to the sound and crouch next to the bush, where a small tangle of reddish-brown fur with large floppy ears lies.

"Hey, little guy, what are you doing here?"

The puppy lifts its head slightly and gives another whimper. It doesn't have a collar, doesn't look familiar.

I hold my hand out to him, letting him sniff it, and stroke his soft head. "Are you injured?" I don't know a whole lot about dogs. My only real experience with them comes from my colleague's dog, Mojo. Jayden's dog is a Bernese mountain goofball who likes to hang out at the office and soak in as much attention as possible.

I scan the sidewalk, searching for the puppy's owner. With the exception of several cars driving past, there's no other sign of life.

I gently scoop him up and cradle him against my chest. He releases a soft, pained sound at the movement, but then he snuggles closer to me.

"There's a twenty-four-hour vet clinic on the way to my office. I'll drop you off there on my way to my meeting."

I carry him inside the house, locate a box big enough to hold him, and cushion it with a towel. The puppy whimpers and licks my hand when I lower him into the box.

The clinic isn't busy when I arrive—other than a talking

parrot that keeps saying, "Spank me naughty boy," two cats eyeing him with distrust, and a snoozing golden retriever.

The parrot's owner is a woman in her midtwenties. Her blush deepens every time he speaks. "Would you quit saying that?" she mutters to the bird, sounding more than ready to stuff a cracker down his beak to shut him up.

While I wait for the puppy's turn, I fire off a text to Liam, letting him know something came up, but I'll be there as soon as possible.

Five minutes later, the puppy and I are in the exam room, and the vet is checking him over.

"He's a little malnourished, and his front leg is sprained," the man explains. "But he should fully recover in no time. I'd like to keep him for twenty-four hours to monitor his condition; then you can take him home."

"He's not my dog," I remind him.

"He didn't have a tattoo. Let me see if he has a microchip."

The vet checks the puppy's neck with a handheld device and shakes his head. "Either the owner didn't get around to having the microchip inserted, or it's not functioning."

"What do I do now?"

"I can look if there's space available in a foster home. Otherwise, you can drop him off with the SCPA and hope someone claims him or adopts him soon."

"What would you do?"

He chuckles. "Keep him. But unfortunately, my house is already full of pets, so that counts me out. I don't suppose you know anyone who would love to give him a home in the meantime, and potentially permanently."

"Not really. I can ask my colleagues if they're interested, though."

"Let me know. And if not, I'll look into the foster care situation, and I'll let you know what I find out when you pick him up tomorrow."

"I hadn't planned on coming back for him. I was just going to pay his bill and was hoping you could find him a new owner."

"Unfortunately, we don't have room for him once he's no longer a patient."

The furball flashes me his puppy eyes, gives a little whimper, and licks my hand.

"He definitely likes you," the vet says.

Likes me or not, I'm not looking at adopting a dog.

But despite that, I can't help but stroke the soft fur on his head. "What kind of dog is he anyway?"

"He looks like a cockapoo."

"A cock-a-what?"

"It's a designer breed. One of his parents was a poodle and the other a cocker spaniel."

"Isn't that the definition of a mutt?"

"Not in this case. It's when two different breeds are mated to produce an animal that hopefully includes the best attributes of both breeds. That's why they call it a designer breed."

I shoot the puppy's picture with my phone to show the guys and Isabelle at the meeting. Maybe I can convince one of them to adopt him, because one thing's for certain, I don't want to drop him off at the animal shelter. The poor little guy deserves better.

LIAM, CONNOR, AND ADAM ARE SEATED IN THE CONFERENCE room when I arrive at our office.

"Jayden and Isabelle aren't here yet?" I ask, taking my seat next to Adam. A coffee from The Coffee Nut is waiting in front of me. I nod my gratitude to Connor.

"They're on their way," Liam says.

"Do you think he's asked her?" Adam is referring to Jayden's plans to propose to Isabelle this weekend. His girlfriend. The woman who used to be our kickass office manager before she finally proved to both Liam and Jayden that she deserved to be the company's first female operative.

But while she was proving herself capable of the job, she and Jayden were falling in love.

Well, truth be known, they were in love prior to that...but they were both too blind to see for themselves what the rest of us already knew.

"I guess we'll find out soon enough," Liam, the only married member of the team, says. "What took you so long to get here?"

I tell them about the puppy and show them his picture. "I don't suppose any of you would like a dog."

Liam shakes his head. "I've already got my hands full with Cassie. I don't think I could handle a puppy thrown into the mix."

"I'm more of a big-dog lover," Adam says. Connor agrees with him.

"Why don't *you* adopt him?" Adam asks.

"Same deal. If I adopt a dog, it'll be a big one. But I'm not looking to adopt a dog or a cat or any other animal."

Liam opens his mouth, as if to say something, but doesn't get that far. Jayden and Isabelle enter the room, holding hands.

"She said yes," are the first words out of Jayden's mouth. A wide grin spreads on his face.

"We told you she would," Liam says, pushing himself out of his chair.

We congratulate them. Hugs are exchanged.

"You called us in to see if Jayden went through with the proposal?" Isabelle asks after we're finished. From her expression, I'm guessing the two of them were celebrating the proposal with some horizontal action when Liam called them.

"No, I called everyone in for another reason." Liam gestures for us to take our seats. "We've been asked to help, once again, with the Orlov case. Even though Vadik and his men at the winery were arrested—and are currently facing life in prison— the Feds have yet to locate his grandson, Nikolai Orlov. As long as he's still free, the Orlov family will continue to commit crimes. He was marked to take over the family business once his grandfather stepped down, and it's suspected he's doing just that. Only now, he's deep underground."

"And the Feds want us to flush him out?" Landon asks. Vadik Orlov was the leader of a Russian crime family we helped the FBI with several months ago.

"That's exactly what they want us to do. But we're doing it through his cousin, Chloe Reinhart."

"Chloe? Isn't she the owner of that winery?"

"Yes, the winery that the Feds suspect she has no idea she owns. Her name is on the legal documents, but the Feds have nothing beyond that to indicate she's ever been on the property. They interviewed the employees, and none of them have actually met her. Or at least, none of them have met the woman in the photo they were shown."

"They're hoping she knows where her cousin is hiding, or at the very least, he'll attempt to contact her."

"Would he really take that risk if he believes the Feds are looking for him?" Isabelle asks.

"It's possible. As kids, the two were close. Back then, Nikolai would do anything for Chloe and was super protective of her. The Feds don't know why, but it's clear there was a special bond between them. They're hoping it's still there, even though he has yet to reach out to her—as far as they're aware."

I pick up my coffee. "So they want us to do surveillance on her?"

"It's more than that. They want someone to get close to her. Get to know her and gain her trust. But they're also concerned for her safety. They have reason to believe one of Orlov's enemies has issued a contract on her.

"The Feds obviously can't put her under witness protection because then Nikolai won't be able to contact her, and they won't be able to nail him."

"What do we know about her?" Jayden asks.

"She's an elementary school teacher. Single." Liam pushes the manila folder in front of him toward me. "And she's about to become your girlfriend…"

2

___

CHLOE

"There's our favorite ray of sunshine," Lawrence says as I approach his table in the recreation room of the seniors' retirement residence. His voice is like antique paper—brittle but at the same time, full of wisdom.

His friends are sitting with him in the brightly lit room, as is usually the case when I volunteer here. Half the tables are filled with various groups of individuals, gossiping, knitting, or playing chess.

"I don't suppose your little ray of sunshine brought a bottle of whiskey to really brighten our day." Samuel flashes me a hopeful grin.

I pat his weathered hand and smile at him. "You know I'd never do that. It's not what the doctor ordered."

His grin transforms into a disgusted grunt. "What the hell does that kid know about medicine anyway?"

The kid he's referring to is at least fifteen years older than me. And at thirty, I'm hardly a kid myself.

"Given that he has a medical degree on his office wall," I say, "I'm guessing he knows a fair amount about the topic."

The other three men snicker.

"But I can get you some yummy lemonade if you'd like." I'm not being sarcastic. It really is delicious.

Although from what I've heard, it was especially popular during the Fourth of July celebrations last year, when someone spiked it with vodka, and the seniors showed everyone how to really party.

Even Mrs. Witherspoon with her walker.

Some of the residents are still talking about the conga line.

The men agree that a glass of lemonade wouldn't kill them —but only if I'm heading that way.

I return a few minutes later with the pitcher and glasses. I fill the glasses and hand them out, then sit on the empty wooden chair between Frank and Ivan. "So, what game are we playing today?"

"Monopoly," Ivan says on a sigh. "Why they won't let us play poker is beyond me."

Frank guffaws, and his belly jiggles like Santa's does when he laughs. With his long white beard and large girth, he reminds me of the jolly old man himself. "That's because strip poker's against the rules. Which is why they made us stop playing it."

I feel my eyes widen. "You guys were playing strip poker?" Now that's something I'm glad I didn't witness.

"Not here in the rec room. We used to sneak into Hattie's suite and play it there."

"We? You mean Hattie and you four gentlemen?"

"Not at all," Lawrence says with a cheeky grin. "By the time the nighttime staff figured out we were up to no good, we'd been holding weekly strip-poker nights for a few months, and there was a fair number of us." He lists around twenty names, which includes an equal number of males and females. And I must admit I'm surprised by some of them.

"And we would've gotten away with it if the nighttime staff

hadn't checked on Agatha and found her missing." Frank grunts.

Samuel removes the lid from the Monopoly box. "The way they acted, you'd have thought she was the Queen of England. I'm surprised they didn't call in the secret service to locate her."

"They practically stormed the room," Lawrence adds, "surprising the shit out of us."

Frank laughs even louder this time. "Which wasn't a bad thing for the individuals dealing with constipation."

I smile at the four men who, in the past year, have become more like grandfathers to me than my own grandfather ever was.

I'm referring to the one on my mother's side. I never got to know my other biological grandparents. Nor did I get to know my stepfather's parents.

As for my remaining grandfather, the last I heard—according to the news—he's currently facing the possibility of life in prison. The list of charges is long and includes activities associated with the Russian mafia.

That's right, I'm a mafia princess. Or I would've been if I hadn't escaped that life, thanks to my mom. But leaving it came at a price. I had to walk away from my entire family, including my mother.

Squashing down the pain of missing her that perpetually bubbles beneath the surface—along with the pain that my family so easily turned their backs on me—I help Samuel set up the board and hand out the game pieces and money. Because Samuel worked in the financial industry before he retired, he's always the banker.

"Do you have any plans for Christmas, Chloe?" Ivan asks after we've been playing for several minutes.

Frank rolls the dice. "Christmas? That's not for another six weeks. We haven't even had Thanksgiving yet."

"I have no plans," I say, "other than visiting the residents who'll be spending the holidays here."

"Why not spend it with your family?"

"Or with a husband?" Lawrence adds.

I don't answer, pretending both were rhetorical questions, pretending to be super enthralled with the game.

The men aren't fooled. I can feel their curious gazes on me.

"Do you realize," he says, "we've all shared about our past lives, and about our families and loved ones, but we really know nothing about you, young lady? Other than you're a kindergarten teacher, you love your job, you volunteer here several times a week, and you're single. That's it."

"And you're an artist," Frank adds.

"A graphic artist," Samuel clarifies, "who would one day like to illustrate children's books."

All of that is true. I went to art school and had planned to have a career illustrating children's books and creating kid-friendly artwork. I ended up taking some art therapy courses, worked in a summer day camp for a few years, and decided I wanted to be an elementary school teacher.

And I couldn't be happier.

Happier than I ever would've been as a mafia princess.

"Then you know everything there is to know about me," I say, adjusting my property cards on the table, ensuring their edges are all even, so I don't have to make eye contact with the men.

"What about your family?" Lawrence asks. "Do they live in San Francisco, too?"

"No." Or at least I'm assuming none of them still live in the city. I haven't heard from any of them in seven years. Not even my cousin Nikolai, who I was close to growing up.

My grandfather had explained to my family that due to my decision to not be a part of the family business, they weren't to contact me anymore.

But despite that, I had hoped that Nikolai would've contacted me at some point over the years—other than sending me the occasional birthday and Christmas card, which I'm positive our grandfather doesn't know about. I still have them. They're my only link to the family I was once a part of. They're the only link I have to the man who was once my best friend.

"They don't live anywhere near me," I lamely say. The truth is, I have no idea in which jail my grandfather currently resides, and I have no intention of finding out.

"What about a special someone in your life?" Lawrence asks.

"You mean like friends? Yes, I have those."

Okay, I mostly have colleagues with whom I'm friendly. And a couple of close friends. Kiera and Ava are both teachers where I work.

Lawrence raises his eyebrow. "That's not what I meant, and you know it. You're a sweet, generous, smart, and beautiful woman. Any man would be lucky to have you."

Tell that to the men who were once in my life.

My father.

My stepfather.

Mark, my ex-boyfriend. He didn't even have the guts to break up with me to my face. He texted me a week after he told me he loved me, with nothing more than a "Sorry, babe. It's not going to work out between us, after all." He'd never called me babe before.

The impersonal nature of the breakup gutted me.

But that's okay. I returned a stronger Chloe.

A Chloe with her heart locked away in a security box—the key currently swimming with the fishes.

I smile brightly at Lawrence, like a firefly—if fireflies could smile. "I don't have time for a relationship. I'm busy with my work, volunteering here, and my artwork. I don't have the energy for anything more than that."

"Don't you want kids one day?"

"I have twenty-five kids in my life right now. That's more than enough." And I love every one of them.

Including the little troublemakers.

Especially the troublemakers. They always make life more interesting.

"What about you four?" I ask. "Any plans for the holidays?"

Trick #1 when you don't want to talk about yourself? Redirect the questioning to the other person—or persons, in this case.

"My son emailed to tell me he won't be able to get away from work over the holidays. He has a huge project he's responsible for, one that could make or break the company. That means I won't get to see my grandkids after all."

I give Lawrence's hand a light squeeze. "I'm sorry you won't get to see them."

"Me too."

"What about you three?" I asked Samuel, Ivan, and Frank.

"My daughter and I are estranged," Frank says. "Have been for about ten years now. Which means another Christmas without seeing my grandkids. But that's okay. I'm used to it."

My heart tightens to the size of a stepped-on Christmas bauble. I know how he feels, and I ache for him.

"You can borrow my grandkids if you want," Samuel volunteers. Under his breath, he adds, "Maybe they'll at least notice *you're* alive."

We all wait for him to elaborate.

He doesn't.

"How's the game going?" Mathilda asks behind me, startling me.

"Great," we all tell her, even though we haven't been paying attention to it for the past few minutes.

"We were just talking about the holiday season." A devilish smile slips onto Lawrence's face. "I don't suppose Cook's gonna whip up more of her delicious eggnog again this year for the Christmas party?"

The other three men cackle, and I do my best to keep the grin off my face.

Instead of vodka in the lemonade, it was a bottle of rum in the eggnog. And again, let me repeat, these seniors know how to party.

"In light of what happened last year, we've removed it from the menu."

This results in a round of protests. "You can't get rid of the eggnog," Lawrence grumbles. "That—along with the kids' concert—is the best part."

Mathilda releases a long sigh—the kind you hear before someone shares bad news—and I brace myself for what's coming next.

"Unfortunately, the school had to cancel. The principal just phoned to tell me the sad news."

"So, no concert?" Samuel asks.

Mathilda shakes her head in a drawn-out movement. "Sorry, no concert."

"What if we get someone else to do it?" I ask.

"I don't know who else to ask. Millwood Elementary School has been doing it for as long as I can remember."

"I might have an idea," I say, my mouth moving faster than my brain can keep up. I really hadn't meant to say my thoughts out loud.

The four men look at me like I've just promised them ice cream with a whiskey chocolate sauce for dessert.

Oops.

3

LANDON

"Principal Woodnut will see you now," the school secretary tells me. I've been sitting in the office waiting room for the past five minutes.

Long enough for memories of my childhood to power skate through my thoughts. Although back in those days, I wasn't waiting to see the principal because of my job.

And detention was often the outcome.

The secretary nods at a door across from her desk. I push myself to my feet and walk over to it.

The door's opened a crack. I open it farther and step inside a bright and cheery office. The furniture is a dark wood veneer. That's the only noncolorful item in here.

A woman who looks like she's been teaching since dinosaurs went extinct sits behind the desk, a sparkle in her eyes.

Behind her, on the bookshelf, are hardback editions of numerous kids' books I recognize. Liam's wife is both a teacher at the school and a New York Times bestselling author of middle-grade fantasy.

"I take it you know Ava." The older woman gestures to

Liam's wife. Ava's been teaching second grade here for the past four years and was able to provide me with more information about the woman I'm supposed to be dating than the FBI shared with Liam...only Chloe doesn't know that.

The plan is for me to get to know Chloe as quickly as possible and become her boyfriend. But she's not supposed to know the plan. It's got to look real.

Ava smiles at me, but her thoughts are clearly conveyed in her eyes. She's not thrilled I'll be keeping the real reason I want to date Chloe a secret from her friend. Chloe will get hurt if she falls for my irresistible charm.

Ava's words, not mine.

But she also doesn't want anything bad to happen to her friend, so she's going along with the lies. Liam did mention, though, that she threatened to stick thumbtacks in my balls if I hurt Chloe.

Good to know—since I happen to be quite fond of my balls.

I shut the door behind me and give Ava a quick hug. She's like a sister to me—only a lot less annoying than my biological ones can be.

"I spoke with your boss this morning," Principal Woodnut says, "as well as the FBI. I'll admit this is highly unorthodox. Do you even have teaching experience?"

Plenty, just not in the way she's hoping. "No, but I do have a degree."

"In what?"

"Electrical engineering."

"Hmm. Not exactly useful when it comes to working with kindergarteners."

Tell me about it. I don't know the first thing about dealing with that age. I'm hardly admitting that to her, though.

But really, how hard can it be?

"Because you'll be substituting for Zoe Bryant's class while she's on maternity leave, your classroom is right next to Chloe's.

I can arrange it so the adjoining door between the two rooms is left open, should you need help. Plus, then you'll have easy access to Chloe."

She doesn't state what all three of us know to be true. Zoe isn't officially on maternity leave. But since she's Ava's best friend and Liam's team knows her, we were able to convince her to start her maternity leave a month sooner than planned—at the FBI's expense.

"Sounds good," I tell Principal Woodnut.

"You're really not going to tell her what's going on?"

"It's best she doesn't know."

The reality is, Principal Woodnut doesn't know the full truth either. She only knows that I'm there to protect Chloe. That much we could tell her. She doesn't know about Chloe's connection to the mafia crime family that's continuously been on the news over the past five months.

Principal Woodnut nods, deferring to the arrangement.

"I guess there's nothing left to say. Welcome to Dalhousie Elementary School; if you need anything, be sure to let Ava, Chloe, or me know." The corner of her mouth twitches for a brief moment, and I try not to wonder what the hell that's about. "Ava will escort you to your classroom." Some more twitching of her mouth and she stands up. "Good luck, Mr. Reed."

I've been doing this job long enough to interpret body language and speech patterns. It comes with the territory. Which is why I catch the you're-royally-screwed, barely suppressed laughter in her tone.

Not exactly reassuring, but a bunch of kindergarteners is hardly a big deal. I've served overseas, been shot at, taken down the enemy.

There's nothing these kids can dish out that I can't handle.

"Okay, soldier, let me show you around," Ava says.

We step out of the office.

"Ava, there's a call for you on line two," the secretary tells her. "You can take it in Mr. Hauge's office. He's not in until later this morning, so he won't care if you take the call there."

"Thanks, Jeanine. I'll be right back," she tells me and disappears into the room.

The main door to the office swings opens, and a woman enters. Her wavy, shoulder-length hair is the color of a new penny, and she's wearing a cream knit top with tiny blue flowers and black slacks. Her makeup is on the minimal side, natural.

Christ, she's fucking gorgeous.

A thick stack of books sits perched in her arms, and her purse dangles from one shoulder.

She takes a step forward as her bag slides down and hooks on the door handle. She continues her forward momentum, but the bag has other plans. Half her body jerks back, and the books tilt precariously in her arms, threatening to crash to the floor.

I spring forward, grabbing for the books as they begin their descent.

Realizing she's about to lose her precious load, she attempts to hug it to herself and stumbles into me. Forgetting about the books, I instinctively grab her around the waist, bringing her hard against me.

The books hit the floor with a series of loud bangs.

A shocked gasp releases from her soft pink lips, and I loosen my hold on her—much to my body's annoyance.

"Sorry." I step back and start collecting the books from the floor.

She crouches to do the same. "You have nothing to apologize for. It's my bag and the door handle who owe us an apology." A strand of hair falls in her face.

She shoves it behind her ear as I chuckle at her comment. We both stand up, our arms full of books.

"Where do you need these?" I ask.

"My classroom, but I need to talk to Principal Woodnut first."

"She's expecting you, Chloe," Jeanine says.

Chloe?

This is the woman I'm supposed to be dating? She looks nothing like the picture in the folder Liam gave me yesterday when he told the team about the mission.

Chloe's a fairly common name. For all I know, there's at least two of them in this school.

"Hey, Chloe," Ava says from behind me. "I see you've already met Landon—Zoe's replacement while she's on maternity leave." To me, Ava says, "You'll be teaching in the classroom next to Chloe's." She flashes me a meaningful expression.

I guess that answers my question. This is the Chloe Reinhart whose grandfather is facing life in prison.

"Today's his first day," Ava adds.

Chloe's eyes widen. "Zoe's on maternity leave? I thought she was working until winter break. Is she okay?"

"She's fine. Just a slight change of plans. I'm giving Landon the tour; then he's all yours."

I turn back to Chloe. "Since I'm headed that way, do you want me to drop the books off in your classroom?"

"That's okay. I can manage." She reaches for them.

I jerk the books away from her.

"Are you sure? I can at least help and take those two." She points to the ones on top of the pile.

"I'm positive."

She nibbles her lip in a move that's so goddamn sexy.

Get your mind in the game, Scorpio.

"Okay." She scurries off to Woodnut's office, leaving me with Ava.

A short time later, after Ava has shown me all the sights and explained the ins and outs of our day, we step into an empty classroom.

"And this is where you'll be spending the next few weeks... less, if you're lucky." She walks to the teacher's desk—my desk —and picks up a folder from it. "This is your attendance list."

I survey the territory. A fucking rainbow exploded in here. The drawers against the walls, the rug in the corner of the room, the stout bookshelves, the posters with cartoon illustrations, the half-dozen squat tables with pint-sized chairs—it's all a multitude of bright colors, and it makes Principal Woodnut's office look dull.

Shit. What the hell have I gotten myself into?

4

CHLOE

I enter Principal Woodnut's office, and at her request, take a seat, pushing all thoughts from my head of the incredibly sexy substitute teacher.

The sexy teacher who will be in the classroom adjoining mine for at least the next four weeks.

"Jeanine said you wanted to talk to me," Principal Woodnut says, breaking me from my thoughts.

"That's right. I don't know if you've heard, but I volunteer several days a week at Golden Sunshine Retirement Village. And well...they need our help. Or rather, the students' help."

She leans forward, planting her elbows on the desk. "You have my attention."

"Every December, Millwood Elementary School puts on a concert for the residents. They love it. For some seniors, it's the only real interaction they have with kids. Their own grandkids aren't in their lives much." *If at all.* "Unfortunately, the school had to cancel for this holiday season, which means the highly anticipated Christmas concert won't be part of the residence's tradition this year. The seniors are extremely disappointed."

"And you're hoping our students can perform at the Christmas concert instead?"

I nod.

She leans back in her chair, her expression soft but unreadable. "Unfortunately, the decision for something like this isn't completely in my hands, even if I do believe it's a marvelous idea. I can give my stamp of approval, which is the first step."

"Whose hands is it in?"

"Tabitha Windhouse's."

At the name, my heart spirals downward and hits my stomach with a loud *oomph*.

Tabitha Windhouse. The president of the PTA.

And the woman who, for some reason, doesn't like me—although heaven knows why. I've never taught either of her kids.

"Why's it in her hands and not yours? You're the school principal."

"The woman has clout with the school board you can't even begin to imagine." Principal Woodnut leans forward again as if to share a national secret. Her next words come out in a hushed whisper, barely heard over the heater whirling in the background. "Sometimes, I swear the woman has ties to some sort of mafia. I've learned to pick my battles; otherwise, she finds loopholes that work in her favor if she's against the idea."

At the detested word, "mafia," my entire body feels as though Elsa from *Frozen* has turned it into a block of ice. "Surely she can't be that bad."

Principal Woodnut releases a long yes-she's-that-bad sigh and nods. "But I'm sure she should be fine with you doing this —except for one problem."

"What's that?"

"Zoe's the one who organizes the school performances, and she's now on maternity leave."

"I don't suppose her replacement has the same musical theatre experience and the expertise to pull the show together?"

A barked, raspy laugh escapes Principal Woodnut. "I can guarantee Landon doesn't have that kind of expertise."

Before I can think things through, I blurt, "I can do it. I can organize the show."

Please say yes. Please say yes. Please—

"Absolutely, if Tabitha and the PTA are on board with it, and you're willing to organize the show yourself—with the help of any faculty who volunteers to assist you—then you have my blessing. But remember, we don't have much of a budget for this, so you'll have to figure out how to keep it within the allotted amount. And that includes transportation to and from the seniors' residence."

"Perfect. I can do that." Buzzing with relief and excitement, I stand.

Principal Woodnut glances at the Mickey Mouse clock on her desk. "You'd better get to class. Kiera will be letting the students in shortly."

Right.

I head for the door.

"Oh," she adds before I get there, "and can you help Landon since he's new...to teaching elementary students?"

"He is? What age group has he worked with?"

"High school."

High school? God, I can only imagine what a disaster that would've been, with impressionable teenage girls falling in love with him because he's good-looking. Talk about awkward.

"Does he have any experience working with kinder-garteners?"

"No, that's why he might need your assistance from time to time. You might consider keeping the door between your classrooms open, so you can hear if the kids prove to be a handful for him."

That causes me to startle. Why would she hire him if she didn't believe he was capable of dealing with that age? He can't be the only available person who could cover for Zoe. "Okay. I can do that."

"Attagirl."

I enter my classroom a few minutes later and open the adjoining door. Ava's laughing, and Landon has a big grin on his face.

She spots me and waves me over to join them. "I was giving Landon a few pointers, and we were catching up a little."

"Catching up?"

She nods. "That's right. We went to college together."

"Back when she and her husband were first dating," Landon points out.

I vaguely know the story about how Ava and her husband were college sweethearts, but then something happened, and they broke up until a few years ago when they bumped into each other and quickly fell in love again.

Romantic Me sighs dreamily. Their story sounds like a Hallmark movie.

Nothing close to mine.

"Well, good luck, Landon," she says. "But I'm sure you won't need it."

"And I'm next door," I tell him. "If you have any questions or need my help, just ask."

"I'll see you two at lunch." Ava hurries out the door.

"Good luck," I throw out at Landon and return to my classroom. Thoughts of how I can convince Tabitha that the Christmas concert is a great idea perform the *Dance of the Sugar Plum Fairy* in my head.

Humming the music to myself, I walk to the side cabinet and look inside the large cage on top of it.

"What the heck are those?" Landon asks from behind me.

A surprised gasp breaks free from my lungs. "Wow, way to sneak up on a girl and give her a heart attack." I clasp my hand against my heart in mock exasperation. "What were you in your former life? A ninja?"

"Something like that. So what are those things?" He points at the three sleeping hedgehogs cuddled together in the corner, his eyebrow raised in jest or quizzical concern.

"My classroom pets. This is Pinecone." I point to the hedgehogs in question. "And this is Thistle, and Tumbleweed."

"I don't have any classroom pets, do I? No snake I failed to notice or some sort of rodent." His tone is laid-back, as if nothing scares him.

"No, Zoe doesn't have any pets. I have these three because a friend of mine was moving, and she wasn't allowed pets in her new apartment. There was no way I could let them go to a shelter. Who knows what would've happened to them?"

"So you adopted them?"

"I figured they would make great classroom pets, and the kids love them."

"You love animals, then?"

I grin. "I do. Pets are wonderful for reducing stress. That's why dogs make great therapy animals and reading companions for kids who struggle with reading."

"Do you have any? Dogs, I mean?"

"No. These three are the only pets I own. I'm not home enough to be a dog owner."

"Have a busy social life, do you?"

"I wouldn't exactly call it a social life. I volunteer several evenings and on the weekend at a local seniors' residence." The school bell rings, echoing through the building. "You should go into your classroom now. The herd will be stampeding in there any minute, and the last thing you want is to be in here when they do."

He salutes me, and I watch him go, pretending it has nothing to do with the view.

He really does have a nice ass—I mean shoulders.

Nice *shoulders*.

5

LANDON

The classroom silence dissolves into chair scraping and chatter, along with squeals and laughter, as pint-sized beings tumble in through the door from the hallway.

"Where's Mrs. B?" one little girl asks, her long red hair in two pigtails. She's wearing a purple sweat shirt with a sparkly pink elephant on the front.

"She's on maternity leave, and I'm taking her place until she returns." Or until Chloe is no longer in danger and the FBI has her cousin in custody—both of which I'm hoping happens long before Zoe's maternity leave ends.

"What's ma-tur-me-key leave?" a blond-haired boy with black-rimmed glasses asks.

"Ma-ter-ni-ty. It's when the mother-to-be stops working for a few months, so she can take care of the baby."

The two kids and several others stare at me with blank expressions. Another kid comes running into the room, his arms held out like he's an airplane, and he's making loud engine noises.

"You're big," Pigtails announces, looking up at me as though I'm a skyscraper. "You're bigger than my daddy."

"He's bigger than a mountain," someone else says. I don't know which one because I'm too busy watching the kid pretending to be an airplane climb onto the table.

"Mister."

I feel someone tug on my shirt sleeve. I look down to find a kid attached to it.

"Mister." Tug. Tug. "He's not supposed to be on the table, and I need to go to the bathroom." Tug.

"Okay, take your bathroom buddy with you, but come right back once you've finished."

He doesn't wait for me to say anything else. He goes charging from the room, buddy in tow.

"What's his name?" I ask Pigtails and point to the kid on the table.

"Trevor. Has Mrs. B had her baby yet?"

"No." I walk to the table. "Trevor, we don't climb on the table. Both feet on the floor, please." I help him down.

A loud shriek rips through the air from the other side of the room. I turn to witness water spraying from the sink, soaking the two kids standing there.

"Is everything okay?" Chloe asks, her head poking through the adjoining doorway.

"Hi, Miss R," the boy with glasses says. "Did you know that Mrs. B is on ma-tur-me-key?" He looks pretty proud of himself even though he mangled the word again.

"Yes, I did, Tommy." Chloe walks over to the two shrieking kids and turns the water off. Neither had bothered to move out of its range of fire. Water drips from their clothes, forming a puddle on the floor.

"I'm wet," the little girl whines.

Chloe smiles sweetly at them. "You certainly are. But I'm

sure we can find something in my forgotten-clothes box for you to wear while your clothes dry."

To me, she says, "There's a mop around the corner. You can use it to dry the floor." She points to the corner she's referring to.

"All right, everyone," she says to the class, her voice loud enough to be heard over the noise. "Time to take out your writing practice book and sit in your assigned seat. What letter did you learn to write on Friday?"

Most of the kids answer "H"—with a few other letters called out.

"That's right," she says. "For the next few minutes, I want you to practice writing the letter H." And like magic, the rowdy bunch of kids hustle to the small, colorful plastic drawers, pull out their writing books and pencils, and march themselves to their seats and sit.

Chloe winks at me and escorts the two soaked kids into her classroom.

"I'm going to clean up the mess," I announce to the class, "and then we'll get started. I don't want to hear any talking while you practice. *Capisce*?"

"What does ka-peesh mean?" Pigtails asks.

"Do you understand."

She shakes her head. "No, that's why I asked."

"No, that's what *capisce* means. Do you understand." And because I want to show who's in control of this pony ride, I walk away, having the last word.

Five minutes later, the two soggy kids are in dry clothes, the entire class is busy practicing Hs in their workbooks, and I've taken attendance.

Chloe is back in her classroom with her own kids. The morning goes by relatively fast, once I get the general gist of what the hell I'm doing. It's pretty easy actually—walking-through-a-pit-of-hungry-alligators-without-getting-eaten-alive kind of easy.

But I've got this. I didn't survive the SEALs just to be taken down by a bunch of kids.

Chloe and I are assigned the first recess duty. We get the kids dressed for outside and funnel them out the rear door of the building. The other two kindergarten classes join us, but the teachers stay inside and shoot back whiskey—or whatever they do to get through the day with the incessant questions and fidgeting.

"You seem to be doing okay so far," Chloe says as we watch the kids run around the field. Some of them are chasing soccer balls. Others are climbing over the playground equipment like ants on a piece of pastrami. "Kindergarteners must be quite a shock to the system after working with high school students."

"High school?"

"Principal Woodnut mentioned you used to teach high school, but then decided to be an elementary school teacher. That's why she asked me to help you. She figured you might feel a little overwhelmed at first by how different this age group is compared to what you're used to."

Well, isn't Principal Woodnut the crafty one?

"Right. But I'll admit I like this age. They're fun, and they ask the funniest questions." All the truth.

They also asked questions that thank Christ Chloe didn't witness, like "Why do I have a penis but my sister doesn't?" and "Where do babies come from?" and "What does intercourse mean?"

Seriously, what kid knows the word "intercourse"?

"So, what about you?" Chloe asks, looking adorably sexy with her rosy cheeks and the end of her nose pink. Her hands are hidden in her coat pockets. "Do you have any pets? I never had the chance to ask you before you had to go to your class-room this morning."

"I kind of have a puppy."

"How do you *kind of* have a puppy? Does your wife or girl-friend half own it or something?"

"Nope. I'm single." I slide a glance at her to check her reaction and catch her studying me. She shakes her head as if mentally answering a question I'm not privy to. "I found the puppy outside my town house yesterday morning and took him to the vet because he was injured."

She gasps, and her eyes fill with concern. Like she wants to march down to the clinic and give the puppy lots of hugs. "Will he be all right?"

"He should be. So now I'm looking for a home for him. You don't by any chance know anyone who would like a dog, do you?"

"Sorry. I wish I did. You could ask the staff here. They might know of someone."

"I'll do that, thanks."

"Is he staying with you while you find him a new home?"

It would seem so. The clinic called last night to let me know that there are currently no foster homes available to take him in until a forever home can be found.

"I'm picking him up at the clinic after work."

Chloe looks at me as if I'm her hero. Guess she must really love animals.

"What kind of dog is he?" she asks.

I show her the photo on my phone.

"Oh, God, he's so cute. What's his name?"

"He never mentioned it to me. Maybe he told the vet techni-cians." The corner of my mouth slides up to one side.

"You have to give him a name. You can't just call him The Puppy. It might give him a complex later on."

I study her for a second. Hell if I know what to call him. The Puppy works for me.

Several boys run past us, chasing each other and laughing.

One of them tags his friend and yells, "You're it."

"Any suggestions on what I should call him?" I ask her.

She takes my phone from me and studies the picture for a moment. Her light floral scent teases me briefly before she leans away again. Something inside me stirs. I ignore it, unable to put a name to it.

They say some pets look a lot like their owners. I don't know how much truth there is to that. Jayden and his dog don't bear much resemblance to each other. Plus, Mojo is more on the lazy side. The same can't be said about Jayden.

When it comes to Chloe's hair color, she and the puppy have that in common.

But that's where the similarities between them end. The puppy is...well, he's just a puppy. Chloe is sexy as all hell.

But not sexy like the women I've been known to hook up with in the past. Those women were more blatant with their sex appeal.

Chloe is sexy in a sweet, wholesome way.

And that thought reminds me exactly why I'm here, in the playground, watching kids during recess.

I'm supposed to be her boyfriend—the man who's going to protect her sexy ass. The man who's charged with discovering where her cousin is hiding so the Feds can finally nail *his* sorry ass to the wall.

"Whiskey. That's what I think you should call him."

A barked laugh erupts from my lungs. "You think I should name him after an alcoholic beverage?"

"Sure, why not? The color of his coat reminds me of a glass of whiskey. I mean, you can call him Jack or Daniel, but Whiskey sounds cuter...and he's definitely a cute puppy."

"Do you like whiskey?" She looks more like a wine drinker to me. A wine drinker who owns a winery she might not know about.

"Can't say I've ever had it. But the elderly gentlemen where I volunteer have hinted quite loudly that they would love it if I sneaked some in for them." She grins. "Anyway, it seems like the perfect name."

"Okay, Whiskey it is." Because it's not like the little dude will be with me for long, so I don't really care one way or another what he's called.

After recess, I spend the morning playing math games with the kids. This is followed by them working on their math coloring pages while I walk around checking on how they're doing.

"Does anyone have any questions?" I ask at one point when some of them start to get restless, squirming in their seats like they're sitting on an ant nest.

Wrong thing to inquire.

"Have you kissed a frog?" Jessica asks. "My sister told me if you kiss a frog, it turns into a prince."

"Nah ah," Kathleen says, shaking her head so fast I wouldn't be surprised if she gets whiplash. "If he kisses a frog, it'll turn into a princess 'cuz he's a man."

Twenty-five pairs of curious eyes turn my way. "Is that true?" Ryan asks. "If you kiss a frog, it'll turn into a girl frog?"

"A princess," Kathleen corrects.

"Same thing," Ryan retorts.

"No, it isn't," Pigtails—officially known as Patty—says. "Princesses live in big palaces." She stretches her arms out wide, demonstrating how big these palaces are, and almost pokes Ryan in the eye.

"Good point," I say because I assume that's true. The girls here probably know a helluva lot more about princesses and royalty than I'll ever care to know.

"Have you kissed a frog?" Jessica asks me again.

"Can't say I have or that it's on the agenda."

Twenty-five heads nod, apparently satisfied with the answer.

Until...

"Why haven't you kissed a frog?" she asks.

"I'm selective of who I kiss. You can't just go around kissing anyone." That's pretty close to the truth.

I haven't kissed everyone.

But I have kissed a fair number of women over the years—and that's not including the girls horny teenager-me kissed after I discovered the joys of the opposite sex.

"Now, let me rephrase my earlier question. Does anyone have any questions about math?"

Ryan's hand shoots up. I nod for him to ask it.

"What is one million and ninety-eight times fifty-five?"

"That wasn't the kind of question I had in mind. Any questions about the coloring page you're working on?"

Note to self: Be as specific as possible when asking the kids a question.

The bell rings, announcing lunchtime. I direct the kids to get their lunch bags and return to their tables to eat their food.

Chloe pokes her head into the classroom. "How's it going so far?"

"Good."

The kids are still alive anyway, and they're not hanging from the lights.

Whether they've actually learned anything remains up for debate.

But that's really none of my concern.

My only concern is the woman standing in front of me and her deadly excuse of a cousin.

"They'll eat inside for fifteen minutes, and then Tracy will take them outside to play for the rest of the lunch break. That's when we'll get to take our break in the lunchroom."

With that, Chloe disappears back into her classroom.

And I contemplate how to get to Step B—asking her out on a date.

6

CHLOE

"I've got a sticky dilemma," I tell Ava and Kiera as I enter the staff room with Landon behind me.

Several other teachers eating lunch look up from the other end of the long table. They smile at me and return to their conversation. Outside the closed window, excited kiddie shrieks and laughter leak in from the playground.

"Did Joey dump glue in his hair again?" Kiera asks.

Landon and I take a seat across from them.

"Thank God, no." Trying to get it out was a nightmare enough as it was, but that was nothing compared to when his mom saw the mess. Let's just say it took me several days to get over the hissy fit she threw when she came in to see me the next morning. "This is possibly worse."

"What could be worse than that?"

While we eat our food, I tell them about the canceled Christmas concert at the seniors' residence and about my plan, and that I have to get Tabitha's approval if I want my class to perform for the seniors.

"I take that back," Kiera says. "That *is* worse than Joey dumping glue in his hair."

"It would help if Tabitha at least liked me. Then it probably wouldn't be an issue. For some reason, she acts like I'm poison ivy."

"You know why, don't you?" Ava says.

I shake my head.

"She caught her husband masturbating to your photo. She kicked his sorry ass to the curb and divorced him." Well, that's beyond disturbing.

"Seriously, how did I get so lucky when it comes to the men in my life? Is it any wonder I want to stay single? I should just join a nunnery."

Ava's gaze darts to Landon as Kiera says, "I think you might have to be Catholic to become a nun."

"Good point."

Dear Mom, I mentally write in a letter that will never be sent.

Why couldn't we have at least been Catholic? That might have made my life somewhat easier.

Miss you greatly,

Chloe

"You really want to remain single for the rest of your life?" Ava asks.

"Given my history with men, that's probably a smart thing to do. It's not like they stick around forever." I give Kiera a sad smile. "Sorry."

She shrugs and gives me an it's-okay smile that's weak at best. Her husband died last December in a skiing accident. She understands firsthand about the lack of forever.

"Yes, your boyfriend ghosted you and then dumped you via text," Ava says, "but that doesn't mean you should give up on love."

I laugh—not because what he did was particularly funny, but because... "I bet you didn't expect to spend your lunch listening to girl talk on your first day of teaching kindergarten,"

I say to Landon.

"I have two sisters. I'm used to it."

"I don't think staying single for the rest of my life is a bad thing," I say to Ava. "Think of everything I can accomplish without having to worry if I'm doing something to scare the man away. And I can spend more time on my art."

"You draw?" Landon asks and continues to devour his sandwich.

"I have an art degree, which is why I love art time with the kids." And because I really don't want to talk about my love life, I say, "Speaking of dogs, you have to see the picture of Landon's puppy."

Ava's eyes widen. "You have a puppy?"

"Technically, I'm just his foster parent until I find him a new home."

"Show them the picture of him. He's absolutely adorable," I tell Kiera and Ava.

Landon pulls up Whiskey's photo on his phone and hands it to Ava.

"Ohmigod, he *is* adorable." She passes the phone to Kiera, who also gushes over the puppy.

"So, what are you gonna do about Tabitha?" Kiera asks as I sneak another peek at Whiskey while she hands the phone back to Landon.

"Good question. Do any of you have any suggestions? Maybe I could send her on an all-expense-paid trip to the Bahamas." I'm kidding, but given what Ava told me, even that might not be enough in Tabitha's eyes after what her husband did.

Even though that had nothing to do with me.

It was all on him.

Kiera smiles sweetly at Landon, flashing her dimples. "Maybe you could seduce her into granting her permission for the Christmas show. You know, take one for the team."

I beam at him. "Oh, that's a great idea. You're hot. She's bound to say yes if you ask her."

One of his eyebrows raises. "You think I'm hot?"

I wave off his comment and pick up a cherry tomato from my salad. "Of course. We all do, right?" The last part is directed at Kiera and Ava.

"She does make a good point," Kiera says. Ava doesn't say anything, but the corners of her mouth twitch with barely contained mirth.

Of course, she won't say anything. She's in love with her husband. In her mind, everyone pales in comparison to Liam.

And pretty much in reality, too.

The man is damn hot.

Just not as hot as Landon, but I'm not admitting that to anyone. They might get the wrong idea.

"And once you've seduced her into giving me permission to do the show," I say, "I'll arrange everything. Zoe is the one who usually organizes the school concerts and performances, but since she's on maternity leave, that falls on me."

Somehow I keep my voice even, not a hint of panic coloring my tone.

Perhaps there's an actress inside me, after all.

Way, way, *way* deep inside me.

"I can help you with the concert part," Landon says.

"Do you know anything about organizing performances?" Hope swirls inside me like a chocolate-and-vanilla soft serve ice cream.

"Not exactly, but I'm willing to do whatever I can to help you."

"And that includes the seduction of Tabitha?" I flash him what I hope are convincing puppy dog eyes, channeling the ones in Whiskey's photo.

"I don't seduce women I don't want to be with."

"Even if it's for a great cause?"

"Not even for that."

"How about a little harmless flirting? Just pour on that natural charm you have going for you. You don't have to seduce her. Flatter her a little, and she'll be more than happy to oblige your requests."

From the corner of my eye, I catch Ava cringing.

"You look like you work out regularly," Kiera says.

Landon nods. "That's right."

He's wearing a button-up shirt, but it's clear from the way it fits his body, he's in great shape. His exposed muscular forearms confirm that, too.

"Then, I suggest you remove your shirt while talking to her." Kiera waves her empty fork at him. "That's bound to work. Just don't be obvious about it—that way she won't get the wrong idea."

Ava covers her mouth with her hand as though she's trying to hold back a laugh. The corners of her eyes crinkle, giving it away.

"Can't you just ask her?" he says. "She might surprise you. Tell her exactly why you want to do the concert. How can she say no?"

"Do you not remember the part about why she hates me? It's not like I can even apologize for what happened. I didn't do anything to encourage him. I've never even met her ex-husband."

"Okay, I'll ask her, but I'm not seducing her, and I'm not removing my shirt." He directs the last part to Kiera, and I grin.

"*Thank you. Thank you. Thank you.* And the seniors thank you, too." I'm so giddy with excitement, I'm practically bouncing in my chair. "And if there's anything you need help with, just ask me." It's the least I can do.

"I wouldn't mind getting more pointers about working with elementary school kids. And we should talk about the production sooner rather than later."

"I can definitely do that."

"I have to pick Whiskey up at the vet after school—"

"Chloe can go with you," Ava says. "And you can talk about all those things afterward."

Landon unfolds himself from his chair and gathers up his empty lunch containers. "Sounds like a plan. And then I can make you dinner."

He strides from the staff room before I can respond.

"What the hell just happened?" My head feels like it's spinning after the abrupt turnaround of that conversation.

Kiera grins. "I believe you got yourself a date with the hot teacher."

7

___

LANDON

Well, that was easier than expected.

Several hours later, I'm still thinking that as the final bell rings.

I don't mean that being a teacher is easier than I'd expected. Because it isn't. And anyone who says otherwise is an asshole.

I have a whole new respect for kindergarten teachers. I probably owe mine a huge apology—if she's still alive.

What I hadn't been expecting was how easy it was to get Chloe to agree to go out on a date with me, especially after she made it clear she wants to stay single.

"Oh boy, what happened in here?" Chloe asks after the last of the kids are skipping down the hallway to the front entrance.

She surveys the damage, then picks up a picture book from the floor and heads to the bookshelves in the corner. "A hint for tomorrow...get them to start tidying up about thirty minutes before the end of class. And if they're finished in time, they get to listen to a story. The longer they take to clean up, the less time there is for the story."

"Great advice. Thanks."

"How about I put away the books, and you can clean up the art supplies?"

"You've got yourself a deal."

I gather the plastic plates from the tables and carry them to the sink. Fifteen minutes later, everything is back where it belongs.

"How long have you been teaching?" I ask Chloe as we walk to the staff parking lot. The cool wind tumbles dried leaves across the ground.

"About five years. I got my art degree, but then I realized I didn't want to be a starving artist. So I returned to school for my teaching certificate, and the rest is history."

"But why kindergarten? Why not be a high school art teacher?"

"I thought about doing that. I taught teens as part of an extracurricular program at the art center near where I lived. But as much as I loved doing it, I wanted to work with little kids more.

"I still teach art classes for teens, but I save that for the summer when I have more time."

"Teaching during the school year and volunteering at the seniors' residence must keep you busy."

"It does—especially since I volunteer with the seniors several times a week."

"Wow, you must really enjoy it."

She points to what looks like a 2016 red Honda Civic. "That's my car. And yes, I do really enjoy it. I don't have any grandparents, or at least none who are still part of my life. The residents at the seniors' home are like surrogate grandparents to me. I love them as if they *are* my grandparents. And they treat me like I'm their granddaughter."

She smiles at me. It's a gorgeous smile—one that causes a spark deep in my gut, two live wires briefly touching.

"What about you?" she asks. "Are your grandparents still part of your life?"

"They are. My granny lives with my parents. And is always keeping them on their toes." I mentally laugh at how much she does that. "She told me once that it's how she keeps herself young. My grandfather, her husband, passed away a few years ago."

"I'm sorry for your loss."

"Me too. He was a great guy. I'm positive you would've liked him. My other grandparents live in Texas, near one of my sisters and her family....Did you want to come with me in my vehicle or follow me?"

"I'll follow you. But in case I lose you, what vet clinic are you going to?"

I tell her the name. It's not exactly close to here. My home is on the other side of the city from the school.

For a second, I think she's going to change her mind, and maybe she would have if we weren't both friends with Ava. Ava has already vouched for me, which makes my life a helluva lot easier when it comes to the mission.

We eventually arrive at the clinic where Whiskey has spent the past thirty-two hours.

"Do you have any supplies for him?" Chloe asks as we enter the building.

"I picked up some stuff for him this morning." The convenient thing about having a colleague who's a dog lover is that Jayden could tell me what to get. He also gave me pointers when it comes to taking care of a puppy.

Rule #1 when it comes to puppy obedience: Show him who's boss—which works for me.

I approach the front desk. "Hi, I've come to collect the injured puppy I dropped off yesterday morning. The cockapoo."

The receptionist's mouth breaks into a soft smile. "Ah yes,

the sweet puppy who has stolen everyone's heart here. Have you come up with a name for him yet?"

"Whiskey. And if he's stolen everyone's heart, does that mean someone wants to adopt him?" I smile hopefully at her, pouring on the charm like hot fudge over a sundae.

"Sorry, we're all maxed out on pets right now. Otherwise, I'm positive one of our staff members would. Interesting choice of name, but it's also very fitting."

She tells the woman behind her, wearing cartoon cat scrubs, that we've come for the puppy. The woman disappears through the doorway and re-emerges a minute later, carrying him in her arms.

"Oh, aren't you the just the cutest bundle of fluff?" Chloe coos, letting him sniff her hand, then scratching him behind the ear.

The puppy releases a little bark and attempts to lick her face.

"Looks like you've already won him over," I say. Now I just need him to win her over enough so she takes him off my hands.

The vet assistant gives me directions on how to care for Whiskey's wound and answers all my questions.

"And you'll let me know if the situation changes and a foster home becomes available?" I've already left a description with the humane society in case someone turns up there, searching for the puppy.

"Yes, we have him on the list."

"And if you hear of anyone looking to adopt a puppy..."

"We'll give them your contact information. But are you sure you don't want to keep him? Given his rough start, he really is a sweet little dog. And this breed is a great family pet." The woman's gaze shifts to Chloe.

"I'm positive." I'm the kind of man who likes to be in full

control of his life—and something tells me Whiskey is the opposite of what I need.

I take him from her, and after the woman has said her good-byes to him, Chloe, Whiskey, and I head out for the next part of my mission: a date with Chloe.

Whiskey's going to be the perfect sidekick for that. Chloe will have a hard time saying no to being my girlfriend when I have him in my life. She's already opened her heart to him, so the rest of this should be easy.

I practically high-five myself for the stroke of genius in rescuing the little dude and deciding to be his foster home for the short term.

Chloe helps me put Whiskey into his crate, and I load it into the back seat of my jeep. It only takes ten minutes to arrive at my place, and I park in the garage.

Chloe parks on the street in front of my town house and joins me in the garage.

"Look familiar?" I ask Whiskey. "I found him by the bush," I tell Chloe, pointing to the plant. "I have no idea how long he'd been there or where he came from. I only know he doesn't belong to any of my neighbors, and they didn't recognize him." I lower his crate to the ground and open the trunk to collect his supplies.

"Let me help," Chloe says.

"That's okay, I've got this."

She doesn't listen and grabs the big bag of puppy food.

"I can get that. It's heavy."

"It's not that bad. I can manage. I'm stronger than I look."

Strong isn't the word I'd use to describe Chloe. She's all soft, warm woman.

"I'm sure you are, but how about you bring his bed instead? Or maybe the bag with the toys I bought him?"

She shifts the oversized bag to one arm, grabs the handle of the cloth bag containing the puppy-friendly toys, and tosses me a smug, get-over-it-caveman grin.

Shaking my head to myself, I remove the rest of the supplies from my vehicle and close the trunk.

Once we get everything into the town house, I put Whiskey's crate in his temporary bedroom and open the wire door. Happy to bail on it, he climbs out and places his paw against my calf.

"You're supposed to rest," I tell him. Vet's orders.

I scoop him up, taking care not to hurt his leg. He gives me a little puppy bark, and I carry him into the living room like he's a football, one hand supporting him under the belly, the other carrying his dog bed.

I set it on the hardwood floor and carefully lower him on top of it. "Stay here while I get dinner started," I tell him. To Chloe, I ask, "Would you like some wine?"

"No, I'm good."

"You sure? I've got an open bottle of Zinfandel from Enchanted Springs Winery."

If the winery name sounds familiar, Chloe keeps the recognition off her face.

"I love wine, but I prefer to save it for the weekend."

"Do you have a favorite brand?"

She shrugs. "Not really. We might be in wine country, but I really don't know much about wine. I always order Riesling from whatever mid-range wine is listed on the menu."

"Riesling? That's your favorite white wine?" It's not one I remember being part of the Enchanted Springs inventory.

She nods.

"What about red wines?"

"Syrahs." Another wine that isn't part of the Enchanted Springs inventory. "But I'm more of a white-wine girl."

You would think if you owned a winery, you would favor the wines you produce.

So maybe the Feds are right, and she really is clueless about the winery in her name.

"Do you do your own taxes?" I ask.

"That's kind of an odd question to ask someone you haven't known for long."

"Maybe tax talk turns me on."

That makes her laugh. "How can anything to do with taxes turn anyone on? I mean, I get it if you're an accountant, tax season might *possibly* make you horny. But for most people, that's not the case."

Whiskey gets off his bed and limps toward me.

"Stay," I tell him in my SEALs tone.

He doesn't listen. He just looks at me, head cocked to the side, and keeps hobbling forward.

Chloe crouches next to him and scratches behind his ear. This causes him to stop and flop onto his side, a happy puppy grin on his face.

"But to answer your question," she says, "no, I don't do my own taxes. A family friend has been doing them for years. Math isn't my thing, so I'm happy to hand everything over to him during tax season."

Whoever's filing them knows about the winery Chloe isn't aware she owns. And the person might know a lot more about her family's dark side than she's aware of.

And this includes the truth when it comes to Nikolai.

"My accountant retired a few months ago, and I'm looking for recommendations." The lie forms easily on my lips. "Is your family friend accepting new clients?"

"I'm not sure. I can ask him if you want."

"That would be great. Assuming you're happy with him, of course."

"I can't say I have any complaints. The IRS hasn't been knocking on my door, so I guess he's doing a good job."

I walk to the kitchen. "So we've established you like Riesling and Syrahs, and you don't do your own taxes. That's probably more than I know about most of my dates."

She laughs, stroking Whiskey's fur. "Yes, we're definitely getting into deep territory. But that's more than I know about you. All I know is that you used to teach high school math, and you're now a substitute teacher and a puppy foster father."

I remove the chicken breasts from the fridge, along with the other ingredients I'll need to make dinner, and set them on the counter. "I also play hockey whenever I can."

When it comes to going undercover, the closer you can keep to real life, the easier it is to maintain your story. You're less likely to slip up and say something that will give away that you're not who you're claiming to be.

"Are you on a team?"

"Yep. We play in a competitive adult league. We all grew up with aspirations of playing in the NHL, but then reality didn't quite pan out that way." All that is true. But what I'm not going to admit is that we're all in the same field when it comes to our careers.

My teammates are comprised of FBI agents, cops, and former military who still work at keeping the bad guys at bay, including one who's a prosecutor.

"Kiera's husband used to play hockey. She and I went to his games all the time and cheered the guys on. They were really good."

"He doesn't play anymore?"

"He died last year, around the holiday season. He went skiing with some friends, lost control, and hit a tree."

That sounds familiar. "Stephen Ashdown was her husband?"

She nods. "You knew him?"

"Not very well. He was a great player, and as far as I could tell, a nice guy."

"He was a very nice guy. Sweet. A real romantic. Those guys are a rare breed."

The corner of my mouth twitches. "You saying I can't be a romantic, too?"

Because if that's what she's saying, she's not too far from the truth.

I'm about as romantic as the next guy.

Chloe shrugs. "In my experience, most guys aren't that way." She pauses fussing over Whiskey; he whimpers, begging for more. "You're too adorable for words," she tells him.

"I'm not used to being called adorable, but I'm sure my masculinity can handle it," I say on a laugh.

She looks up from Whiskey and shakes her head, a grin on her lush lips. "Adorable is definitely not how I would describe you." She returns her attention to the puppy. "I'm going to help Landon with dinner, but as soon as I can, I'll be back to fussing over you. Okay?"

Whiskey gives a little bark.

"I've got everything under control here," I tell her. "You don't have to leave him just yet."

"Are you sure? I'm more than happy to help."

"You are helping. With him."

She smiles softly at me and then at the puppy. "All right. I'll stay with you while Landon makes dinner."

"I take it you've never had a romantic boyfriend?" I ask, mostly because the more I know about Chloe, the more I can use it to gain her trust. And if she trusts me, maybe I can eventually discover where Nikolai is hiding.

"I did. Or at least I thought he was romantic until he one day decided he'd had enough of being my boyfriend. He didn't love me like he'd thought he had. A few days later, he texted me to tell me he didn't love me after all. And that was the last I heard from him. So that kind of trumped the romantic stuff."

"He's the only romantic boyfriend you've had?" The guy sounds like a douchebag.

"I had a boyfriend in college—years before I dated Mark—but that boyfriend was more like a frat boy. He wasn't known for being romantic. I've dated a few guys since Mark, but I've pretty much decided having a boyfriend isn't worth the time. I'm so busy with my job and my artwork and my volunteering, I don't have time for a boyfriend." Her gaze returns to the puppy, and she scratches him behind the ear. "Isn't that right, Whiskey?"

He gives her another little bark, and I inwardly cringe—and curse her fucking ex-boyfriend. He's making my job a lot more challenging.

"What about you?" she asks. "Has a girlfriend ever broken your heart?"

I shake my head—since it's mostly true.

"Are *you* the heartbreaker, then?"

And this is where I'm suddenly royally screwed. Because my answer might ruin the mission—or at least my part of the mission. I don't expect Chloe's the kind of woman who likes dating a man who was at one time a player. And I'm not referring to the type that plays hockey.

"I'm not a heartbreaker. I've been in relationships that died out over time, and we mutually agreed to go our separate ways."

Again, all a lie.

I begin chopping the vegetables.

"Have you had many girlfriends?"

"Just three. My last girlfriend had a great job offer in New York City, and there was no way she could turn it down. I wasn't interested in...I wanted to remain in San Francisco and teach here. So we went our separate ways and remained friends."

"Has she been back to visit?"

"Yes...with her fiancé." No point in having Chloe believe I've got some sort of fuck-buddy arrangement with my fictitious ex-girlfriend.

"Are you interested in falling in love and having a family one day?" she asks.

That's the kind of question women who are looking to adorn their ring finger ask. They don't want to waste their time with a man with commitment issues. But since Chloe's made it clear she isn't interested in having a boyfriend, I have no idea what she's hoping to hear.

"Yes, one day."

I assume being a kindergarten teacher doesn't give you superpowers...like the ability to tell when someone's lying.

"And there's no special woman in your life you're hoping to one day be the mother of your kids?"

"Not yet." I give her a meaningful look. "But I'm hoping that changes soon."

An adorably sexy blush spreads across her cheeks. At least my not-so-subtle hint didn't go right over her head.

Whiskey places his paw on her lap, requesting her attention.

"I think he's hoping the same." I cluck my chin at him.

"And what's that exactly?"

"That you'll agree to see if this thing between us will go further than dinner."

8

CHLOE

At Landon's hint that he's hoping things will progress beyond dinner, my body turns Arctic cold. I wouldn't be surprised if tiny polar bears are playing tag in my gut.

It's not what you think, I tell it.

"You mean you want to have sex with me?" I didn't intend to say it out loud, but that's got to be what he's thinking.

His eyebrows tug up his forehead. "I'm not the kind of guy who has sex on a first date."

I manage to hold back a snorted laugh. He looks exactly like that type. He exudes sexuality.

"That's good to know." My girlie parts have the opposite opinion—they want to jump him now—but they don't have a say in this conversation.

"So, are you interested in having a second date after this?"

"Technically, this isn't even a first date."

"Sure, it is. I'm making you dinner, right?" He gestures at the food spread out on the counter. "That counts as a date."

I laugh—he really is funny. "But talking shop kind of negates that. And shop talk is the reason I'm here. We're discussing the show, and I'm sharing tips on how to deal with kindergarteners."

"Well, how about we have a date tonight and not talk shop?"

I shake my head. "I don't date."

"Not at all?"

"Nope. Not at all. Men tend not to stick around in my life for long."

"You've obviously gone out with the wrong men."

"Oh, it's not just the men I've dated. My biological father and my stepfather weren't any different."

A frown creases Landon's brow. "They both actually told you they were leaving your mother because of you?"

"No, but after they left us, they never tried to contact me. I thought they loved me. I was wrong. So clearly, I'm a terrible judge of character." Although in the case of my father and stepfather, it was my mother who'd been the terrible judge of character.

I'm just the one who (eventually) learned from Mom's mistakes. I'm the one who decided to be a lot more cautious when it came to giving my heart away again.

I scoop up Whiskey and cuddle him.

The little furball licks my chin. I can see why dogs make good emotional-support animals. His unconditional love is a great balm for the battered soul.

I grin at him and kiss his fuzzy little head. Then I look over to Landon. "I'm not interested in dating you. But I'm more than happy to be your friend."

Since you can never have too many friends.

Landon doesn't say anything more on the topic, which, fortunately, switches to something I'm happy to discuss. While he cooks dinner, I continue cuddling Whiskey and sharing my teaching tips.

At one point, I walk over to the bookshelf against the wall and study the photos on it. Most of them are of different outdoor locations—some I recognize from the US, others from South America. In each of them, Landon is with a group of men, all wearing backpacks.

I pick one up and study it. "You've hiked Machu Picchu?" I can't keep the excitement out of my voice at the thought that he's been there. We have that in common.

"I have."

"I love hiking, and that's one location I've been lucky to visit. Along with the Grand Canyon." I nod at the bookshelf. He's also been there.

"Do you hike often?"

"I try to go as often as I can during the spring and summer. I love getting lost in nature and forgetting all my problems waiting for me at home."

"I feel the same way. There's something about hoisting on a backpack and hiking."

I return the picture frame to the bookshelf. Part of me wants to tell him that if he's ever looking for a hiking partner...

But I don't let the thought go too far. As much as I would love to go hiking with someone as passionate about it as I am, we've only known each other for a few days.

That doesn't, though, stop us from spending the next hour talking about the different locations we've been to and comparing notes.

TOP SECRET

AFTER DINNER, WE'RE PUTTING THE DISHES AWAY IN THE dishwasher when Landon asks, "When are you talking to Tabitha?"

"Tomorrow night. There's a PTA meeting then."

Although after what Ava and Kiera told me, I don't have a

good feeling about that plan. I have no idea how I'm going to convince Tabitha to throw in her support for the Christmas show.

"What time's the meeting?"

I tell him.

"I'll be there."

"Ahh, so Kiera convinced you to go shirtless for the cause after all?" Score one for my best friend.

He laughs, the sound deep and delicious. Like a warm hug on a chilly fall morning. "No, but I figure the more support you have behind the idea, the better your chances of her approving it."

"And if that fails, you'll go with Plan B?" I gesture at his upper body with a wave of my hand.

"How about this...if I remove my shirt for the cause, you agree to go out with me for our second date."

"First date."

His mouth tugs to one side. "So, you're agreeing to go out with me?"

I roll my eyes. "Fine. If it comes down to you removing your shirt to encourage Tabitha to agree to the Christmas show, I'll go on a date with you."

[TOP SECRET]

THE NEXT EVENING, LANDON, KIERA, AND I HEAD TO THE GYM, where the PTA meeting is being held. The three of us stuck around after the bell rung, prepping for tomorrow.

Tabitha is talking to a fellow PTA mother when we enter the gym. She's looking as elegant as always: blonde hair pulled back in a sleek bun, a camel-colored pencil skirt skimming her slim body, her white blouse no doubt from a high-end designer.

I, on the other hand, look as far from elegant as you can get. My pale-pink knit top has a red paint splotch on it from the Thanksgiving art project we were working on in class today. One of my students accidentally sent his paintbrush sailing across the room, and it hit my boob.

And no amount of dabbing it with a wet paper towel would remove it.

Quite the contrary.

The moment Tabitha spots us walking toward her, her gaze drops to the stain. Her mouth tilts to the side.

Landon's smirk is wickedly sexy; Tabitha's just spells trouble.

"It's nice to see you again, Chloe." Her tone implies the opposite. "What do we owe the pleasure of your company? You don't usually attend our humble meetings." Her gaze cuts to Landon and travels lazily down his body.

Trust me, I wouldn't be here if it weren't necessary.

I smile sweetly at her while dreaming about chocolate. Rich, creamy Lindt chocolate. The kind that leaves you groaning with pleasure. That does the trick. "I volunteer at a residence for the elderly, and their Christmas party is at risk of being canceled." All right, that part isn't entirely true, but close enough. "The school that usually performs had to back out. I thought it would be a positive experience for my kindergarteners to perform for the residents. Principal Woodnut asked me to let you know about it." *So that you don't pull any strings to prevent it from happening, even though you, as the president of the PTA, shouldn't have any say in the matter.*

The sweet smile returns to my face, contorting my cheeks to the point that they're aching.

"Where is it?"

I tell her the address.

"Isn't that awfully far from here?" She makes it sound like we're talking about the North Pole.

"I can arrange for a school bus to transport the kids to and from the place."

She eyes me, lips puckered as if she'd licked an unripe grapefruit.

My stomach starts to free-fall, a parachuter minus the gear.

"I'm not sure it would be the best use of our resources," she says.

Landon steps forward. "Perhaps you should put it to a vote and see what the other parents here think."

"I'm confident I can speak on behalf of the PTA members. Unlike you, Mr.—"

"Landon Reed." He holds out his hand to her. "I'm the kindergarten substitute teacher while Zoe Bryant is on maternity leave."

She shakes his hand without missing a beat. "Unlike you, Mr. Reed, my children have attended this school for the past few years. And during that time, I've had the pleasure of getting to know most of the parents. I know their wishes enough to be able to speak for them."

Kiera shoots Landon a look that Tabitha misses, one eye raised in an I-told-you-so gesture.

He winks at me, and without a word, raises his hands to his collar and unbuttons it. Tabitha doesn't say anything. She just watches him, a deer mesmerized by the oncoming truck lights.

She's so busy taking in the show, she misses the comical eyebrow dance Kiera levels my way. I have to squish my lips together to keep from laughing out loud.

Landon keeps unfastening his shirt, revealing his abs. And hot damn, they're a work of art.

I steal a quick glance at Tabitha. If her expression is anything to go by, she agrees with me one hundred percent. Her gaze is glued to the PG-rated strip show playing out in front of us.

"Sorry, weren't we discussing the Christmas show?" Landon casually says, as if it's normal for him to strip in front of a bunch of gawking women.

A few moms run their tongues along their lower lips. I wouldn't be surprised if they rush to sign up for parent-teacher conferences once they find out he's a teacher here—even if he isn't teaching *their* kid.

"Like I already told Chloe, I'll have to put it to a vote." Tabitha's gaze remains locked on his well-honed abs.

"Works for me."

Tabitha drags her eyes away from Landon and excuses herself to start the meeting.

Grinning, he leans in close to me, his warm breath brushing against my cheek. "Looks like you owe me a date."

"You've got yourself a deal." It's the least I can do, especially if the vote goes in favor of the Christmas show.

Landon re-buttons his shirt, and we take our seats in the front row.

Tabitha walks up the stage steps and turns on the mike. "Hello, everyone," she says in her take-charge voice, and everyone sits. "Thank you for coming tonight. We've got a busy agenda for this evening since we have to talk about a few fundraisers still planned for the school year. But first, I'd like to welcome Dalhousie Elementary's newest teacher, Landon Reed."

She points to where we're sitting. Excited murmurs spread through the gym.

"Landon is covering for Mrs. Bryant's kindergarten class while she is on maternity leave. First on our agenda is the Christmas show. Zoe is the one who usually organizes the event, but now that she's away, we don't have anyone with a theatrical background to do it. But Miss Reinhart has asked us to allow the kids to entertain the residents at Golden Sunshine Retirement Village during their Christmas party.

"Since we don't have Zoe's skills to help us with this, I thought we should put the idea to a vote first. Hands up if you believe we should risk the school's reputation within the community and organize a Christmas show for the retirement home."

Landon shoots up out of his seat. "That's not entirely true about not having anyone with a theatrical background to help Chloe. I happen to know someone who might be willing to help."

"You do?" I ask him, keeping my voice low so Tabitha doesn't hear me.

He nods but doesn't elaborate.

"Might?" That comes from Tabitha.

"I'd have to check with her first. But I'm sure she would be delighted to help. She loves kids."

Tabitha doesn't look too sold on his comment, but she gives him a slight nod of acquiescence. "All right. Raise your hand if you think Miss Reinhart should organize the Christmas show."

I look over my shoulder to see how the vote goes. Tabitha's groupies exchange a glance as if trying to figure out how she wants them to vote. Over two-thirds of the remaining teachers and parents raise their hands.

"Well, it looks like the show will go on," Tabitha declares with as much enthusiasm as a kid faced with liver and onions for dinner.

I lean toward Landon and whisper, "Thank you!"

"You're welcome," he replies, voice low and rough, the sound igniting mini fireworks between my legs. *Damn, the man's dangerous.* "Are you free after this for our second date?"

"First date."

He laughs under his breath. "All right, first date, if believing that helps you sleep better at night."

"First date...and only date," I remind him, hoping I don't regret agreeing to it. In the world I left behind, when a man performed a favor, it always came at a cost.

A steep cost.

Like in *The Little Mermaid*, when Ariel gave up her voice to be with the prince. My grandfather was no different from Ursula, who demanded Ariel's voice in payment. I mean, sure, he didn't turn anyone into seaweed, but I wouldn't be surprised if someone actually did go swimming with the fishes and never resurfaced after asking for a favor and failing to pay the price.

Granted, all Landon is expecting is a date. But I hope I'm not making a mistake by letting a man help me, something I haven't done since escaping my family.

[TOP SECRET]

"Do you like country music?" Landon asks as he and I walk to our cars in the parking lot. The PTA meeting finished a few minutes ago.

"I can't say it's something I listen to regularly, but I don't mind it."

He grins at me with that cocky smile of his. "I'm driving. I'll drop you off at your car afterward."

"I can drive." I really don't mind.

He throws me a caveman look that says, "Sorry, not happening."

It's clear he's a man who's used to being in control, so I let him have his way. On this. It doesn't matter who drives—and it's not like he's a stranger I've just met.

Well, mostly he's not a stranger I've just met.

Thirty minutes later, we're climbing out of his jeep in front of what looks like a giant red barn in a parking lot. Lively country music pours from inside. A neon sign on top proclaims the building is Brodie's Barbecue & Bar.

"This isn't what I was expecting." But I'm all for an adventure...as long as the adventure gets me to bed at a decent time. It is a school night.

"I figure you're the kind of woman who appreciates a great meal and a good time. And you can't do much better than this place."

"I'm not exactly dressed for this." Not that the red splotch of paint on my top spells "dressed for this" in most dating situations...unless you're going to a paintball center.

"You look great. No one's going to judge your clothing. But if you want to go somewhere else..."

"No, this is fine."

We enter the building. It's everything I imagined it would be. Almost.

Like with most restaurants, it has a lounge to one side. It's the dance floor in the middle of the restaurant that's unusual. Several people are partner dancing, including an elderly couple and a few kids who are bouncing around to the upbeat song.

"Hi, y'all," a woman in a black dress and cowboy boots says. Her dark hair is pulled up in a perky ponytail. "How many are in your party?"

"It's just the two of us," Landon tells her.

She glances at her device and grabs some menus from beneath the podium. "Follow me. How are y'all doing tonight?"

We tell her we're doing fine, and she seats us at a table not far from the dance floor.

"Will Whiskey be okay with you gone so long?" I ask Landon.

"He'll be fine. A friend of mine has been checking on him."

The waitress comes to the table soon after that, and Landon and I both order burgers and fries.

The song changes, and there's a stampede of people rushing to the floor. They move into position and start line-dancing along with the music.

Landon stands and offers me his hand. "Let's dance."

"I don't know how to do that." I gesture to the individuals, their movements perfectly synchronized.

"I'll show you."

I hesitantly take his hand and let him drag me to an empty spot on the floor. It's obvious this isn't Landon's first time doing the dance. He moves to the music as if he were born doing the line dance.

Me? Not so much.

I've never been super coordinated. If there's one word to describe me when it comes to sports and things like line-dancing, it would be awkward. Clumsy.

I bump into the man next to me because he went right and I went left. "*Oof*. Sorry."

He dips the rim of his cowboy hat at me and grins. "Not a problem, miss."

I move in the opposite direction and crash into Landon. He chuckles.

"Sorry," I tell him.

It takes me another few minutes to finally figure out the moves.

Too bad that's as the song ends.

Another one starts, and Landon takes my hand. He puts his other hand on my upper back and leads me through the upbeat song as best as he can, given my lack of coordination.

By the end of the dance, I'm laughing so hard at how bad I am at this, my cheeks ache. I can't remember the last time I've smiled this much.

"Wow, you're really good at this," I say, still giggling.

The music switches to a slow song. I expect Landon to release my hand and for us to return to our table. Instead, he pulls me closer, and his free hand slides south, along my spine. More couples join us on the dance floor, and he and I sway to the music. His gaze drops to my lips, and for a moment, I'm positive he's going to kiss me.

A longing stirs deep inside me, sweet and spicy and full of promise. I can't remember the last time someone kissed me.

I drag my gaze from his mouth and focus on the wall on the opposite side of the room. Anything to distract me from his lips, his eyes.

His thumb brushes against the curve of my back, setting off a series of delicious tremors along my skin. My gaze flicks to his.

He leans in, and I have no idea what to do. Despite what he claimed, this isn't a date.

My breath stalls in my chest, and I deliberated my options.

"Our burgers are here," he says, completely throwing me for a loop. That wasn't what I was expecting.

The air in my lungs escapes in a smooth *whoosh*.

"Oh, good," I lamely say. "I'm super hungry." Without waiting for him, I hasten to our table.

9

LANDON

"How's teaching kindergarten going so far?" Adam asks with a snicker, his voice coming through the speaker on my phone.

I dropped Chloe off at her vehicle after our date less than two hours ago, and then inconspicuously followed her home to make sure she got there okay.

Now, I'm sitting on my couch, watching a hockey game on TV while Adam is parked in his SUV outside of her apartment building, keeping an eye on the place.

It's not an ideal situation since we have no control over who enters and exits the building.

And that thought churns sourly in my gut.

It's another reason why Liam wants me to be Chloe's boyfriend and push the agenda of spending nights together. Clearly, it's been a while since he was single and dating.

Given that Chloe and I didn't kiss after our first date, I'm not sure how likely his plan will come to pass. The closest I got to a kiss was the one I planted on her cheek.

That was my choice—to leave her wanting more.

Things would be a lot easier if we could just tell her the truth, but I have no idea how to do that without revealing our true identities.

And that's a bridge we don't want to cross yet.

We want to draw Nikolai out, and this is the best way.

"Let's just say, I owe my kindergarten teacher a huge box of chocolates for putting up with me at that age," I say to Adam.

The laughter of my five teammates comes through the phone.

"That bad, huh?" Jayden asks.

"It wasn't what I was expecting, that's for certain."

I get them up to speed on the Christmas concert and my date with Chloe.

"She's already falling for your charms?" Adam asks. "Nice job, man."

"It's more about Whiskey's charms than anything. This little guy can charm the shit out of anyone." The little guy in question is snoozing contently on my lap while I watch the San Francisco Rock game.

I cringe as the Calgary Flames score. The Rock are now down two in the second period.

"Any word yet on who has the contract out on Chloe?" I ask them.

"No," Liam says. "The Feds can only say that whoever's interested in her also wants to locate Nikolai. The sole difference is, whoever has the contract on her wants to take him out. The Feds just want to lock him up for the rest of his life and destroy the mafia kingdom he inherited."

"Is it really that big of a deal if someone kills him instead?" Connor asks. "It would certainly save tax-payer money."

"If the Feds can lock up Nikolai, they can also take out other players in the crime family. That's their ultimate goal."

"Sounds great—except for the part where whoever has the contract out on Chloe will sweep in and deepen their network in the area," I say. "The reason they haven't so far is because the Orlov crime family is too deeply entrenched in this part of the world. The only way to gain control of the territory is to take out the entire family."

"Including those members who have nothing to do with the criminal activities?" Connor asks.

He's right. Chloe can't be the only innocent in this game.

"The Feds are working on that, too," Liam says as a Flames player lands in the penalty box. "It's a never-ending battle. But for the most part, it's *their* battle until they ask for our help."

"Well, who do we have here?" Adam says, voice on full alert.

"Who?" I ask, my heart suddenly pounding unexpectedly in my chest.

"It's a woman who doesn't live in the building." He describes her as best as he can due to the distance and lighting.

"Whoever it is, she isn't purposely hiding her face. So she's probably some innocent visiting the building."

"Can you tell what apartment she buzzed?" Connor asks at the same time I say, "Are you able to send us a photo?"

"I have no idea. Her body was blocking the panel, so I couldn't see which button she pushed. But I'm sending you her photo now."

A moment later, the image comes through on our phones.

What the fuck?

"Her name is Tabitha Windhouse. She's the president of the Dalhousie Elementary PTA." I give them the CliffsNotes version of what I know about her.

"Too bad we can't bug Chloe's apartment. Then we could hear if that's who Tabitha is visiting."

This is where being the good guy is problematic. You can guarantee the mafia has no issues bugging people's homes, vehicles, or phones if it suits their purpose. The same can't be said about the Feds or us unless there is approval from the higher powers. If they're caught illegally bugging someone, any evidence they collect could be inadmissible in court.

Which means the bad guys might win.

And no one wants that—except for the bad guys and their greedy lawyers.

I can't even ask Chloe the next day about Tabitha's unexpected visit. There's no way for me to explain how I know about it without drawing suspicion.

"Maybe Ava can get her to talk about it at lunch. She could ask her how tonight's PTA meeting went." I might not specify it, but the comment is directed at Liam—Ava's husband.

And Liam knows it. "I'm not comfortable dragging my wife into our case. It's enough that she talked to Principal Woodnut first to get permission for you to be at the school even though you're not qualified to be a substitute teacher. The less Ava's involved, the better.

"But I'll make sure she knows to tell me what Chloe says if she confides in Ava about why Tabitha was there."

That will have to do.

"Otherwise, I'll have to hope Chloe brings it up at lunch," I say.

"Connor, what can you tell us about Tabitha?" Liam asks.

Connor's our information guy. If there's anyone who can find out anything, it's him. Depending on the mission, he can often get information from his FBI contacts if the info isn't available to him through his normal channels.

I'd be surprised if he hasn't already done a background search on Tabitha while we've been talking.

"She was married to Tim Atkins, a prosecutor and a vocal advocate for giving white-collar criminals longer jail time. They've been divorced for a year now."

Apparently, Tim's creepy pastime when it came to Chloe didn't damage his career.

"They have two kids, both attending Dalhousie Elementary School. They share custody. She's the president of the PTA, which you're already aware of. She ran a high-end catering company before she married Atkins, and she's currently a full-time mother." He lists a bunch of other things, none of which set off any alarms.

"She could be here simply to talk to Chloe about the show," Adam says.

I wince at the hit made on the Rock player, which sends him flying to the ice. "Assuming that's who she's there to see."

"Keep us updated if you see anything else pertaining to Tabitha's visit," Liam tells him.

"Will do."

"Speaking of the show...Isabelle," I say, since I have her on the line. "What are the chances of your Grandma Josephine giving me advice about planning a Christmas concert for seniors?"

"Are you asking because she's a senior and knows that demographic, or because she's an Academy and Tony Award-winning actress?"

"Let's go with C: all of the above. Zoe's the one who's usually responsible for the school performances. But since she's on maternity leave—thanks to us—the planning all falls on Chloe. I've volunteered to help her, but I know as much about that sort of thing as she does. So I figured—"

"You'd get extra brownie points when it comes to becoming her boyfriend?" Isabelle asks, putting the puzzle pieces together.

"Yep, that pretty much sums it up."

"You do realize my grandmother doesn't like to do things half-assed, right?"

I laugh. "Yes, I do realize that."

"Chloe's probably thinking something along the lines of the kids singing a few songs. My grandmother will be envisioning something more along the lines of a Broadway-style production. But I can still ask her if you'd like."

"Yes, please." That should buy me more than enough brownie points.

Hopefully.

10

CHLOE

I pull into my parking spot at the school and turn off the engine. Before I have a chance to climb out of my car, Landon steers into the empty spot next to me.

He waves and gestures for me to wait a moment. I slide out of my vehicle and collect my purse and bag of supplies for the day.

"Mornin'," he says, coming around to where I'm standing.

"You ready for this?" This being his third day at school.

"Definitely. Isn't the number one rule when it comes to bears to never let them sense your fear?"

The corners of my mouth twitch. I'd hardly compare kindergarteners to a ferocious forest beast.

They're more like a combination of Pooh and Tigger: always eager for something sugary and ready to bounce off the walls.

"Good point," I say. "They'll be swinging from the lights if they sense your fear. And I'm sure William, the janitor, wouldn't appreciate that."

He laughs, and we walk toward the building. The crisp November air is heavy with the promise of rain, and I can almost feel my waves frizz in the lingering dampness.

"Did you have a good night after I dropped you off at your car?" he asks.

"It wasn't too eventful. I talked to my accountant for you. Sorry, he's too busy to take on new clients."

Landon's expression says my news doesn't surprise him. "That's okay. Thanks for asking. What else did you do?"

"I came up with a list of Christmas songs the kids can sing for the concert. Now, I just need to find someone who can accompany them. You don't, by any chance, know anyone who plays an instrument, do you?"

"Sorry, I don't. So other than coming up with the list of songs, did you do anything else exciting last night?" He doesn't sound particularly disappointed by the extent of what I've told him. It's more like he's expecting there to be something else.

"I watched some TV"—an old episode of *Outlander* because Jamie Fraser's accent is damn sexy—"but that's about the extent of it. What about you?"

Landon opens the side door, and we step inside the building. "My evening was pretty much the same. Except I worked on my teaching plans and watched hockey."

I laugh. "You sound as boring as I do."

After checking in at the office, we head to our classrooms.

"I heard the good news," Ava says, coming toward us down the hall. "That Tabitha agreed to let you do the Christmas performance." Her gaze flicks momentarily to Landon before returning to me.

"More like the parents and teachers at the meeting agreed it would be a good idea. She was outvoted. So it looks like she won't be pulling any strings to get the school board to prevent it from happening."

"And she was okay with that?"

"She kept whatever she was thinking off her face, but I suspect she's waiting for me to screw up with the show so she can say 'I told you so.'"

Landon and Ava exchange glances again. "Which is why we won't give her that satisfaction," he says.

I SWEAR IT MUST BE A FULL MOON...OR WHATEVER IT IS THAT turns cute, curious kids into abominable monsters.

Even my typically sweet little angels have sprouted horns in the past few hours.

And I'm not referring to unicorn horns.

Melissa goes racing around a table, squealing as Anton chases after her with a blue monster puppet on his hand.

I remove it. "Is there any particular reason you're chasing Melissa around the classroom when running inside is against the rules?"

He lifts his chin, the confidence of a cutthroat attorney oozing from him. "She took my pencil."

"Did not."

"Did too."

"Did not."

"Did too."

Melissa's closing statement involves sticking her tongue out at him.

"All right, you two." I remove a pencil from the holder on my desk and hand it to Anton. "Go sit down and practice writing the letter L. Both lower and upper case."

"But—" Melissa starts to say.

"No buts. We don't run in the classroom, and you both know that. You save it for outside. And you don't use poor Wilfred here for terrorizing other students. He's a happy monster and doesn't like to be wrongly stereotyped to be something other than what he is."

"What does ste-re-type mean?" Jackson asks, his eager face peering up at me, even though he wasn't part of the initial conversation.

"It means believing that everyone from the same group has the same characteristics. For example, assuming a really tall man is a great basketball player. For all you know, he doesn't like sports. Or maybe he's a talented hockey player and doesn't know the first thing about basketball."

At "hockey player," Landon's image pops into my head.

Nope, not happening, I tell my brain, my body, and anything else that's listening.

I'm not going there. Being a single woman is a good thing.

I'm independent.

I'm strong.

Okay, the lack of sex in what feels like a lifetime sucks, but there's definitely more to life than being in an intimate relationship with a man.

Besides, that's why God invented vibrators.

"Wilfred might be a blue monster," I say, "but that doesn't mean he's scary because the monster stereotype says he's mean and scary. He can be a giving monster who likes to help everyone he sees. And just because he's a blue monster doesn't mean he loves cookies. Does that make sense?"

All three of them nod and return to their tables.

By the time the final bell rings, I'm more than ready to go home and soak in the tub. But before I can do that, I'm scheduled to volunteer at the retirement village. I haven't told Mathilda yet that the Christmas show doesn't have to be canceled after all.

The kids all leave, and I pack up my stuff to work on at my place.

Landon pokes his head in the classroom, like he's done several times during the day. "Are you going home now?"

"No, I'm volunteering first at the seniors' residence. I'll see you tomorrow."

"I'm almost finished in here. Wait for me, and I'll walk you to your car."

I brush him off with a wave of my hand. "You don't need to do that. It's not like the school's in a bad neighborhood."

He opens his mouth, as if he's going to say something, but whatever that was is interrupted by the ringing of his phone. He glances at the screen, gives me the universal sign for "wait a second," and answers it.

He turns around, talking to whoever's on the other line, and strides back into his classroom.

Not wanting to stick around and feel like I'm eavesdropping, I grab my purse and coat, and leave.

The weather isn't any better since this morning. The air is chilled and damp from the earlier dump of rain, and large puddles dot the near-empty parking lot.

At my car, I glance at my front tire, and a silent curse rushes through me like a gush of wind.

Fuckadoodle.

My tire is flatter than a stepped-on chunk of Play-Doh.

I let out a hard breath and crouch to examine the wheel.

Footsteps approach from behind. Before I have a chance to turn around to see who they belong to, a gloved hand covers my mouth and nose. My heart rate screeches to a halt, and a surprised scream jostles loose from me, the sound muffled by the hand.

I'm roughly yanked to my feet, and a thick arm pins me to a large, hard body.

Even without seeing who it belongs to, I know the man holding me isn't Landon.

I struggle and squirm and kick at him. He tightens his grip, squeezing the air out of me like the coils of a giant serpent.

A giant serpent with feet.

My attempts to escape are getting me nowhere, so I lift my foot and stomp it. Hard.

My shoe makes contact with the instep of his foot.

"Fucking bitch," he hisses in my ear.

But alas, the attack on his foot isn't enough for him to release me.

It is enough, though, to surprise him, and his grip loosens slightly. So I do it again.

"Fucking stop that," he growls.

"Go to hell."

That's what I say. All he hears is a muffled noise that sounds unrecognizable at best. For all he knows, I've just asked him to color in a picture of a friendly dinosaur.

I keep squirming...

Until I feel the cold press of metal against the side of my head.

I freeze.

"That's fucking better." His palm on my mouth shifts, allowing me to breathe a little easier.

Literally, not metaphorically.

"I'm going to remove my hand from your mouth, and then we're going to take a little walk to my van. You're not going to struggle or call out for help. If you do, you're a dead little lady. Am I perfectly clear?"

I can barely hear him, my pulse pounding loudly in my ears, but I nod my head, understanding a lot more than he realizes.

As promised, his hand disappears from my mouth—and my lungs plead for me to take a long drawing breath of the soothing cool air. To ease my throat, which is sore from screaming.

Dampness rolls down my face, but I can't tell if it's from tears or random raindrops that are beginning to fall.

The gun moves from my head, and he pushes me forward. I

can no longer see it or feel it, but it's there all the same.

I'm not a religious person—but that doesn't stop me from praying to God or any other deity who can help me. Praying that I'll get through this.

That I won't become another statistic.

There are so many things I have left to do on this planet, like the Christmas show.

If I don't survive this, there won't be a Christmas show. Not unless the teachers go through with it to honor my final wishes.

Maybe God will let me return to earth to watch it.

Or I could be an angel and help with spreading good deeds.

I could live with that (no pun intended).

The man tells me where to go—which isn't the same place where I'd like to tell *him* to go.

When faced with death, people go through many phases before acceptance kicks in. They bargain with God. They promise they'll be a better person if he lets them live.

They'll give up smoking or drinking too much coffee or whatever their vice is.

I'm too busy for that.

I'm planning all the things I can return to earth to do as an angel—like Clarence in *It's a Wonderful Life*.

I'll probably have to start small. Rookie stuff. The bigger good deeds are no doubt delegated to the more experienced, senior angels.

This is assuming I'll return in human form. Maybe God has a sense of humor and will send me down as a dog.

A cute dog like Whiskey.

The thought that I'll never see Whiskey again clenches my heart in an invisible fist. It tightens when I realize I might never again see anyone I love.

My friends.

My mother.

My cousin Nikolai.

What are the chances if I return as an angel, I'll get to see the people I love again?

That's the last thought I have before I'm suddenly free of the man's arms and stumbling to the ground.

My hip lands hard on impact with the asphalt, breath jolted from my lungs.

For a stunned moment, I lay sprawled on the ground, attempting to make sense of everything.

Landon is a few feet from me, fighting the man who grabbed me. His fist flies toward him. The man ducks back, avoiding it.

I glance around, searching for something that might help level the odds in Landon's favor.

A gun lies on the asphalt a few feet from me. But I have no idea how to use one, and I don't want to accidentally kill Landon or seriously injure him.

I scramble up and push the gun aside with my foot, hiding it behind a garbage can in case the tables should turn to the bad man's advantage. That's when I spy a tree branch on the ground—a gift from heaven.

I dive for it.

The branch is heavy in my hand, but not heavy enough to keep me from hoisting it up. I adjust my hold on it like it's a baseball bat.

Landon ducks the man's fist and lunges forward. The man reverses a step.

And I swing the branch with every ounce of strength I possess—and then some—aiming for behind the man's knees, relying on momentum to work in my favor.

The element of surprise works to my benefit. He stumbles back. Before his attention can return to Landon, Landon levels a blow at the man's head.

He goes down in a crumpled heap.

For a minute, all I can do is numbly stare at the man passed out on the ground while Landon checks him out. I open my mouth to say something, anything, but the words are too stunned to leave.

Every cell in my body vibrates, and I can feel myself start to shake.

"Thank you," I finally manage to get out as Landon straightens. "He had a gun, and...and he was going to take me somewhere, but I don't know where."

Now that the dam has been torn down by that simple thank-you, the remaining words come out in an unstoppable gush. "He must have dropped the gun when you jumped him. I knocked it away so he couldn't grab it."

Landon slowly approaches me as if I'm some sort of wounded animal that he's afraid will claw him if he gets too close. "Did he hurt you?"

I shake my head.

Landon wraps his arm around my shoulders. "You're shaking."

"Oh, I just thought we were experiencing an earthquake," I joke. Well, attempt to joke. It comes out clumsy and falls flat on its face.

"You're in shock. Let me drive you to my place. Whiskey might help."

Now that he's said it, I wouldn't mind cuddling the bundle of fluffiness. It might help distract me from what happened.

"Shouldn't we call the police?" My voice is still shaky.

"I'll do that now. They can interview you at my home."

"What about the gun? We can't just leave it and him here. A kid might find the gun and hurt themselves or someone else. And he might regain consciousness and escape."

The last thing I want is for him to attack another woman, one who doesn't have a guardian angel named Landon watching over her.

He nods. "Okay, I'll call them now. But you need to sit." He's got a point there. I'm not sure my legs will keep me upright much longer.

He assists me into his jeep and turns on the engine. "This should help warm you up."

He doesn't climb into the driver's seat. Instead, he shuts the door and tracks down the hidden gun while talking on his phone.

He returns to the unconscious man and removes a gun from the holster I didn't know Landon was wearing. It was hidden under his leather jacket.

Standing over him, Landon starts talking to him, the gun pointed at the creep. The man shifts his body slightly. He then stills, probably realizing my guardian angel is packing a weapon, and the man no longer is.

I should be shocked that Landon is standing there holding a gun. I hate guns, especially given their criminal links to my family. But after what I just went through, I couldn't care less that he's packing heat. I'm just thrilled he showed up when he did.

Landon continues talking to the man. I can't hear anything he says over the engine's purr and the heat blasting through the vent.

After what feels like a lifetime, a black SUV and a cop car pull up. A man and woman climb out of the SUV and walk to where Landon's standing, guarding the downed man.

They look like plainclothes police or detectives. All three individuals have what appears to be a discussion with Landon. He does most of the talking and points to where I hid the gun.

I continue watching them, trying to process everything that happened since I left the school. I especially pay attention to Landon. He seems more at ease with everything going on than I would expect from a teacher.

Like this is an everyday occurrence for him.

Like he was a cop in another lifetime.

Eventually, their discussion ends. The cop removes a pair of handcuffs and clicks it onto the bad man's wrist. The entire time he talks to him, possibly telling him his rights. The bad guy doesn't say anything, his expression blank.

The cop and the male plainclothes officer drag the criminal off the ground and shove him into the back seat of the cruiser.

The woman walks to where I hid the gun and bags it as evidence.

Landon returns to the vehicle and climbs into the driver's side. "How are you doing?" His brow crinkles with concern.

"I've been better."

He puts the jeep into reverse.

"Aren't the cops going to interview me about what happened?" I ask.

"I've told them everything I witnessed. But they might be over later to talk to you if necessary. Do you have any idea who the man was?"

I shake my head. "I've never seen him before." And I'd be more than happy to never see him again.

"Okay. Let's get out of here."

"I can't," I say, coming to my senses. "I need my car, and I'm expected at the seniors' home."

"You can let them know you won't be in today. One of my colleagues can fix your tire and bring your car to my place."

"Colleagues?" My state of shock must have addled my brain. Nothing he's saying makes sense.

11

CHLOE

Landon parks his jeep in his garage and helps me down. Even with the heater blasting on our way here, a chill penetrates deep in my bones.

He scoops me up in his big strong arms—a sweet caveman to the core.

"I can walk," I tell him. Not that I mind being in his arms. Maybe I can borrow some of his heat to banish the chill.

"I know you can." He carries me to the door leading to the house.

It's probably just as well, even if it's a short distance. I'm not sure my legs are on speaking terms with me yet.

He lowers me to my feet. I quickly miss his heat.

He unlocks the door, steps inside, and turns off his security alarm. He's five steps above me in that department. The closest thing my building has to security is the buzzer for a tenant to let you inside the front door.

And even that isn't a deterrent for anyone who wants in. Mrs. Rayne is hard-of-hearing and has a tendency to open the door for anyone who presses the buzzer.

A little bark comes from the laundry room.

Just what I need.

I kick off my shoes, and without saying anything to Landon, I head that way. As expected, Whiskey is in his crate. "Hey, little fella. I could use some cuddle time from the sweetest guy around."

"Are you referring to the dog or me?" Landon says behind me.

I laugh. "The dog. Definitely the dog. Is it okay if I remove him from his crate?"

Whiskey answers for Landon with a little *woof* and touches the metal door with his good paw.

Landon chuckles. "There's your answer."

I open the door and remove the puppy, so he doesn't try walking with his injured leg. I cuddle him to my chest. He reaches up and licks my chin.

I smile at him. "Thanks, I needed that."

"I should probably take him out to do his business."

Looking around for Whiskey's leash, I say, "I can take him." It's not like I have anything better to do. Watching the puppy poop might be a great distraction.

Okay, maybe not.

Landon removes the leash from on top of the washing machine. "Go sit on the couch and call the senior center to let them know you won't be volunteering today."

"But I have to go." I want to tell Mathilda that the Christmas concert doesn't need to be canceled.

"No, you don't. You're still shaken. Plus, you and I need to talk about something."

That piques my curiosity. "What?"

"You'll find out soon enough. Now go sit. Or else I'll throw you over my shoulder and take you to the couch myself." The humor in his tone is overridden by the gleam in his eyes of someone who doesn't accept no for an answer very often.

He holds out his hands for Whiskey. I pass him the little furball.

The furball gazes adoringly up at him.

"Are you sure you don't want to adopt him?" I ask. "He really likes you."

"I like him, too, but that doesn't mean I want to keep him for the long term. I'm just the temporary home until he finds something better."

If you ask me, Whiskey has already found something better, and he agrees with my assessment.

Landon grabs Whiskey's leash and heads for the front door. I sit on the couch in the living room and phone Mathilda. I explain why I won't be able to volunteer and tell her the good news about the concert.

"That's wonderful! Thank you so much, Chloe. The residents will be thrilled when they hear the great news."

The warmth from her words fills me—her concern over what happened, the relief about the show. It chases away some of the residual chill that remains even after holding Whiskey.

We talk for a few more minutes until I hear the front door click shut, and I end the call.

Landon enters the living room and places Whiskey on my lap. "I'll be back in a minute."

He heads to the kitchen and returns soon after with two glasses containing an amber liquid. He hands one to me.

I take it from him and sniff it. "What is it?"

"Whiskey."

"When you said whiskey would make me feel better, I thought you meant this little guy." I nod at the puppy in question.

Landon shrugs and sits next to me.

Whiskey—the puppy—settles himself on my lap.

I sip the lukewarm liquid. It burns going down, and I cough.

The movement nearly bounces Whiskey off my lap. "Sorry," I tell him, my eyes tearing up from the drink.

He gives me a happy, unperturbed doggy grin and settles himself again.

"You said you need to talk to me about something," I say to Landon, still curious at what he has to tell me. Happy to talk about anything other than the attack.

Landon takes a long draw of his drink, but unlike me, he doesn't cough. "I'm not exactly an elementary school teacher."

"That's right. You usually teach high school."

He shakes his head, the movement slow and emphatic.

"You don't usually teach high school, either? But you're a substitute teacher, right?"

"Nope. I work for a company that people hire for security purposes."

"You mean you install security devices in homes and businesses?"

He laughs under his breath. "Nothing like that."

"So, like a bodyguard?"

"It depends on the individual client's needs. There are other things we do, too."

I nod as if I understand when in truth, I'm on the opposite end of the spectrum. "Okaaay. If you're not a substitute teacher, why are you at my school pretending to be one?"

"Because our client believes your life is in danger."

"Danger? I teach kindergarteners. How can my life be in danger? I mean, other than what happened at school. But that was a random attack. It could've happened to anyone."

And that's when I get it—helped along by Landon's serious expression. "It wasn't random, was it? Is this because of my family?"

Well, doesn't that just poop all?

And to think that all this time, I'd thought that by turning my back on my family, I would be free from the lifestyle I wanted nothing to do with. But in the end, it had been little more than an allusion.

Once you become part of that family, there's no escaping.

I'd heard stories over the years that people who worked for my grandfather but then wanted out ended up swimming with the fishes—or the sharks.

At first, I'd thought it was nothing but a myth, like Greek gods, dragons, and Cyclops.

I was wrong.

Just like I was wrong in believing I had truly walked away from my family.

Nothing could be further from the truth.

"My client found out a contract had possibly been placed on your head. After what happened today, it's no longer a possibility. It's very much true." Landon doesn't seem too thrilled about that.

That makes two of us.

"Your client? Who's your client?"

He doesn't answer right away. "When was the last time you talked to your cousin Nikolai?"

That gets a startled response from me. "Nikolai? What does this have to do with him?" My words come out soft, little more than a whisper, as memories of my cousin flood me.

Of his parents dying fourteen years ago when one of our grandfather's enemies blew up their car. Nikolai's brother and sister were with them at the time. They were going to see the Philharmonic Orchestra, but Nikolai backed out at the last minute, more interested in attending a hockey game with his friends than attending the concert with his family.

He was sixteen years old at the time.

I was also supposed to be in that car. This was one of those rare times when being hit with the flu was a good thing.

Before Landon can answer, I guess, "*That's* who your client is? My cousin?"

It actually makes sense. Nikolai was always looking out for me when we were kids. If I got hurt, he would try to make the pain go away, even if it just meant bringing me cookies and watching my favorite show with me.

When a bully decided to pick on me at school, Nikolai was the one to put him in his place.

And when Nikolai heard a rumor about me that was going around school, he was the one to set everyone straight.

Landon hesitates for a brief second, then nods. "That's right. He wants to keep you safe. You weren't supposed to find out about it, though. We thought it'd be best if I become your boyfriend, so I'd have a logical reason for being with you all the time. Practically twenty-four seven."

"Twenty-four seven? You mean not only are we supposed to work together, I'm also supposed to *live* with you?" Nikolai and I haven't seen each other in years, but he should know me better than that.

I would never move in with a man I've only known for a few days.

That would be crazy.

"That's right," Landon confirms. "It's the best way to keep you safe until all the individuals associated with the contract on you have been arrested."

"Arrested? Since when did anything related to my family result in arrests? I mean, other than when members of my family are the ones who are being arrested. This is nuts." I'd start pacing while thinking things through, but that's not exactly feasible with Whiskey on my lap.

Not unless I want to remove him.

Which I don't.

"I didn't escape my family and their criminal activities only to end up with a fake boyfriend who's also the bad guy."

Landon's eyebrow quirks up. "Bad guy? What do you think I am, a comic book villain?"

I wave off his comment. "You know what I mean. I have no intention of being yanked back into that family." I'm still confused by his earlier comment. My family does everything they can to avoid the cops and the FBI. They don't try to get people arrested.

They just kill them off.

"Is that's why you wanted me to wait for you so you could walk me to my car?" Another thought kicks me in the gut, knocking it out from under my heart. "That's the real reason you took me out last night to the restaurant, and why you want to help with the Christmas concert?" It wasn't because he liked me and wanted to help me out. It was because he was hired to be my bodyguard.

Landon cringes. Not a whole lot, but enough for me to catch it. "Yes, I'll admit they're part of it."

"So, you don't actually want to date me?" I think I do a pretty decent job of keeping the hurt from my tone and ignoring the real issue here. "And you don't really want to help with the Christmas concert?"

Landon finishes his drink in a swift move and lowers the glass to the coffee table. "That's not entirely true. I might not know the first thing about running a Christmas show, but I do want to help with it. And as for the dating part. Like you, I don't date. So we're all good on that."

"So, you were pretty much planning to use me for sex?" Why else would anyone move in with their new boyfriend or girlfriend after a few dates?

Landon rubs the back of his neck. "Yeah, we didn't exactly think that one through. We were more focused on keeping you safe without you discovering the real reason you and I were a couple."

Well, that's a relief. Kind of.

"You aren't even interested in me that way?" I'll definitely need more whiskey to get through this conversation.

Possibly the entire bottle.

I down the contents of my glass and return it to him. "Can I have some more, please?"

"Are you sure?"

I nod. Between what happened in the parking lot after school and Landon's confession, I require something that will make me...happier.

Dear Mom, I mentally write.

If you were my age and a hot man wanted you to live with him while he was protecting your butt, would you do it?

Oh, and what would you do if you escaped your Russian mafia family only for that family to want to drag you back in again?

Miss you greatly,

Chloe

Landon gets up and heads toward the kitchen. When he returns a moment later, the contents in my glass have been replenished, and he's carrying a bottle.

He hands me the glass and parks the bottle on the coffee table.

Whiskey—the puppy—snores on my lap, oblivious to the conversation and the storm of emotions brewing inside me: Happiness that Nikolai still cares about me and wants to keep me safe. Fear that someone wants to kill me. Disappointment that I'm nothing more than a job for Landon. Like all the men in my life, he had no intention of sticking around for the long run, even before I discovered the truth about who he is.

And those are just the main emotions.

My gaze sweeps over the living room and lands on a picture on the wall. I'm guessing it's Landon's family when he and his sisters were kids. There's something familiar about the lanky, dark-haired boy in the photo.

A soul-deep longing punches me in the gut—a longing for those simpler days, back when I was a little girl who was oblivious to the truth about my family. Back when chasing butter-flies and playing pirates with Nikolai filled my days.

"I'm sorry but I can't do this," I say. "I don't care what's at stake, I'm not being dragged into my family's web of lies and illegal activities. I'd rather take my chances with whoever has the contract on me."

"You're getting this all wrong, Chloe. My team and I don't play on the wrong side of the law. That's why your cousin hired us. He knows you don't want to return to that life, but he couldn't exactly go to the cops either. So he called in a favor with someone he knows, a mutual friend who Nikolai knew wouldn't betray him to the cops. I know you don't have reason to trust me, but you do trust Ava, right?"

"Does Ava know about all this?"

"She does."

I nod. "All right—it looks like I don't have much choice but to trust you. For now, anyway." Because no matter what I said a moment ago, I'm not interested in dying. No more than I am in going back to my family.

Besides, if Landon was known to the cops for being on the dark side of the law, they would've arrested him when they showed up at the school. "So, what now?"

"I continue to do as I've been hired to do."

"Protect me like some sort of bodyguard?"

"Yes—and the part about you being my girlfriend. Like I said before, it'll make things easier when it comes to explaining why I'm with you most of the time. More so than if we were just colleagues or friends."

That makes sense.

"But we've only known each other for less than a week, and we *are* colleagues. No one will believe we went from meeting each other for the first time one day to practically living together a few days later." A new realization hits me. "Does Principal Woodnut know you aren't a real substitute teacher?"

"She does."

"And she has no problem with that?"

"She knows why I'm working undercover. So no, she doesn't have a problem with it."

"Does anyone else at the school know?"

He shakes his head. "No. For now. But given the attempted kidnapping this afternoon, I'll have to bring in my colleagues to help keep an eye on things."

Ah, the mysterious colleagues he mentioned in the school parking lot after I was attacked. He told me he would explain once we returned to his place.

"You mean more substitute teachers? As it is, you were lucky Zoe started her maternity leave early. You won't get so lucky with anyone else. No one is scheduled to take time off prior to the winter holidays."

"I guess we'll find out tomorrow," he says in an equally mysterious tone. "Anyway, back to the girlfriend-boyfriend thing. Will you be okay with that?"

I swallow down more whiskey. The burn is still there, but not as strong as before. "Do I have a choice?"

"Not really, but I thought I'd ask."

I roll my eyes. "How considerate of you."

He chuckles. "If there's one thing you'll learn about me, it's that I'm a considerate man."

Somehow, I don't believe that.

"Well, I'm going to give the plan a hard pass," I say. "Like I said, no one will believe I'm dating you."

"Why not?"

"Because the entire time I've been teaching at the school, I haven't once gone on a date."

"You changed your mind when you met me." He says it so simply, like he really does believe that would be possible.

"No one will believe that either."

"So make them believe it. Consider it a matter of life or death."

"I'm not a good actress," I counter. Clearly, I'm also not a good lawyer. I can convince kindergarteners to not run around the classroom, but I can't persuade Landon that his plan is nuttier than peanut butter.

"You don't need to be. I'm not asking you to make out with me in the middle of the staff room...unless you want to. I wouldn't be opposed to it if you do." He winks at me.

I can't help but laugh at that. "So how do we do this? Just waltz into school tomorrow and declare that we're dating?"

He leans back against the couch. "I have no idea. I'm kind of rusty when it comes to having a girlfriend."

Oh, goodie. An amateur.

Not that I'm a pro or anything when it comes to having a boyfriend—beyond the two-year relationship that left me with a broken heart.

"But you have had one?" I ask, a little surprised by his revelation. Rusty generally means the person has had experience with the given situation.

"I did in college, and then a more serious relationship after that. She was my last and only girlfriend."

"*Only?* What happened to turn you off dating?" She must have really broken his heart or screwed with his brain.

"That's nothing you have to concern yourself with. My past relationships have nothing to do with my ability to be your fake boyfriend."

"I don't know about that. Maybe you were a crappy boyfriend, and you'll be an even crappier fake boyfriend." My mouth tilts to one side in a challenge.

His smile matches it. "I'm sure I'll be a quick study."

"Hmm" is the only retort I have left in me. I down the contents of my glass in one go and hold it out for him to refill again.

He flashes me a doubtful expression.

"The last one, I promise."

With an all-right-it's-your-funeral glance in my direction, he picks up the half-empty bottle and pours the liquid into both glasses.

"How's this living-together thing gonna work?" I waggle my index finger between us. There's a slight slur to my words, but nothing to worry about. "Are we taking turns staying at each other's homes? Maybe alternating nights and weekends?"

"You'll be moving in with me." He says it so matter-of-factly, like there was never a question of this being the case.

"Maybe I don't want to move in here." I give an unsteady wave of my hand to his living room.

It's a lie.

Well, a partial lie.

I love what I've seen of his place so far. It looks like it's been recently renovated, and even though the decorations are all masculine in design and color, the interior really is gorgeous.

"I like my apartment," I say. "Why can't you move in with me?"

"For several reasons. First, you have no security in your building. Anyone can easily get inside and have access to you."

All right, he has me there.

"And what's the other reason?"

"Your building doesn't allow pets, and I have Whiskey to consider."

I frown. "How do you know my building doesn't allow pets?" He's right, though. It doesn't.

"Because we've already looked into it."

" 'We'? Is this the royal 'we'?"

" 'We,' as in myself and my colleagues."

None of this should surprise me. They're associated with my cousin, after all. He's one of those individuals who would never leave a stone unflipped. To do so would be sloppy.

Our grandfather taught us that.

I glance down at Whiskey and gently stroke his soft head. That would be one perk of staying here. I'd get to have this sweet puppy in my life for a spell.

"How long are we talking about when it comes to us living together?" I ask.

"For however long it takes until the individuals who ordered the contract on you are in jail, and the ones who were hired to kill you meet the same fate."

I shudder at his words and sip my whiskey.

Oh, screw that.

I take a long draw of the body-numbing beverage. "So, we're talking a few days to a few weeks?"

"Something like that."

And what happens afterward? He leaves, and a new substitute teacher is brought in to replace him.

And everyone knows that I was dumped.

Oh, joy.

"What if we kept our fictitious relationship a secret?" I suggest.

"Then there's no point being in a fictitious relationship. We could just carry on as is. But we want whoever has a contract on you to know you're not a sitting duck. We want them to know you have a boyfriend who will make their life more challenging if they try anything."

"Wouldn't me having a bodyguard do the same thing?"

"If people think you have a bodyguard, it will result in too many questions. Questions we'd rather weren't asked. Plus, we want to draw out the person who is trying to kill you and put them away. That will be more difficult if they know my team is armed and dangerous. Then they're less likely to make mistakes and get caught."

I mull this over for a few seconds. Everything he said makes sense. But what do I know? I'm just a kindergarten teacher. "How's he doing? Nikolai?"

A shadow of some unlabeled emotion flickers briefly on Landon's face. "When was the last time you talked to him?"

I shrug. "Not for a few years. Not since I walked away from my family because I didn't like what they stood for."

"He's doing fine. That's all I can tell you."

I want to ask him if Nikolai misses me as much as I miss him, but I don't bother.

I'm not really sure if I want to know the answer.

12

LANDON

I hate this.

I hate lying to Chloe, but I don't have a choice. I'm doing this to protect her—or so I keep telling myself.

I hadn't planned on telling her that Nikolai hired us to protect her. She was the one who thought he had, and all I could do was go along with it. It seemed like the best way to discover if he's been in touch with her. But based on her answers and reactions, that would be a big no.

So basically, the one person we were hoping could lead us to him is as clueless about where he's located as we are.

Our only hope now is that he'll try to contact her—since he knows she's hanging out with one of the individuals responsible for his grandfather being in prison.

Note to self: Tell Ava that Chloe thinks Liam and his team are working for Chloe's cousin.

Yep, Liam's going to kill me for dragging his wife further into this mess, but there's not much I can do about that. I'm doing the job we were hired to do.

Chloe gulps down the contents of her glass. I remove it from her hands and set it on the table next to the half-empty bottle. She's already had three drinks, and she doesn't come off as someone who regularly consumes alcohol.

I don't want her to regret it tomorrow when she has to teach a bunch of noisy kindergarteners.

"Since you're moving into my town house for the time being," I say, "we should pick up some of your things from your apartment."

She flops her head against the back of the couch. "God, this is such a mess. How will I explain this to anyone? Kiera will think I've gone insane."

"I don't give a damn what everyone thinks. You're my number one priority. And I bet Whiskey doesn't give a damn either." I nod at the snoring puppy asleep on Chloe's lap. "I can guarantee he'll be happy you're my new roommate."

Chloe laughs. "You might be right about that. He seems to want to adopt me as his personal pillow. He's definitely the single perk in all this." She grins at me, the weariness from earlier after she was attacked fading slightly at the edges.

She might be grinning, but the humor from a few seconds ago vanishes from inside me. The flash of fear that coursed through me when I witnessed the man dragging her to her feet still lingers like the stench of ripe stilton cheese.

But that momentary fear wasn't the only emotion I experienced at the time. Pride had swooped in when she hit him in the back of the knees. Now, *that* was a whole new level of hotness.

She's a whole new level of hotness.

"By the way, thank you," I say. "I was the one who was supposed to save your life, and you're the one who saved mine."

Yes, the caveman inside me grunts at that.

But even the caveman has to concede it was worth it to see Chloe in action.

"You're welcome," she says.

"But how about we don't make that a habit. I'm supposed to

keep *you* safe, and I can't do that if you're going to try to be a hero."

She stares at me for a long second. "So, the next time that happens, I'm supposed to just stand there and watch someone almost kill you?"

I smirk at her. "Didn't realize you like me that way." Then I turn serious. "Do you know how many people die each year playing hero?" My words release as a growl, startling both Chloe and Whiskey.

He eyes me with confusion and barks.

"That's right," Chloe says to him, her tone sweet and silly. "The big bad control-freak has a problem when a woman has to rescue him."

She's partly right. I do like to be in control. When I'm not, it feels like a billion ants crawling all over me, nipping at my skin. Leaving me itchy.

But I'm definitely not a control freak.

Much.

"I've been hired to protect you," I remind her, "not the other way around."

"You obviously don't know me very well. If someone needs help, I'm not walking away and pretending they don't."

Which makes her the opposite of her family. The only ones they're truly willing to help are themselves. If they do help you, it's always at a cost.

I push myself to my feet and offer her my hand. "C'mon. Let's go to your apartment to pick up your stuff."

She peers up at me. "You really must think highly of yourself if you believe a woman will want to move in with you after one date."

"Ha! So you *are* admitting yesterday was a date."

"Given what I now know, I can say, without a smidgeon of doubt, yesterday in no way can be construed as a date." She laughs softly, then her gaze drops to her lap—and the sleeping furball there. "I don't think I can go anywhere. I don't want to disturb him."

"I'm sure he'll get over it, especially once you move in with me." I gently scoop up Whiskey. He peers at me with a doozy expression and yawns. "Bedtime, boy."

AT CHLOE'S APARTMENT DOOR, I TAKE HER KEY FROM HER AND enter first. "Stay right here," I tell her, pointing to where I want her to park herself while I check the rooms.

I return a few minutes later, satisfied the place is safe for now.

"Okay, you can start packing," I tell her.

"How long will I be staying at your place?"

"I'd say to count on it for a few weeks. Maybe a month." Or longer.

"A month?" She practically squeaks it. "I can't live with you for a month."

"If it means keeping you safe, you can live with me for a year if need be."

Her eyes widen, panic shining in them like the powerful rays from a lighthouse. "I never even lived with my ex-boyfriend before he'd had enough of me and vanished from my life."

"Are you afraid you won't be able to keep your hands off me?"

A sexy blush spreads across her cheeks, but she lifts her chin in equally sexy defiance. "I can promise you I won't have a problem keeping my hands off you." She walks into her bedroom.

"I notice you didn't make me promise to keep my hands off *you*," I say, chuckling as I follow after her.

She swivels around to me. "I assumed that wouldn't be an issue."

She's right about that. Not because I don't want to touch her. Because, fuck, there's nothing I want more right now than to see if her skin feels as soft as it looks. But I'm also a professional, which means keeping my hands and all other body parts to myself.

"Did you know Tabitha was in your building last night?" I ask. "Do you have any idea why?"

"She was?" Chloe doesn't even look in my direction when she replies. She removes a suitcase from her closet.

"Has she been here any time other than that?"

She places the suitcase on the bed and opens her top drawer. "Not that I know of. But it's not like I'm watching the front door twenty-four seven."

"Does she know you live here?"

"She might," Chloe says, rummaging through the drawer. "I have no idea what personal information the PTA is privy to."

She pauses what she's doing, arms full of panties and other unmentionables, and turns to scowl at me.

I catch a view of black lace and light pink satin before discreetly turning away. The last thing I need is the image in my brain of her wearing them.

Too late, my brain warns.

"How do you know she was here?" Chloe asks. "Were you stalking me?"

"No. I went home after the restaurant," I say, mentally scrubbing the image from my mind of Chloe in the bra and panties, and shift my attention to the various framed animated woodland animals on the wall. Chloe's artwork. "But one of my colleagues has been watching your building for the past few days. He spotted her going inside."

"Did your spy tell you how long she was here for?"

"About an hour or so."

She dumps the pile of clothing into the suitcase. "She must have been visiting another tenant."

"Can you think of anyone that might be?"

"Not really. There are a few single guys, but I can guarantee they aren't her type. There are also a few single women—again, not her type."

"What about married men?"

"Yes, there are a few married couples, as well as couples living together."

"Do you think she was visiting any of them?"

Chloe scrunches her lips together in thought. "Anything's possible. For all I know, she's having an affair with a married man in the building. Without knowing which apartment she was visiting, there's no way for us to know for sure."

[TOP SECRET]

AFTER CHLOE FINISHES PACKING, I DRIVE HER BACK TO THE TOWN house, keeping my eyes open for anyone who could be trailing us.

Rule #1 when it comes to missions: Keep your eyes on your surroundings—and assume everyone is following you.

Spies and criminals are a lot cleverer than portrayed in movies and on TV. They don't follow you from point A to point B, hoping you don't notice them. The smart ones work as part of a tag team. One individual might turn down a street to look like they haven't been trailing you for the last few minutes, and their partner takes up the pursuit.

Like with hockey players on the ice, communication is key.

So even though it looks like no one is following us, I always assume someone is. I never drop my guard. The moment you do, it's game over.

At my town house, I park my jeep in the garage. Chloe's car is on the street after Jayden fixed her tire and parked the vehicle there. "And just so you know, I'll be driving us both to school tomorrow."

"Why can't I drive myself?"

"Because it's harder to protect you that way."

"So, not only are we dating a few days after we met, I'm also living with you, *and* you're driving me everywhere? You do realize this means I've just set women back a few hundred years? What's next? You're going to tell everyone about our upcoming arranged marriage?" A huffed sigh follows her amusing mini rant, and she crosses her arms with a grunt.

"If it means keeping you safe, then sure."

"Why can't we just tell everyone the truth?"

"It's better they don't know about the contract on you. It'll make people nervous."

"Should they be nervous?"

"No. But my team wasn't only hired to keep you safe. They were hired to figure out who's got the contract on you and take out the man."

"By 'take out,' you mean kill him?"

If Liam's team was truly working for her cousin, then yes, more than likely, that's what would be expected of us—which we wouldn't do. But since we're working with the FBI...

"No, I mean, make sure he's locked away until his dying day. My team keeps to this side of the law."

"Unlike my family," she says under her breath. It's not a question, but I treat it as though it is.

From what I can tell so far, Chloe is nothing like her family —that's why she's no longer part of it, I guess.

"That's right," I tell her.

"Does that mean you've never killed anyone?"

"I used to be with the Navy SEALs. So, yeah, I've killed quite a few murdering bastards during my years of service."

"Doesn't that make you a hypocrite?" Her tone is like syrup, all hints of judgment hidden beneath the sweet layer.

"I'd like to think I'm more of a defender of the innocent and the defender of our right to freedom."

"Like a superhero?"

I laugh. "Minus the cape and superpowers."

She's quiet for a moment before asking, "If you could have any superpower, what would it be?"

"The ability to fly like Superman would be handy. The ability to ward off flying bullets would also be useful." Especially in my line of work. Bulletproof vests can only take you so far. "What about you?"

"I'm not sure if it's considered a superpower, but Wonder Woman's lasso would be great. I could use it to make sure people are telling me the truth. It would save me a lot of heartache."

I inwardly cringe since I'm not exactly innocent when it comes to telling lies. But I'm doing it for her benefit, not mine, as well as everyone else who is at risk because of her family's criminal lifestyle.

I remove the two suitcases from the trunk and bring them inside. I then return for the three boxes she also packed, containing her computer and some art supplies, and everything else she'll need for the next month or so.

"So, where am I sleeping?" she asks once I've piled everything on the foyer floor.

Good question. I hadn't exactly thought that one through—and neither had any of the team. "You can sleep in my room. I'll take the couch."

"Isn't this a two-bedroom town house?" she asks, eyeing the couch.

"The other room is my home office. It doesn't have a bed."

She looks me over and studies the couch. "Have you ever tried sleeping on that?" She points at it.

"Not really." Okay, I did attempt to sleep on it once. It's not exactly designed for someone my height.

"It's doesn't by any chance have a foldaway bed, does it?"

"Nope. What you see is what you get." Or rather, what *I* get.

"How about you take your bed and I'll sleep on the couch. It's the least I can do since you're putting your life at risk for me."

"It's all part of the job."

I don't give her a chance to argue. I pick up her two suitcases and carry them upstairs to what is now her bedroom.

13

CHLOE

The next morning, I round up my clothes and head to the bathroom. The door's shut, but when I try the knob, it isn't locked.

I push the door open...in time to see Landon standing on the bath mat.

Naked.

Beads of water glistening on his tanned skin.

Oh, my.

The polite thing to do would be to turn around or close my eyes—except I can't get my body to do either of those things.

I stare at him. In shock.

The man looks good with clothes on. But—*holy shish-kabobs* —out of clothes is a whole different story.

I figured he was lean and muscular, but I never realized how cut he is. He's like a piece of art.

And that includes his rather endowed nether region.

My face heats to a temperature hotter than hell, yet I'm still unable to get my legs or eyes to cooperate with my brain. "I'm... I'm sorry. I didn't realize you were in here."

Landon reaches for his towel, seemly unbothered by my

staring. His cock stirs to life under my gaze. "That's my fault. I should've mentioned the lock is broken." He wraps the towel around his hips. "I haven't had a chance to fix it. I'll get on that tonight."

The *Mayday, mayday, mayday* message my brain is sending finally makes its way to my legs.

I swivel around and bolt, fully prepared to hide out in his bedroom for the rest of my life.

Possibly for all eternity.

A few minutes later, Landon calls out, "Bathroom's all yours. I'll be downstairs if you need anything."

I cautiously peer around the bedroom door and catch his clothed backside retreating down the steps. Then I scurry into the bathroom and have my shower. The entire time I'm in the bathtub, water sluicing off my body, I try not to dwell on how only a short time ago, the water was caressing *his* soapy body.

Lucky water.

No, no, no—mind out of the gutter, please. It's been a long time since I've seen a naked male body, but that doesn't mean I should lust over him like a horny college-aged girl.

My mind might be on board with that plan, but my body has other ideas. Every inch of it tingles with need.

I chew on my lower lip for a fraction of a second and reach for the body wash. I pour a small amount on my fingers and touch my now-aching core.

My near-quiet moan a minute later is swallowed by the noise of the water raining against the bathtub....

BY THE TIME I STEP DOWNSTAIRS, DRESSED FOR MY DAY WITH kindergarteners, the heady aroma of coffee fills the air.

Exactly what I need after last night.

The knowledge that someone wants me dead wasn't exactly conducive to falling asleep. And it didn't help that I spent the night in a bed that's not mine.

A good portion of it was spent attempting to get comfortable in a bed that would typically be considered heavenly. The other part was spent watching the thin streak of light on the ceiling, willing it to turn into a flock of sheep, so I could count them jumping over an imaginary fence.

In the end, I fell asleep out of exhaustion.

And I'm sure everyone who sees me today will be able to tell I got very little sleep last night. The dark circles under my eyes don't exactly scream otherwise.

"I made you breakfast," Landon tells me, standing next to the stove, a cast-iron skillet in front of him. "There's coffee if you want." He nods toward the coffeemaker.

Two empty mugs sit on the counter, each with a different saying: "Holiday Survival Mug" and "Don't Get Your Tinsel in a Tangle."

I laugh and pick up the tinsel one, fill it, and add the proper amount of milk and sugar.

"I hope you like omelets," he says, expertly sliding the contents of the frying pan onto the plate.

I take a long whiff of the air. "It smells amazing." But that doesn't exactly surprise me. So far, Landon has proved himself skilled in the kitchen.

He hands me the plate and gestures for me to sit. There's already a plate in Landon's place, covered with an inverted metal bowl. He sits next to me and lifts the bowl, revealing another omelet.

I take a bite of mine. "Oh, God, this is incredible," I say around a moan, much like the one I made in the shower not that long ago—only a little louder this time. "What's the plan for this morning? Are we just showing up at school and letting everyone guess that we're a couple?" This is my preferred way of doing things, especially if it reduces the chance of anyone actually believing Landon and I are *together* together.

Of course, thanks to the dark circles under my eyes, everyone will assume I jumped into bed with him soon after he started working at the school, and I spent the entire night lost in hot passion and mind-numbing sex.

"I'm sure everyone will get the hint when we show up holding hands." His tone is all business, as if he says this kind of thing to women all the time.

I feel my lips twitch into a grin. "So no big announcement on the PA system?"

He grins back. "That probably won't be necessary."

We quickly finish breakfast. Landon lives a fair distance from the school, which means we have to leave early if we want to make it there on time.

And then we have to hope we don't get stuck in traffic.

We arrive at the teachers' parking lot at the same time as Ava. Kiera's car is already here, with my best friend sliding out of the driver's seat. Her eyes widen when she sees me sitting in Landon's jeep.

The expression isn't mirrored on Ava's face. She seems more amused than anything.

The two of them wait while we exit the jeep.

"Landon's now driving you to work?" The surprise on Kiera's face is mirrored in her tone.

Before I can reply, Landon threads his fingers with mine.

A move not missed by either Kiera or Ava.

Again, Ava doesn't appear too surprised by any of this. Kiera looks ready to drag me down an alley and ask me what the hell is going on.

She's familiar with my past—minus the part about my connection to the mafia. She's aware I'm gun-shy about relationships because so many men in my life have walked away from me. Men who were supposed to love me unconditionally.

She looks between us. "What's going on?" She turns to me. "Why is he holding your hand?"

"Because we're kinda dating," is my lame reply.

"Not kinda," Landon corrects, pulling me to his side. "We *are* dating." He gives my waist a little squeeze.

"Yes, what he said. We're dating. Nothing kinda about it." And since I don't already sound like an idiot, I add, "Yessiree. Dating. When two people go out together and start kissing and getting all romantic."

Kiera barks a laugh. "Thanks for the reminder of the definition for dating, given it's been a while since I've been on one."

The only way this could be more awkward? If I were standing here naked.

"So when did this all come about?" The skepticism in her tone has been dialed up like a burner on the stove cranked to high heat.

"Last night." Going with the truth never hurts.

She nods, clearly waiting for me to elaborate.

"We...we went out for dinner. Together. And...and we thought we'd give dating a try."

And the award for the worst actress ever goes to...

"Even though you two work together?"

"Well, I think it's great," Ava jumps in, smiling broadly. "I couldn't think of a more perfect couple." She hugs us both, but the hug she gives Landon is longer as she says something to him I can't hear.

He gives her a small nod and winks at her.

She shakes her head as she rolls her eyes.

"Now that we've gotten that out of the way," I say, "can we go inside?"

Judging from Kiera's expression, that was the wrong thing to say. She narrows her eyes at me.

Oops.

"I also moved in with him," I blurt as if someone had given me truth serum.

All things considered, it's amazing that my grandfather didn't banish me from the family as soon as I turned eighteen. Lying makes me squirm, and if the police or FBI had ever questioned me, I would've revealed everything I knew within for the first three minutes of the interrogation.

This is probably why my grandfather made sure I didn't know anything that could get him into trouble with the law.

At my news, Kiera's eyebrows come close to knocking against her hairline. "You. Moved. In. With. Him."

I vaguely hear Ava mutter, "Oh, boy," but I'm too busy trying to convey to Kiera with my eyes that I know what I'm doing to look Ava's way.

"That's right." I glance around me, searching for a rock to hide under.

"You've only known him for a few days."

"You do realize he's standing right next to me? He can hear you."

She whirls on him. "Then maybe *he* can tell me why the rush to live together. Or can I expect a wedding invitation by the end of the day?"

I choke out a laugh. "Definitely not."

Ava puts her hand on Kiera's shoulder. "I'm sure they have a good reason for moving so quickly. But whatever the reason, you can trust Landon. He would never do anything to hurt Chloe." She gives him a meaningful look. "Isn't that right?"

"Ava's right," he says. "Now, I don't know about you, ladies, but I need to get inside to prepare for my students." He doesn't give me a chance to object or stick around to talk to my friends. He tugs me along, still holding my hand.

And I willingly go with him.

Anything to escape further interrogation from Kiera.

"Well, I'd say that went well." My tone is a cross between a grumble and a snorted laugh. "Told you this wasn't going to be easy."

"Trust me, that's nothing compared to being shot at."

Hopefully, that's something I'll never have to find out for myself. Just the threat of it yesterday was bad enough.

I start to head to our classrooms. Landon has different plans and steers me toward the main office. "There's someone I want you to meet first."

We step inside. Instead of Jeanine standing behind the desk, a woman about my age with dark hair—complete with cool blue chunks—pulled up in a loose bun, is there in her place. Her knit dress is classier than you'd typically expect to see in an elementary school.

She's talking to a good-looking man whom I've never seen before.

At the sound of the door clicking shut behind Landon and me, the pair peers over in our direction. The woman smiles at me...then her gaze drops to Landon's hand, which is still encasing mine.

Her smile broadens.

Landon leads me over to the pair. No one else is in the office. Principal Woodnut's door is shut, which means she's on the phone.

"Chloe," he says. "I'd like you to meet Isabelle and Adam. They'll be working undercover with me in the school."

"I'm taking over Jeanine's job," Isabelle explains, in case I hadn't figured it out for myself based on where she's standing.

Adam nods his greeting. "I'm the unofficial assistant janitor."

"Unofficial?"

"That means I'm assisting the janitor, but I'm not getting paid for it, so I'm not on the school board's payroll." I'm sure the union will love that if they ever find out.

"We don't want to take any chances when it comes to the students here," Isabelle says, looking none too concerned about riling up any unions. "But we also don't want to draw any attention to the situation by having uniformed cops in the school."

A winter chill takes up residence in my gut and wraps me in its icy blanket. "Are you sure the students will be safe?"

"We're taking extensive precautions," Landon says. "In addition to Isabelle and Adam, we have two other men watching the building from outside."

Isabelle's lips move into what I'm assuming is supposed to be a reassuring smile. "No one will do anything to harm you or anyone else at the school. We'll make sure of it."

I hope she's right, because I didn't escape my former life only for it to be the cause of my death. That would further add to the suckage of spending Christmases without my mother and Nikolai for the past six years.

Doing my best to lock away my panic in a metal box, I smile at them. If Landon trusts his colleagues can keep me safe, then I need to give them the same level of faith, too.

"Well, it's nice meeting you." I make a show of checking the time on the wall clock. "I should go and set up for the morning."

I release Landon's hand and immediately miss its warm strength. His hand goes to the small of my back, and his thumb lightly caresses the skin under my blouse. Even though we're not talking skin-on-skin contact, a hum of electricity migrates through me from the spot.

It's been forever since my body responded to a man that way.

And look how that turned out.

Oh, well.

Fortunately, I'm aware that what Landon and I have is nothing more than smoke and mirrors. He'll be gone once I'm safe again. There are no expectations of happily ever afters.

Too bad I can't tell my best friend that.

KIERA FLASHES ME A LOOK THAT SCREAMS, "ARE YOU SURE YOU know what you're doing?" It's the fifth time she's done that in the past ten minutes while the four of us—including Landon—eat lunch in the staff room.

"Maybe I'm using him for sex," I blurt, half joking.

Three pairs of eyes—two wide as paper plates, one crinkled with suppressed laughter—stare back at me.

Oops. I didn't mean to say that out loud.

Especially when he and I won't actually be having sex.

Never mind that this sex dry-spell is growing old.

Way beyond old.

I shrug at their expressions. I mean, what can I say? Kiera is going to believe Landon and I are having sex, regardless of what I tell them. That's a perk of being in a relationship.

They know I'm not a virgin.

They know I'm not waiting for "The One" before having sex.

But on the other hand, Kiera also knew that I wasn't interested in having any more men in my life. And she also knows I'm not into one-night stands.

Neither of us is.

"So you're telling me the only reason you moved in with him is for sex?" Kiera looks as though she's not sure if she should be shocked or burst out laughing.

"Of course not. I moved in with him because he's a nice guy."

Ava coughs, which I suspect was to mask the laugh that

erupted from her. She presses her fist to her mouth and pretends to cough again.

"Because he's a nice guy?" Kiera annunciates each word slowly.

"And he has a cute puppy," I add, a small shrug in my tone.

That's all it takes. Ava cracks up, almost doubling in half from laughing so hard.

"Well, Whiskey *is* cute." I fail to keep the touch of defensiveness from my voice.

I look at Landon for confirmation. He's only doing slightly better than Ava when it comes to his suppressed laughter.

"She's right," he says. "Whiskey is cute. But I'm hoping she likes me for more than just my dog."

"Yes, apparently she likes you due to the sex," Kiera says drily.

Is it too late to hide under the table?

"There's a lot more to Landon than that." I gesture to the table currently obscuring his man parts. The man parts I saw on display a few hours ago—in case Kiera needs me to describe them. "He's a good cook. He's funny. And sweet. And good with kids. And is smart."

"Those aren't good enough reasons for moving in with a man two days after you meet him," Kiera says. "If he was merely your roommate because you need a place to live, then fine. I could see that. But the last I've heard, you aren't being evicted from your apartment, the building didn't burn down last night, and the pipes haven't burst, forcing you out of your home."

Damn. Why didn't Landon and I think of the burst-pipe excuse? That would've made more sense.

Right—it still wouldn't have flown with her. I could've easily stayed with her if any of those things had happened.

"I'm falling in love with him, okay?" The words sound as though they're being dragged through extra chunky peanut butter. "And yes, maybe we're moving fast with everything, but you have to trust me when I say I know what I'm doing. Besides, life is short. I could be dead tomorrow"—literally, dead tomorrow—"so what's wrong with living today like it's my last day?"

The cracking of my voice when I point out I could be dead tomorrow seems to be convincing enough. Kiera knows first-hand what I'm talking about.

Landon reaches for my hand on the table and gives it a subtle squeeze. Message clear. He won't let anything happen to me if he can help it.

Kiera gives me an appraising look for a moment and turns to Landon. "Do anything to hurt her, and you'll have me to contend with. Okay?" She narrows her gaze at him, then gives him the universal sign for I'm watching you.

I choke back a laugh.

Landon removes his hand from mine and extends it to Kiera. "You have yourself a deal."

They shake on it.

"Good, now that we have that out of the way, we need to talk about the Christmas performance," I say. We have less than a month to prepare for it.

"Are you free after work?" he asks me. "There's someone I want you to meet."

14

LANDON

"Where exactly are we going?" Chloe asks from the passenger seat of my jeep. School finished—without incident—twenty minutes ago.

All right. That's not exactly true.

There were several incidents. Like spilled paint. One kid testing out his newfound vocabulary—a word he'd heard his much older brother use.

A word that wasn't appropriate for his ears or those of his classmates.

And then there was the disagreement over whose turn it was to pick today's story. For a second, I thought it was going to end in a brawl.

"Sausalito," I reply.

"So, who's the mysterious person you want me to meet?"

"She's Isabelle's grandmother."

"Okaaay. Is there any particular reason you want me to meet her?"

"I figure she can help us with the show."

"So, she's a teacher?"

I grin at Chloe. "Nope." And return my attention to the road.

"What kind of background does she have that will help me with the show?"

"She has an Academy Award for Best Actress and a handful of Tonys."

From the corner of my eye, I see Chloe swivel abruptly in her seat. "Are you kidding me?" Her voice comes out as a squeak.

"I kid you not."

"And she's expecting us?"

"She is. She doesn't know who you are. She knows you're a client, and I'm working undercover as a teacher at the school where you teach. She's not aware of the specifics beyond that."

"Does she know why I need her help?"

"Yes. That part, I could tell her."

"Does she also believe I'm your girlfriend?"

I nod. "For the sake of the mission, it's better that she believes the same as everyone else. But you don't have to worry that she'll be like Kiera. She won't grill you about why things are moving quickly between us."

"Does she know our relationship has progressed at lightning speed?"

"I'm not sure if that part came up in the discussion Isabelle had with her."

"Will you at least tell me her name?"

"Josephine Ashworth."

That results in a squeal from Chloe. "Ohmigod. I know who she is. My grandmother was a huge fan of hers. I've seen every one of her movies at least three times. She's an amazing actress." Compared to a Jaguar, the speed of Chloe's words would've left it in the dust. "I don't even know what to say to her. I'm going to sound like an idiot."

I highly doubt that. If anything, Isabelle's grandmother will fall instantly in love with her.

"Just don't mention who your grandfather is or that you're linked to the Russian mafia," I warn. Josephine had a run-in with that side of Chloe's family not long ago. The less she knows about Chloe's link to them, the better.

Chloe snaps her fingers. "Oh, darn it. I was so hoping to wear my 'I'm an ex-mafia princess' ugly Christmas sweater for the show."

I laugh, keeping my attention still on the road. "Do you really have one?"

"Of course," she says on a laugh. "It's all the craze." Her laughter dies away. "Anything else I shouldn't bring up?"

"No, that's about it. Just stick to talking about the performance, and it will be fine."

I PARK THE JEEP IN JOSEPHINE'S MASSIVE DRIVEWAY AND ESCORT Chloe along the path to the door of the mansion. The late afternoon sunlight is rapidly dwindling with the approaching sunset, which is due in another hour or so. Not that you would know it from the thick cloud cover.

"Wow," Chloe murmurs under her breath. "Are you sure royalty doesn't live here?"

Hollywood royalty, perhaps.

Chuckling, I ring the doorbell. The deep melodic chimes of "Silent Night" play from within the house.

"Josephine doesn't believe in waiting until after Thanksgiving to get into the Christmas spirit," I say.

Chloe examines the huge, elaborate wreath on the door. "I can see that."

The front door opens. Juanita takes one look at us, and a big grin lights up her face. "Miss Josephine and the troops are waiting for you in the living room."

"Troops?" Chloe glances at me.

"She doesn't mean the military." Based on Chloe's expression, that's exactly what she's thinking. "Juanita is referring to Josephine's two closest friends."

"Ooh, you're in for a surprise. There's someone else who has joined them." Juanita takes our jackets, and I guide Chloe into the large living room.

"And there he is," Josephine says, grinning at us from a plush cream-colored couch. As always, the woman is elegantly dressed, as are all three of her friends. None of them lack for money. "And you must be the sweet Chloe my Isabelle told me all about. Have a seat." She gestures at the empty love seat across from her.

In addition to the usual two suspects—Henri and Liza—who are sitting on armchairs, a second man is seated next to Josephine on the couch.

"Chloe, these are my friends, Henri, Liza, and Andrew." She gestures to each of them with a wave; they grin at Chloe in turn. "Isabelle told me you need help organizing the Christmas show with your little tykes. She also mentioned you don't have anyone to accompany them when they sing. So this is where Andrew will be helping us out."

The man in question rubs his hands together. "As you'll soon see, I'm quite an accomplished pianist."

Henri snorts a laugh, an amused gleam in his eyes. "Quite the accomplished pianist?" He explains to Chloe and me, "This is *the* Andrew Stanton, world-renown pianist, and the winner of seven Tonys for the music and lyrics he wrote. Each one for an award-winning Broadway musical."

Chloe's mouth drops open for a heartbeat before she recovers herself. "That's incredible. Thank you."

She might be attempting to look composed on the outside, but I can tell from the way her eyes shine, she's trying not to squeal and bounce on the seat.

"No, thank *you*." His voice is crinkly and fragile like antique sheet music. "I can't remember the last time I got to play in front of an audience. I'm not exactly in high demand these days."

"That's why they call it retirement," Liza points out.

"Since when did retirement mean being sent to the valley to chomp on grass for your remaining days?" He winks at Chloe, who laughs.

And red-hot desire shoots straight to my cock. She really is beautiful, both inside and out.

I turn my head in time to catch Liza soundlessly applauding. Her attention is on Josephine, but she's bopping her head in Chloe's and my direction.

"I'll admit I have no idea what I'm doing," Chloe says, not noticing what Liza is up to. "The teacher who usually organizes the school shows is on maternity leave, and I don't have any musical talent."

"That's where I come in," Josephine says. "While I might not have the vocal pipes of my younger days, I can certainly teach those little tykes a few songs. Which ones are you looking at performing?"

Chloe lists six or seven. All the standard songs that have been around since the beginning of time.

"That's not bad, darling," Josephine says. "If you want to go the more traditional route."

"Or if you want to put those people in an early grave." Henri shakes his head. "What you need are some selections to liven up the party."

"Well, if Agatha York has her way, that won't be a problem," Chloe says. "Assuming she can sneak in the contraband rum for the egg nog. *And* the egg nog."

"Ooh, I'm liking the sound of this party more and more," Henri says. "You can sign me up for smuggling in the good stuff."

By the time Chloe and I leave the mansion, the music arrangement has been finalized. Chloe plans to talk to Principal Woodnut in the morning to expedite the necessary volunteer clearance for Josephine and Andrew.

"Thank you so much," Chloe says after she and I climb into my jeep. "The concert's going to be amazing."

She leans over and kisses my cheek. It's an innocent kiss. Nothing more than a show of gratitude.

Too bad my body doesn't quite see it the same way.

It buzzes with need and desire. Desire for her to do a shit-load more than just kiss me like that.

She pulls away, but the whiff of her light floral perfume lingers, tormenting me further.

WHISKEY'S SITTING IN HIS CRATE, LOOKING ALL SHADES OF hopeful when we walk into the laundry room.

"I'll just take him outside," I tell her. "We won't be long."

"I can start making dinner. Is there anything in particular you want?"

"I'm fine with whatever." I need to get away from her sweet scent for a few minutes and regroup.

Rule #2 when it comes to missions: Never sleep with your target.

Unless it suits the purpose of the mission—like seducing vital information from the individual.

But Chloe isn't technically my target. That honor goes solely to her cousin, Nikolai Orlov.

So when you look at it that way, there's no reason for my need to take a minute.

Try, she's not interested in you that way, dumbass.

I remove Whiskey's leash from the key holder and open the crate door. I fasten it to his collar and carry him outside.

The ground shines from the streetlights in the lightly falling rain. The dropping temperature from the approaching storm helps cool me down a few degrees. Enough so I can return to the town house a little less turned-on than before.

I lower Whiskey to the grass and let him go about his business.

When I step inside the town house a short time later, the delicious smell of dinner greets me. Chloe is busy in the kitchen, her attention on whatever she's cooking on the stove. And for a moment, I watch her swaying to the music from the speakers in the living room. She's caught up in the rhythm, her body moving in a way that makes mine, once again, aware of her.

So much for regrouping while I was outside.

But it's more than that. For a second, my brain entertains the thought of coming home every night to seeing her like that. In the kitchen. Making dinner. Looking incredibly sexy.

Wearing nothing more than my hockey jersey.

A need—one I'm not familiar with—stirs inside me.

Whoa, where the hell did that come from?

I push it away and walk over to join Chloe. "Whatever you're cooking, it smells incredible."

She smiles sweetly at me, causing the hunger for her to swell up like a hot-air balloon. "Thanks. Hopefully, it tastes as good as it smells."

She reaches out and scratches Whiskey behind his ear. He happily soaks up the attention, content to remain in my arms.

"I'm sure it will." Needing to pull my thoughts away from

how her body would feel against mine, I ask, "When are you volunteering next at the seniors' home?"

"Not until Thursday."

I nod. That's good. "I have a hockey game tomorrow night. This place is secure, but I still want one of my colleagues to stay with you while I'm gone."

"You mean like a babysitter?" There's no missing the grimace in her tone, even though it's absent from her face.

"I wouldn't put it exactly like that."

Her face brightens, and the stirring shifts to my chest, warming me up from the inside, in a way I haven't felt in a while. "Can I watch you play hockey instead?"

"Are you sure?"

She nods. "Positive. I haven't watched a game since Kiera's husband died. She stopped watching hockey after he passed away."

"Okay, I'll ask Isabelle and Jayden to join you."

"Jayden?"

"He's one of my other colleagues. He's engaged to Isabelle."

"Ahh, so I'll be the third wheel?"

"Not exactly. They'll be working, so they'll be keeping that disgusting mushy stuff on hold." I screw up my nose like a little kid who sees his parents kissing.

Chloe laughs and goes back to stirring the food in the saucepan. "How did you end up playing hockey? Why not football or some other sport?"

"That might have something to do with my dad originally being from Canada. He grew up playing hockey and was super talented. He just wasn't quite talented enough to be drafted into the NHL. He passed on his love of the sport to my sisters and me."

"Did they learn to play it, too?"

"Kathy, my oldest sister, didn't. She loved watching the game but was never interested in playing it. I don't think it even dawned on my father at the time to encourage her to play hockey. There was no question when I was born that I would participate in the sport. And that led to my little sister, Evie, playing it. Her theory was, if the sport was good enough for me, then it was good enough for her, too."

Chloe's eyes shine and she grins. "Was she good?"

"Definitely. She was as competitive as I was and put a lot of talented guys to shame when it came to skill." I chuckle at the memory of just how many guys she put to shame that were foolish enough to challenge her.

"What are your parents like?"

"They're great. My mom was a pediatric nurse. Now she spends her time refurbishing discarded furniture and selling it. Dad recently retired from his job and helps her. The two of them have created quite the little business." That keeps them both happy and busy.

But not too busy for Mom to ask from time to time about my (non-existent) girlfriends.

"What about your family?"

A cloud briefly crosses Chloe's face. She picks up a knife and starts chopping the parsley on the cutting board. "There isn't much I can say about them. As you know, none of them are in my life anymore." She chews on her lip for a second, as if contemplating whether to tell me something, but then releases it and shrugs. "But before that, my mom and I were close. She's an amazing woman. She always manages to find the bright side in everything."

Chloe grins, and it feels as though a cloud has drifted from the sun and the world is suddenly brighter. "I remember one time when I was eight years old, and I'd painted a vase for her birthday. It was bright and had lots of yellows and reds and oranges. Her favorite colors. I was so excited to give it to her, but I accidentally dropped it and it broke. Mom glued it together, but a piece was missing. It was impossible to use as a vase.

"Mom told me that it didn't matter because she had an even better use for it. She turned it into a plant pot. The hole worked great for drainage. The last time I saw her, she still had that vase with a plant growing in it."

Chloe's eyes grow shinier, but this time for a different reason. It's clear she misses her mom, but unlike me—who can easily hop on a plane and visit mine or any of my family—Chloe doesn't have the same luxury.

And for the thousandth time since I first learned about the Orlov family, I mentally curse Vadik and his criminal activities.

An itch to pull her into my arms bites me on the ass.

But before I have a chance to satisfy the urge, Chloe blinks away the tears and checks the contents of the saucepan. "So, how's the couch working for you? I really feel bad taking your bed." She dumps the parsley into the pot.

"Don't be."

"I can sleep on the couch. I fit it better."

"Yes, but you're the guest."

She returns the lid to the saucepan. "More like your fake girlfriend who's here for protection from the bad guys. That's hardly a guest."

"It's really okay."

"How about we alternate nights? You get your bed tonight, and I get the couch." She has that tone I recognized from Isabelle. It's her don't-even-bother-trying-to-argue tone.

I ignored it. "Look, tell you what, once I grow tired of sleeping on the couch, I'll let you know."

She opens her mouth.

"I've made my decision," I say before she can object.

"God, are you always this stubborn?"

"I like getting my own way."

"I can see that." She looks over at the living room, and a small frown furrows her brow. "Where's Whiskey?"

I follow her gaze and quickly scan the area. "Good question." A scowl takes up residence in my tone.

We both search the living room.

It doesn't take long to find him; you just need to follow the trail of stuffing spewed across the hardwood floor.

He and what was once a couch cushion are having a wrestling match in the foyer, and the cushion isn't coming out the winner.

"No, Whiskey," I say in a firm tone.

He ignores me, attempting to get his teeth into cushion again. He chomps onto the corner and drags it backward, almost colliding with the side table.

"Whiskey, drop."

Again, he ignores me, and I grunt.

Chloe laughs softly next to me. I scowl at her, which makes her laugh harder.

She bites her lower lip, holding in her laugh. "Sorry," she whispers, attempting to arrange her face in a serious expression but failing spectacularly.

She walks over to the puppy. "No, Whiskey." She disengages what's left of the cushion from his mouth. "We don't chew on pillows."

Whiskey barks at the cushion as she takes it away and hands me the drooled-on remnants. "I hope this didn't have any sentimental value."

"I'll live," I grumble, throwing the little troublemaker a stern glare.

Grinning a puppy smile, he wags his tail, not at all threatened by my expression.

15

CHLOE

A player from the opposite team slams into Landon, sandwiching my fake boyfriend between the plexiglass and himself.

"Ouch, that's gotta hurt," I say. The other team is currently down a point, which is making them rather testy.

"Landon's tough," Isabelle tells me. She's sitting on one side of me while her fiancé flanks me on the other side. Her very hot fiancé, may I add.

Jayden's super friendly, too. They both are.

"This is nothing compared to when he and I were serving in the SEALs," he says. "And some of our missions now aren't exactly about cuddling kittens."

Isabelle snorts a laugh. "When have *any* of your missions been about cuddling furry baby animals?"

I snicker and sip my hot chocolate, appreciating the skill level on Landon's team. Not that the opposition are slackers either.

"Landon's really talented," I say, stating the obvious.

I don't know a huge amount about hockey, but I do know

enough to appreciate the game and some of the intricacies of the sport. I learned from the best—Kiera's husband.

"He spent his childhood training for it," Jayden says. "And like most kids who train hard for a sport, his goal was to become a professional athlete. It didn't pan out in the end, but that hasn't killed his competitive nature."

"I bet he has a lot of girls after him because of that." All right, there's a slim chance I'm fishing for information.

Not that I'm interested in him that way.

Nope, not at all.

But there's something about Landon that has me curious to learn more about him.

From a purely professional standpoint, of course.

"He's had his fair share of them. But he's not a player, if that's what you're wondering."

I feel my eyebrows pinch together, and I look back at the ice. "He looks like a player to me. Isn't that the idea of him being out there? To play the game?"

"What I meant is that he's not a player when it comes to women. He doesn't hook up with a lot of women. But he's also not looking for someone to settle down with."

"Ahhh. Got it." I have no idea why Jayden's telling me that. As far as I'm aware, I don't have "Looking for a future husband" stamped on my face.

I subconsciously lift my hand to my forehead, as if searching for a message I didn't realize was there.

"Of course, I'm sure if he found the right woman," Isabelle says, "he'd be more than happy to be in a long-term relationship, maybe start a family. It's like anything. You don't realize you need something until you have it. And then you wonder how you survived without it." She smiles at him.

He returns it and winks at her.

I pretend they aren't having a moment, and I turn my focus to the game.

A player passes the puck to Landon, who races down the rink with it.

The goalie gets into position. Just as I figure Landon is going to shoot at the net, he passes the puck to his teammate.

The goalie had been thinking the same as me. He was prepared to block Landon's shot, and can't move fast enough to prevent Landon's teammate from scoring.

The puck flies into the goal, and Jayden, Isabelle, and I are on our feet, yelling our appreciation.

We aren't the only ones. The seats are filled with girlfriends and wives and kids, all cheering for someone they love on the ice. All being part of something meaningful to their boyfriend, their husband, or their father. All sharing something that gives them great joy.

They could've been at home, doing something else. But they chose to be here.

Just like Isabelle and Jayden chose to be here. I mean, sure, they're here as my bodyguards. But there's so much more to it than that. From the way people say hi to them or nod at them in recognition, it's clear this isn't the first or second or fifth time the pair have been at one of Landon's games.

This—their coming to his games to support him—is a normal part of their lives.

I can't remember the last time I've experienced something like that with a boyfriend. And strangely, it makes me feel like I belong here. That, for a few hours, I'm part of something bigger than just being a job for Landon and his two colleagues.

By the time the game is finished over two hours later, I'm bouncing with excitement. Things got tense in the second period when the opposite team's luck turned around. But in the end, Landon's team won—with Landon scoring the winning goal.

He eventually joins us at the main entrance, his dark hair damp. "So what did you think?" he asks me.

I fling my arms around his neck, surprising us both, temporarily forgetting we're not alone. Isabelle and Jayden are with us.

But as his girlfriend—okay, fake girlfriend—it's my duty to show him how amazing I believe he is.

"It was great. *You* were great."

Before I have a chance to release my arms from around his neck, he wraps his free arm around my waist and pulls me close. "Glad you enjoyed it."

"Definitely. I can't wait to see your next game...." The enthusiastic words quickly fizzle in the air.

Because of what they imply.

Naturally, I'm hoping whoever wants me dead will be caught ASAP. But once that happens, Landon will move on to his next mission, and I'll move on with my life.

A life without him in it.

And that includes no more of his hockey games.

"When's your next game?" I ask, only too aware that my body is tingling where we're touching. I release my arms from around his neck.

My body shouldn't be reacting this way. Landon works for my cousin, and as much as I love Nikolai, he's still the one who's no doubt taking over my grandfather's role of crime boss. He's still the bad guy.

Which makes Landon the bad guy by default. Right?

Except Landon has already told me that he and his team work on the right side of the law—and that's why Nikolai hired them.

Plus, Landon is nothing like the men who associated with my grandfather. Those men always left me with the sensation of a thousand tarantulas crawling over my body.

But with Landon, that's not the case. Nothing about him has set off my "bad guy" alarms.

"Saturday," Landon says, answering my question.

"Do...do you think by then you'll have caught the person who wants me to disappear?"

"That would be preferable. The sooner everyone involved is in prison, the better. Is it likely?" He shakes his head.

For some strange reason, relief rushes through me at his words, like a warm summer breeze.

But the relief isn't from the thought of having my life back, which, according to Landon, isn't going to happen soon. It's for a reason I don't want to put a name to.

"Can I see your next game?" I ask.

Landon threads his fingers with mine. "That can be arranged."

"You really were great out there."

"I think you brought me luck."

From beside me, Isabelle snickers.

"What?" I ask her, confused at why she's laughing.

"I...Jayden just told me something funny?"

I look at him, waiting for him to explain. He doesn't say anything. He stares at his fiancée with the same level of confusion that I feel.

"What are your plans for Thanksgiving?" Isabelle asks as we head to the vehicles. I drove to the arena with her and Jayden, but I'll be returning to Landon's town house with him. "Are you spending it with family?"

"I don't exactly have a family anymore. Or at least not a family that I'm part of," I say. "Which means I don't get to spend the holiday season with them. It was part of the deal I made to gain my freedom from that life."

I don't need to mention what life I'm referring to—they all know.

"What do you usually do for Thanksgiving and Christmas?" Isabelle asks.

This why I don't usually tell people about my holiday plans. Being on the receiving end of their pity is never fun.

"Watch a lot of bad Christmas shows and drink eggnog." I laugh. It's neither forced nor faked. If there's one thing I don't feel when it comes to my lot in life, it's sorry for myself. So many people in the world are doing so much worse than me.

"And I hang out at Golden Sunshine Retirement Village," I add, "spending time with the seniors who aren't visiting with family during the holidays. It's a lot of fun." And that's the truth.

"You're more than welcome to spend Thanksgiving with us," Isabelle says. "Well, more like with my grandmother. And her friends. Some of whom you've already met. She already told me she would love it if both you and Landon joined us."

"I wouldn't want to impose."

"You wouldn't be." A mischievous smile spreads on her face. "In fact, you don't have a choice in the matter. We've been hired to keep you safe, which means you have to do what we tell you. And that includes joining us for Thanksgiving dinner. Isn't that right, sweetheart?" The smile this time is directed at Jayden.

Grinning at her, he shakes his head as though trying not to laugh out loud. To me, he says, "That's right. You don't want to make our job harder than it already is, do you?"

Landon chuckles. "I don't think she's giving you a choice," he tells me.

"He's right about that," she says.

I laugh. "How can I say no then? I'm helping at the senior home with their Thanksgiving lunch, but I'm free after that."

Landon lightly squeezes my hand. "You really like that place, don't you?"

"That's because they're like family to me."

The best kind of family. The family who's always there for you.

16

LANDON

Thanksgiving Day, I find myself at the seniors' residence with Chloe.

"You know what would make me truly thankful?" a man whom she introduced as Samuel says. His sorrowful gaze is directed at the glass of milk she set in front of him.

"What's that?" I ask.

"A scotch neat."

Chloe smiles sweetly at him. "Unfortunately, that isn't on today's menu."

"Or any day," Frank grumbles. "I miss the good old days when we got to drink whatever we wanted. Even when I was a kid, I managed to get some of the good stuff."

"Kid?" I park the glass of milk in front of him. "How young are we talking?"

"Twenty."

"That's hardly a kid."

Frank guffaws. "It is when you're my age. Anything under forty makes you a kid, *kid*."

That has all six men at the table laughing heartily.

Once their laughter dies down, Frank looks me over. "So you're our Chloe's new man, are ya?"

I nod.

"What makes you so sure you're worthy of such a fine young lady?"

They all regard me with the same look a lion gives an antelope before toying with it.

Christ. I've had all kinds of expressions leveled in my direction over the years, both on this job and while in the SEALs. Many were enough to strike fear in the hearts of plenty of men, myself included.

But all that pales compared to how I feel about the way these six men are scrutinizing me.

"Because I care about her and couldn't imagine not spending a single day without her in my life. Because she makes me laugh and makes me want to make her laugh. And because I want to be the man who's there for her, protecting her."

All right, I'll admit some of that comes from a cheesy romance Mom made me watch with her and Dad a few years ago. He and I got into trouble after we burst out laughing when the love interest said it.

I have no doubt she busted Dad's balls after that.

I got away with the standard line of how one day a girl will break my heart, and I'll be too much of an idiot to realize those cheesy lines I was making fun of were the ones that would've saved the relationship.

I highly doubt that.

But right now, those same corny lines appear to be working wonders with the six elderly men.

And Chloe. Her eyes have adopted a dreamy look, which works perfectly for our cover.

"If my dear Sophie were here," Samuel says, "she'd be tearing up something fierce. She always was a romantic."

"There's nothing wrong with being romantic." Lawrence narrows his eyes at me. "That's the problem with the young men these days. They don't know the first thing about romance."

I laugh. "I'm not too sure about that. I've got plenty of male friends who have no problem in that department."

By plenty, I mean two: Liam and Jayden.

And maybe a few guys on my hockey team.

"What do you do for a living?" Samuel asks me.

"I'm a substitute teacher right now. That's how Chloe and I met. I'm currently on assignment at her school."

"You don't look like no elementary school teacher," Frank says.

The man's more perceptive than he realizes.

I study him for a second. "What did you do before you retired?" I ask in a casual, shooting-the-breeze tone.

"Spent my whole life in the Navy."

That would explain it.

"We'll be right back with your meals, gentlemen," Chloe says in what seems like an attempt to rescue me from the interrogation.

Not that I mind. The fact that they *are* interrogating me means they're buying my cover. It also means they care for Chloe the same way she cares about them.

"Sorry about that," she tells me as we return to the kitchen. Around us, the chatter of conversations from the tables drowns out our own from prying ears. "They're super protective of me."

"In that case, I like them already. It's nice that you have so many people looking out for you." Unlike her family.

Although in the case of her family, that's probably a good thing.

My mouth curls to one side. "I don't suppose if I smuggle in a bottle of the finest scotch, they'd give me their blessing when it comes to being your boyfriend?"

"You mean my fake boyfriend." She laughs—and the sweet sound of it causes something deep inside me to stir awake. A something that I don't want to examine too carefully. "But that might work. They can't say you're not worthy enough after that."

We return to the table a few minutes later with dinner plates filled with turkey and all the fixings.

After we finish serving all the other tables, we return to the one with Chloe's pseudo grandfathers, to see if they need anything else.

Other than alcohol.

Before I realize what I'm doing, my hand migrates to her lower back. The move isn't missed by the six men. All wear smug smiles.

"You do realize, if you hurt her," Frank says between mouthfuls of mashed potatoes, "we will go after you."

"Of course, you won't have to worry too much about that." Samuel stabs a piece of turkey into the cranberry sauce on his plate. "Not unless Frank here takes out your kneecaps with his walker first."

He might have been joking, but there's no missing the way Chloe's stiffens under my hand. Unwittingly, he's come too close to what her mobster grandfather, Vadik Orlov, might have done if he was still in the picture.

Fortunately for me, he's facing jail for the rest of his life.

Unfortunately for me, his grandson Nikolai isn't.

I have a feeling if Nikolai ever discovers I've been lying to Chloe, Frank taking out my kneecaps with his walker will be the least of my problems.

Agatha waves Chloe and me over to her table. "My granddaughter sent me pictures of my eight-month-old great-granddaughter. Would you like to see them?"

"I'd love to," Chloe says, smiling.

Agatha passes her several print photos. In the first one, a

baby is sitting on a pink blanket, smiling. Her hands are pressed down on her teddy bear's belly, and her pale-blonde hair sticks up in all directions.

Chloe's smile widens. "She's adorable." She moves the photo to the bottom of the pile, revealing a picture of the baby in a bathtub filled with bubbles. She's clearly having fun splashing and squishing them.

"What about you two?" Agatha asks. "Do you want to have kids one day?"

Chloe is still studying the photos when she answers. "I would love to have kids." Her voice sounds distant, as if she's daydreaming about something and not really here.

Her answer also surprises me, considering she's been adamant about remaining single.

Agatha looks at me, her expression expectant. I'm not sure what to say.

Agatha's question must have suddenly sunk in because Chloe's head shoots upright. "I mean, we've only started dating." Chloe fires me a panicked look. "We're not thinking about those kinds of things yet."

"But you both want kids, right? Now's probably the time to discuss it. You don't want to waste time dating a man who doesn't want kids. My granddaughter did that and didn't find out until a week before the wedding that her fiancé wasn't interested in starting a family. It caused quite the scandal." Agatha chuckles.

Chloe looks at the photo again of the baby in the bathtub, confusion creasing her brow.

"The best part," Agatha says, "was that Beckie still went on their honeymoon, just minus the groom—because why waste a perfectly good plane ticket to Hawaii?—and met the man who is now her husband, and the father of my adorable granddaughter."

"I guess she didn't wait quite as long to ask him about his stance on kids, huh?" I ask.

Agatha laughs. "You got that right. The topic came up about five minutes after they first met on a dinner cruise his ex-girl-friend had booked—prior to deciding an affair with her boyfriend's personal assistant was a great idea. Beckie got a little tipsy on mai tais and blurted the entire I-was-such-an-idiot-for-not-asking-sooner story to the man.

"She asked him if he wanted kids—although I don't think at the time she was planning to marry him. But things worked out great in the end." Beaming, Agatha points to the stack of baby photos in Chloe's hands. "So, Landon, do you want to have kids one day?"

I open my mouth to answer, not exactly sure what to say. I guess, yes, if Sarah and I had been able to marry, we would've had kids.

"Oh, I'm sorry, Agatha. Looks like Mathilda needs us." Chloe grabs my wrist before I can answer, and drags me away from the table, toward the kitchen. Mathilda's nowhere to be seen.

I'm not letting Chloe get away so easily. "Is what you said to her true?"

"About what?"

"That you want to have kids one day?"

She shrugs, the movement drawn-out. "Just because I want to remain single doesn't mean I don't want to have kids. But whether I'll have kids is a whole different topic." She flashes me a glance that warns me she doesn't want to talk about it.

Fair enough.

17

CHLOE

After Landon and I finish helping at the seniors' home, we swing by Landon's town house to shower and change before heading to Sausalito.

Several vehicles are already parked on the driveway by the time we arrive.

We're not precisely fashionably late. Things ran later at the Thanksgiving lunch than expected. So between that and having to clean up afterward, we're well beyond the fashionable part of the equation.

We climb out of the jeep. Landon takes my hand, and we walk to the front door. Even though we're playing make-believe when it comes to our relationship, that doesn't stop the zing humming through me at the feel of my hand in his.

Clearly, we're doing a great job. We've even fooled my body into believing this fake relationship is real.

This time when he rings the doorbell, the sound of Jingle Bells greets us. A moment later, Juanita lets us into the grand house. She takes our coats and directs us to the living room.

Isabelle and Jayden are standing next to the massive

Christmas tree, talking to Henri and an elderly woman I don't know. Several other groups of people are mingling around the room, drinks in hand. Isabelle's wearing a gorgeous royal-blue cocktail dress. Landon and Jayden are wearing black suits. Both men look incredibly handsome.

"What can I get you to drink?" a man in his early twenties asks, a silver tray in his hand.

"I'll have white wine, please," I tell him. Landon requests a red wine.

"I'm so glad you made it, darlings," Josephine says, shuffling toward us. Even her shuffle is elegant. The black-and-silver ball gown might have something to do with that. "You look absolutely stunning, my dear," she says to me. "Don't you agree, Landon?" Her gaze roams down my black sleeveless dress. It's dressy but nothing like her gown.

"She does." He smiles at me, and my breath hitches. I've seen him smile a number of times since he first landed in my life. But this is the first time it's caused my breath to catch this way, this unexpectedly.

Heat spreads across my cheeks. I duck my head, hoping he doesn't notice.

"I love your hair," Josephine adds. "It's such a beautiful color."

I look up and thank her, my face still heated.

"Did your principal tell you my volunteer status has been approved? As has Andrew's."

"She did." And I couldn't have been more relieved than when Principal Woodnut called to tell me that.

"We're both looking forward to working with the children next week," she says. "Nothing makes you feel younger than working with kids."

A papery chuckle comes from behind me. "Don't you mean they remind you how old you are?" Henri's standing in a tux, grinning with an easy gleam in his eyes and holding a cane with *fleurs-de-lis* etched in the bronze handle. "Just last week, one little guy asked me what dinosaurs were like. He honestly thought I was alive when they roamed the earth."

Josephine bursts out laughing.

"What did you tell him?" I ask.

"That most of them were mean and conniving, but I was smarter than them"—he taps his temple—"which is why they've long since vanished, and I'm still walking the earth."

That has us all laughing.

"So tell us about your Thanksgiving lunch," Josephine says. And for the next few minutes, Landon and I tell them all about our afternoon with the seniors and how they're so excited to see the show.

Juanita approaches Josephine and says something to her. Josephine smiles broadly at the woman, who isn't much younger than her. From what Landon told me, Juanita is more like Josephine's companion than a housekeeper.

"May I have your attention?" Josephine calls out to everyone in the room.

Despite her voice being nowhere near as loud as when she was younger, the room goes quiet. The woman has a presence about her you can't ignore.

"Dinner is ready," she announces. "As per tradition, mistletoe is hanging in the doorway to the dining room. All of you with a special someone in your life who's here tonight must kiss under the mistletoe before entering the room. And as you know, I'm a real stickler for that rule."

A wave of soft laughter spreads through the room.

"And this year, I'm excited that my granddaughter, Isabelle, will finally be granting me the wish of seeing her and her handsome fiancé kiss under the mistletoe." She lifts her wineglass to the couple in question. "I was beginning to think you two would never get your act together and notice what was right in front of you."

There's a sprinkling of "*Hear, hears*" from several individuals, most notably Henri and Liza. Beaming like proud parents, the pair raise their glasses at Isabelle and Jayden.

Jayden apparently can't wait until it's their turn under the mistletoe. He gives his fiancée a kiss that has me mentally fanning myself.

I can't remember the last time a man kissed me that way.

Landon and I join the end of the line into the dining room. My palms grow damp at the thought of kissing him. At no point during our discussion about me being his fake girlfriend did we talk about being intimate that way.

When it came to convincing everyone that our fake relationship was real, holding hands in public had seemed like enough.

Jayden and Isabelle kiss again, but not quite as enthusiastically as last time. Isabelle glances over at me, and I give her a thumbs-up. I'm not really sure why. Something in her expression had me wanting to reassure her that everything's fine.

And it *is* fine. The kiss is part of Landon's and my cover.

Well, his cover. I'm just the person he's protecting at the request of my cousin.

Landon and I step under the mistletoe, and I glance up at him and his highly kissable-looking lips.

Lips that I might've wondered how they would feel, how they would taste.

I sense that he wants to ask me if I'm okay with this, but Josephine's standing near us, waiting for us to kiss.

I don't want her to think I've been lying to her, that I'm a deceitful person. She's been so amazing with her offer to help me with the Christmas show. So I smile reassuringly at him, telling him without words that I'm more than okay with him kissing me.

Landon lowers his mouth to mine. He lingers there for a heartbeat; then he lightly presses his mouth against mine.

The instant our lips touch, it's like all the air in the room has been sucked out, leaving me breathless.

Our lips don't touch for long before he pulls away. But it's enough to tilt my world in a way I don't ever remember experiencing.

The moment ends, but the tingling of my skin where he touched me remains. I lift two fingers to my mouth as if that will lock the memory of his lips against mine for longer than a few seconds.

The kiss might be over, but neither of us makes a move to step into the room. We stare at each other for several rapid heartbeats, searching each other's eyes.

A polite cough from the living room jerks me back to the here and now.

I glance at Andrew, who's grinning at us. "Unless you're planning to kiss me," he says to me, "you might want to move along so I can kiss our delightful host."

My face heats up, my insides melt, and I smile to the point where my cheeks ache. "I'm sorry."

We step into the dining room, and I peek over my shoulder in time to catch Andrew kissing Josephine.

And if the kiss is anything to go by, those two are more than just friends.

Oh, that's so sweet.

"What's so sweet?" Landon asks, turning around to see what I'm looking at.

"Did I say that out loud?"

He nods. "Are you going to tell me what's sweet?"

"Those two. Josephine and Andrew. Are they married?" I didn't notice a wedding ring on her finger.

"No. Josephine's husband—Isabelle's grandfather—died about six or so years ago."

"Then I believe they're dating. I know this sounds silly, but I didn't think people in their eighties dated." She's definitely doing better in the romance department compared to me. Maybe she can give me some pointers.

Not that I'm looking for a relationship. But maybe I can share her wisdom with someone looking for love that lasts the ages.

Landon and I sit together at the dining room table. After we're served and Josephine says Grace, we begin eating and drinking, sharing stories, and laughing. The food is delicious, and the company even better.

I can't remember the last time I spent Thanksgiving or Christmas like this.

I'm not referring to the fancy dresses or the suits or even the waitstaff. I'm referring to what it was like when I was a kid. Mom and I would go to Granddad's house—the grandfather who'll be spending the rest of his life in prison—every Thanksgiving and Christmas.

All my extended family had been there.

My cousins.

My uncles and aunts.

I later learned that some of those "uncles" were really his associates. A number of them are currently living out their final days in various penitentiaries around the country.

Before I understood what my grandfather did for a living, family gatherings had been a lot of fun.

It was also when Nikolai and I would sneak off and talk without worrying about our parents or his nosy siblings or our equally nosy cousins overhearing us.

"My teacher wanted my class to write about what we want to be when we grow up," Nikolai tells me one night.

We're sitting in the treehouse that my father and Uncle Aleksi had built. Both Dimetric and Nadia declared a few years ago that they were too grown-up for such a childish thing, so Nikolai and I are the only ones who ever use it.

"What did you write about?" I ask.

"How I want to be a cop. Then I get to lock up the bad guys."

"I think you'll make a great cop. My friend's father is a cop. He came to school one day to talk about his job. He told us how he'd been given an award for being a hero."

Nikolai puffs out his skinny chest, as if proud that one day he, too, will be a hero. "What did he do?"

"He helped pull a woman and her baby from a burning car. Like a superhero."

"Well, that's what I wanted to do."

"Wanted? You mean you changed your mind after you wrote about it for your teacher?" I pick up the brown leaf that had blown in through the glassless window and crinkle it between my fingers. It disintegrates at my touch, the pieces scattering on the floor around my feet.

"My father saw the report and got mad. Told me I couldn't be a cop. Not if I wanted to be part of the family."

I can almost hear Uncle Aleksi saying that, his Russian accent shaping his consonants in a way I could never replicate.

Pretty much the same way all my attempts at Russian had gone. I might have Russian blood pumping in my veins, but I inherited my daddy's inability to speak the language.

At least that wasn't why my father left Mamma and me last year. He's actually proud that I can't speak the language.

He and my grandfather didn't get on very well together. It made Mamma sad.

"Why can't you be part of the family if you're a cop?" I ask Nikolai.

It wasn't a problem for Bethany's family. Why should it be any different for Nikolai's?

He shrugs.

"Don't they want you to be a hero one day?"

Now that I think about it, that was the first time I got the inkling that my family wasn't like the typical family—beyond the obvious part where I didn't have a father anymore.

"Are you okay?" Landon settles his hand on my knee. There's something grounding about his touch.

I smile softly at him, threading my fingers with his. "I'm fine. It's been a while since I've been part of a holiday celebration. I'd forgotten how much fun it can be."

"More fun than having those men at the seniors' home grill me about why I think I'm worthy enough to be your boyfriend?"

I laugh, a little drunk on my overwhelming happiness and the momentary wistful nostalgia. "I'll admit that was one highlight of this afternoon."

"They really care about you. It's obvious you're like a granddaughter to them."

The smile on my face shifts to a full out beam. "I guess that makes me luckier than most people. Forget about having only one or two or four grandfathers, I have a busload of them."

After dessert, Josephine insists we return to the living room, where we can be more comfortable. It's fun watching her tease her future grandson-in-law.

"Since you're going be a married man next year," Liza says to him from her armchair. "I vote you spend the rest of the evening shirtless." She winks at him.

And Isabelle groans. "Haven't we had this discussion before? He took off his shirt that one time because the sprinkler started up while he was walking to the door, and he got soaked. It wasn't to turn you on." She narrows her eyes at Liza and

Josephine. "You two didn't have anything to do with that, did you?"

"Who, us?" they chorus, their innocent expressions as real as Henri's teeth.

Isabelle rolls her eyes. "I should have known better. So much for the temporary malfunction you claimed to be the culprit."

The two women laugh, as do the rest of us.

A few guests leave, but no one else seems to be in a rush to go anywhere. Josephine gestures for Landon and me to sit on an empty chair. "Don't be shy. I'm sure you sit on his lap all the time," she says at my hesitation.

Landon doesn't seem to have any qualms about this cozy arrangement. He pulls me over to the empty armchair and tugs me onto his lap. Jayden and Isabelle aren't sitting any differently than we are, but she looks more at ease than I feel.

But for different reasons—and possibly for the same ones.

I'm becoming more and more aware of Landon, and I was pretty damn aware of him before. Add the kiss from earlier, and my body is buzzing from pent-up desire, pent-up need.

Landon's thumb caresses the spot above the waistband of my panties. That almost does me in. I squirm slightly, trying to relieve the building heat between my legs and low in my belly, while at the same time, attempting to look cool as an English cucumber.

Yep, no problem what-so-ever.

The conversation turns to how things were different in the olden days of Hollywood, but don't quiz me on what was said.

I'm too focused on the way Landon's thumb is lazily tracing circles against my hip. And with each caress of his thumb, my body temperature climbs a degree. There's something sweet and tender about the move.

If I stay here any longer, I'll combust.

I make a move to shift off his lap. His hold on me tightens.

"I'll be right back," I tell him.

He releases me.

I head toward where the washroom is located and spot the door to the balcony. Through the French doors, thousands of tiny dots of lights are visible across the bay.

I open the door and step outside.

The chilled air greets me, wrapping itself around my bare arms. Above the bay, in the inky black night, thousands of stars twinkle like miniature Christmas tree lights. The fog and clouds that usually blanket the sky are absent for now.

God, it's beautiful.

Several minutes slip quietly past before I hear the balcony door click open and shut again. I don't bother to see who's there. I don't have to. In the short time he and I have been together, my body has become attuned to Landon and is tingling with awareness again.

"It's so beautiful," I say on a hushed breath, still staring up at the stars. "I could probably stay out here all night."

He doesn't say anything at first, but I sense his presence draw closer. "What are you doing out here?" His voice is rough and fireworks-exploding-between-my-legs sexy. Not a single cell in my body is immune to it.

I should probably be concerned about that, but I can't seem to drum up even an ounce of resistance. "Watching for shooting stars."

"I didn't realize you're into astronomy." He doesn't sound like he believes that.

"I'm not. Not really. But maybe I should rethink that."

"Why do you want to see shooting stars?"

I shrug—because it feels stupid to say my reason out loud. But I do anyway. "I thought maybe I could make a wish, and it'll come true."

"And what wish is that?"

"If I tell you, it won't come true."

Never mind the part where I haven't had a chance to utter it yet.

He places his hand on my shoulder. The cold November air doesn't affect me. His touch does. Goose bumps prickle along my arms. I shiver.

"You're cold."

"Not at all." Just the contrary.

He turns me around to face him. In the soft light spilling from between partially closed curtains, I make out the heat in his eyes and the fullness of his lips—lips I can't tear my gaze from.

Landon lowers his head closer to mine. "I want to kiss you again." His voice comes out low and gravelly, but he makes no attempt to shorten the distance between us.

"I want that too." More than anything.

This time he does lower his mouth all the way.

Like before, the touch of his lips against mine is barely more than a brush, but it's enough to ignite fireworks in my belly.

However, it's not enough to chase away the goose bumps. Just the opposite.

He pulls back slightly to look into my eyes. Whatever he sees must be the only answer he needs. His mouth returns to mine, but this time it's more than the gentle meeting of flesh.

This time it's electric.

My lips part, allowing his warm wet tongue to invade my mouth, seeking, exploring. Tempting.

My tongue greets it, welcomes it with a slow dance of my own. Nothing about this kiss is fast and greedy. It's about savoring the moment, not knowing if it's the first and only real kiss we'll share—or the first of many more to come.

I lift my hands to his neck and burrow my fingers in the short, soft strands of his dark hair, keeping him from ending the kiss too soon.

The fireworks in my belly from a few moments ago are nothing compared to now. I've experienced numerous firework displays over the years, from the big city ones of New York City ringing in the New Year, to the smaller ones, celebrating the Fourth of July.

None of them compares to the ones currently going off deep inside me.

Landon wraps his arms around me, pulling me closer. Our mouths are not the only parts touching. The full length of my body is pressed against his.

For the first time in forever, I feel wanted and protected.

I feel more than I should, and that scares me.

Because if there's one thing I've learned, it's that it's dangerous to feel this way.

It's dangerous to bring my heart into things where it can so easily be broken. But right now, it doesn't seem too concerned about that.

Maybe it should be.

What difference does it make? This isn't a real relationship. Just enjoy the perks while you can.

They won't last forever.

I have no idea how long Landon and I have been kissing when he finally pulls away. Possibly a few minutes. Possibly a few hours. I just know that the instant he steps back, both my body and mouth immediately miss him.

I also notice for the first time how cold the night air is. But I'm not willing to end this moment just yet.

I allow my gaze to drift to the sky as I search for that elusive shooting star.

If I could make a wish—a wish that would come true—it would be for this moment to never end.

It would be so that I'd never feel the bitter sting of rejection again from sharing my heart with a man.

But since the latter will never come true, I might as well hedge for something else.

Something that doesn't matter which side of the law Landon is on—it's only temporary.

I turn back to Landon and peer into his beautiful brown eyes, warm with flakes of gold. "I want you."

18

LANDON

It takes a second for Chloe's words to sink in, and then I'm kissing her like we've just found out the world's about to end—and this is the last kiss we'll ever have. With anyone.

Eventually, we pull away and let everyone know that we're heading home.

Like her, I'm eager to return to my place.

Eager to see what happens next.

But that's the thing—nothing should happen next.

I'm an idiot.

Those three words keep thundering in my brain as I drive Chloe back to my town house.

Sure, we kissed. We had to—it was part of my cover as her boyfriend.

Or at least the kiss under the mistletoe was part of my cover. The kiss on the balcony? Not so much.

No one was watching us.

No one was expecting us to kiss.

The decision to do that was one hundred percent ours.

It's wrong—but at the same time, it doesn't feel wrong. Just the opposite.

We don't say much on the drive home. Chloe found a radio station that's already playing Christmas music, even though Thanksgiving isn't officially over yet.

I try to focus on the music and not on what she and I will be doing soon, assuming she hasn't changed her mind by the time we arrive. And it's okay if she has.

It would probably be a good thing if she has, because hell if I can bring myself to deny her if she still wants me.

Chloe sings along with a Christmas song. She hits a few notes wrong but doesn't seem to care. She sings her heart out like the world will be a better place for it.

And maybe it will.

"You can sing along, too," she tells me, still keeping with the melody of the lyrics...mostly.

"That's okay. I'm enjoying listening to you sing them." Mostly because she's fucking adorable.

"Now you see why I'm not the one teaching the kids the songs. Thank God. I was getting nervous I'd have to do it, and that would be an epic disaster."

"But you were still planning to do the show even if Josephine hadn't agreed to help out." It's not a question. It's just fact. Chloe's that kind of person. She wants to make everything around her better, even if she stumbles while doing so.

"That's right. But luckily for the seniors, that won't be the case."

My attention's on the road, but I can't miss the grin in her tone that's no doubt reflected on her face.

She goes back to singing. I'm getting the idea that this beautiful, sweet, and generous woman is a massive fan of Christmas.

"So, now that the holiday season has officially begun," she says in between songs, "when are we decorating your place? You'll have to take into consideration that you have one super curious puppy, who could get into all kinds of trouble, but other than that..."

"I don't exactly decorate for Christmas."

That gets a loud gasp out of her. "How can you not decorate for Christmas? That's a travesty."

"I'm just not the kind of man who cares about decorating for Christmas."

"You do like Christmas, right?"

"I'm not some Scrooge who has no use for it and the days leading up to it. I have young nieces and nephews whom I love sending Christmas presents."

"But you just don't like putting up decorations, is that it?"

"Pretty much."

That's not entirely true, but I'm not going to go into my reason for not bothering with any of that stuff.

"What about a Christmas tree? Is that allowed, or are you against them too?" The shock in her tone has been shoved aside, replaced with curiosity.

I shrug.

She slumps back in her seat. "Wow, I might have to rethink this fake relationship with you. I suppose that was a question I should've asked before agreeing to be your fake girlfriend."

"You can't retract it now. You're committed to making our fake relationship work in a completely fake way."

She laughs. "No one can accuse me of not sticking with my commitments. I'll just have to readjust my expectations....Are your parents and sisters like you? Are they also averse to decorating for the holidays?"

The way she says it doesn't sound like she's judging any of us. She's just curious. Not nosy-curious. More like the curiosity that led Sir Isaac Newton to discover gravity.

It's what makes her such a great teacher. She fills her students with the same level of wonder, leaving them questioning everything around them—the way a great teacher should.

"No, my mom and sisters are more like you. They love everything about the holiday season, except they usually wait until December to start decorating. Plus, Mom loves to bake. Cookies. Cakes. Pies. You name it, she bakes it. Evie and Kathy like to give her a hard time and call her Martha Stewart's lost sister—only nowhere near as anal."

I can see that. If my mom makes a mistake, she claims it gives whatever she's working on character. She doesn't get upset.

"That's so sweet. Did she make you fancy birthday cakes when you were kids, like Martha would have?" My gaze is still on the road but I can hear the grin in Chloe's tone.

"Hell if I know what Martha's cakes are like." She laughs at my gruff *I'm-a-caveman-what-do-I-know-about-girlie-cakes?* voice. "But yes, she did decorate our cakes. She was really good at it. I think she took some sort of cake-decorating class with her friends at one point."

"My mom was the opposite. I remember one year she made me a cake with rolled fondant butterflies on it. But for some reason, they kept sliding off the cake and landing in an undignified mess on the plate." Chloe laughs warmly at the memory. "Nikolai's mother, my aunt, always ordered his and his siblings' cakes from a fancy pastry chef. So not your typical birthday cake with whatever licensed children's entertainment or Disney Princess was big at the time. I'm talking about cakes that would outshine most wedding cakes.

"Mom's cakes were a symbol of her love for me. My aunt's cakes symbolized wealth and power."

I'm beginning to see why Chloe is nothing like the rest of her family. And from the sound of it, her mother doesn't have a lot in common with them either.

I ignore the voice in my head pointing out that my mom

would love both Chloe and her mother—as long as she never found out about their Russian mafia connection.

"YOU WANT TO WATCH A MOVIE OR A SHOW ON TV FIRST—OR DID you want to just rip each other's clothes off?" I murmur in her ear as soon as we're inside the town house. My arms are around her waist.

She twists around with a laugh. "Do you mind if we watch something first? I'm just going upstairs to change into something more comfortable."

"While you do that, I'll take Whiskey out. We won't be long."

His paw is doing better, and he decides he would rather walk himself instead of being carried. I click on his leash, and we head outside.

"What's your opinion on decorating for Christmas?" I ask him as he sniffs the ground.

He gives a little bark and lifts his leg to pee.

I guess that answers my question.

"Yeah, that's pretty much my opinion, too."

Sarah, my girlfriend who was in a coma, died two weeks before Christmas. Like Chloe, she loved decorating for the holiday season. Her apartment. Her car. Even her clothes and her hair.

After she died, decorating for the holiday season didn't have the same meaning for me anymore.

Whiskey finishes his business, and we go inside. He heads for the living room. I go upstairs to change.

When I return a few minutes later, he's lying next to Chloe on the couch. I plonk down on the other side of her.

"What are we watching?" I ask before checking the screen.

It takes less than a second to figure it out. The San Francisco Rock hockey commentator's voice is the dead giveaway.

"You're watching hockey?" I ask, even though it's obvious she is.

She smiles and nods.

Without realizing what I'm doing, I wrap my arm around her shoulder and pull her closer. She cuddles into me, her head on *my* shoulder. It feels nice. Better than nice.

At one point during the game, a Rock player is in the penalty box for high sticking. A Vancouver Canuck player passes the puck to his teammate, but Travis Hamilton intercepts it. Then he and his fellow teammate, Elias Lawson, race to the other end, narrowly missing being called offside.

It's a battle between them, the Canuck goalie, and a defenseman. The final seconds of the period tick down. *Eleven. Ten. Nine.* Hamilton shoots the puck at the goal, and Lawson tips it in.

The Canuck fans groan while the splattering of Rock fans jump to their feet, cheering.

They aren't the only ones cheering.

When Hamilton and Lawson stole the puck from the Canuck player, Chloe had shifted to the edge of the couch, body stiff.

As soon as the puck flies past the goalie and the red goal light indicates that the puck went in the net, she's on her feet, cheering. "Did you see that? Ohmigod, that was amazing." She settles herself on the couch next to me, her face glowing in the dim light.

I barely register the horn signaling the end of the period. My gaze is locked with Chloe's, the goal quickly forgotten. All I can focus on is the woman cuddled next to me.

Her lips separate slightly, and I lower my head. I press my mouth against hers. With a stuttering sigh, she lets me in.

The sigh goes straight to my cock.

The tip of my tongue traces her lower lip. A needy gasp releases from her, and her mouth opens to me.

I sweep my tongue inside. She tastes like the sweetest wine. *So good*.

She leans back, resting her head on the couch cushion. Enabling me to deepen the kiss.

I take full advantage of it.

Faint puppy snores on the other side of her tell me that Whiskey won't be complaining about this anytime soon. I shift slightly and lift my hand to just below her chest, tracing my thumb along the band of her bra hidden under her light-knit sweater.

When she doesn't protest, I move my hand up an inch and brush my thumb across her nipple.

She moans in my mouth, giving me the signal I so desperately need. I continue teasing the bud as it tightens under the fabric.

I'm not the only one making the most of the intermission. Chloe tugs the hem of my T-shirt up and slides her warm hand under the fabric. Her fingers graze across the ridges and valleys of my abs.

I suck in a sharp breath and go back to kissing her mouth, her jaw, her neck. "Maybe we should take this upstairs to your room," I say, the words low and rough between panted breaths.

"You don't want to watch the rest of the game?"

"Not at this particular moment. And I don't exactly want an audience for what I want to do to you next." I look pointedly at the snoozing puppy. "Let me put him in his crate, and we can continue upstairs where I think we're headed next." I look at her for further confirmation.

Without a word, her hand drifts to the noticeable bulge in my jeans, and she gives it a light squeeze.

Message received.

19

CHLOE

Landon leaves the room to put Whiskey in his crate. While he's gone, I listen to the hockey commentators and turn off the TV once I hear Landon returning from the laundry room.

My heart rate accelerates, like the two Rock players who just scored the goal. But unlike them, my heart feels out of control, unsure what to expect next.

It's been an awfully long time since I last had sex. I have no idea if it's like riding a bike: you never forget how to do it.

I'm hoping that's true.

I push myself to my feet and close the distance between Landon and me. The heat in his eyes causes me to stumble.

He reaches out to me, and I take his hand. He then leads me upstairs to his bedroom. My heart practically races us there, the party planner for the end of the sex-dry-spell celebration.

In his room, the pale moonlight glows softly on the walls and white sheets. An image of us bathed in the light of the moon as it witnesses me cry out Landon's name as I come floods my thoughts.

Well, hopefully, I come.

It wasn't that way with the last two men I slept with.

As if sensing my hesitation, Landon wraps his arms around me. "We don't have to do this if you don't want to." He plants a soft kiss on my jaw.

"No, I definitely want to. It's just…it's been a while since I've been with a man that way." My chest tightens, and my face tingles with a rush of heat. It feels like embarrassment—and also regret. Regret that I sound like a clueless, sacrificial virgin.

I bite my lower lip.

He tenderly runs his thumb along it, loosening my hold. "Then, we'll go slow." His hand cradles the back of my head and his mouth brushes against mine.

My body melts at his touch. This man, who has risked his life to protect the freedoms we hold dear, has complete command of my body.

And I wouldn't want it any other way.

The fingers of his other hand inch the hem of my sweater up. The dizzying touch of his fingertips skims across my belly, and I shiver.

My fingers reach for his T-shirt, and I help him remove it.

He strips me out of my top, and I shimmy out of my yoga pants.

A languid smile spreads across Landon's face. His gaze drifts down my partially naked body. I'm standing in nothing but my deep-purple lace bra and matching panties, and from the way he's smiling, he clearly approves.

"Christ, you're fucking gorgeous."

No sooner are the words out, than he's kissing me.

This time the kisses aren't tentative. They're hungry.

Possessive.

Consuming.

They feed every part of me with a need I've never experienced before. With a need I might never experience again.

My breath comes in so fast, so unevenly, if I didn't know

better, I'd think *I* was the one racing down the ice, desperate to get to the goal.

Since one of us is more undressed than the other, I seek to remedy that. My fingers stumble on his button, working hard to slip it through its hole.

Luckily, the button takes pity at my efforts and goes through without further resistance.

Landon's hand covers one of my breasts. He runs his thumb across the hard peak hidden under the purple lace. I moan into his mouth.

Somehow, I quickly unzip his jeans, unapologetically rubbing my fingers along his hardening length. Landon hisses into my mouth.

I smile, smugly, my lips still attached to his.

Even more so when I slip my fingers through the opening of his pants and feel his warm cock through the fabric of his underwear. He's wearing either briefs or boxer briefs. I can't tell which, but I'm dying to know. Now.

I remove my hand from his jeans and tug the waistband over his hips, hinting very clearly what I want him to do.

He wisely takes my hint.

A moment later, he's standing in nothing but a pair of sexy black boxer briefs. His socks were ripped off his feet at the same time he removed his jeans.

His well-endowed cock strains against his underwear, to the point where I'm expecting him to rip through the fabric.

Let me help you with that.

I reach for them at the same time Landon lowers the cup of my bra, exposing my nipple to his eager mouth.

And all thoughts of getting him out of his boxer briefs are temporarily derailed.

With his tongue teasing my nipple, he guides me to the bed behind me and makes it clear that he wants me to lie down.

Before I have a chance to do just that, his talented fingers have me out of my bra in record time. He reaches for the lamp on his bedside table and turns it on. A soft glow fills the room, washing away the one from the moon.

While he's busy opening his drawer, I move to the center of the bed.

He removes several square metallic wrappers from a box, shucks off his boxer briefs, and climbs onto the bed to straddle my calves.

I groan in my chest at his perfection, the cut of his muscles in his abs, chest, shoulders. His arms and legs are pretty damn fine, too.

His fingers make deft work of removing my panties, sliding them along my legs. They disappear somewhere over the edge of the bed.

At the way he openly appraises my body, an awkwardness shimmers through me. It's been a while since a man has seen me naked.

On instinct, my hands move to cover me, but I don't get that far. Sensing what I'm about to do, Landon grabs them and returns them to the bed.

"No covering yourself." His low, gravelly voice leaves me squirming on the bed, all shades of turned-on. "Fuck, you're gorgeous, Chloe." He doesn't say it as though he's surprised by that.

His tone implies that he never expected otherwise—no matter how I looked naked, he would've felt the same way.

A small whimper escapes my lips, too soft for him to hear.

He moves back slightly, grabs my ankles, and spreads my legs open. His hungry eyes devour every inch of me. The whimper that escapes me this time is louder, more demanding. Heat and wetness rush to my core, leaving me writhing on the bed, desperate for relief.

The lazy smile returns to Landon's face. He knows exactly

what he's doing to me—and he doesn't appear too repentant about it.

He gently plants a soft kiss midway between the apex of my legs and my knee. The kisses continue northward, each one eliciting a shiver through me.

At the junction between my legs, he plants one final kiss. This one is on my clit.

He licks it, and my hips jerk up off the bed. He parks his hand on one hip, pinning it down. His tongue continues working on my mound, driving me into a frenzy. I'm writhing and moaning and knotting my fingers in his hair.

He laughs softly, his breath brushing my swollen clit, pushing me closer to the edge.

"*Oh, God,*" is the only coherent phrase I manage to say, if you can call it coherent.

And because he apparently hasn't finished driving me insane with need, Landon pushes a finger against my opening and adds another one.

As his tongue has its way with me, Landon pulls his fingers out a few inches, then plunges them inside me again. He curves them slightly, finding the spot that causes all the tight threads to unravel. Hard.

A blinding white heat rushes through me, searing me to the core, and I cry out his name.

At first, I'm floating like ash in the air after a volcano explodes. All the tiny pieces separating in the breeze, unable to find any real form again.

But bit by slow bit, my body resumes its previous shape, and I skink back to the bed. I give Landon my own liquid smile, too boneless to do much else for the moment. He chuckles, pride clearly stamped on his face.

He rips open the condom wrapper and smoothly rolls the rubber onto his thick length. I run the tip of my tongue along my lower lip, imagining what it will taste like if I lick the head of his cock. Picturing in my head the sounds he would make if I took it into my mouth.

He rejoins me on the bed and positions himself between my legs. He then slowly enters me, letting my body adjust to his width. "Christ," he murmurs into my shoulder. The rest of his words are lost against my bare skin.

His warm breath tickles, and I laugh softly.

He moves off my shoulder and grins down at me. "I hope that isn't a reflection of what you think of my cock inside your sweet heat." His gaze shifts to where his member is seated deep inside me. "Because if you want my opinion, your pussy wrapped around my cock is looking pretty magnificent." He grins at me, and I laugh louder this time.

"Don't worry, your manhood is perfectly safe with me." Finished with the conversation, I thrust my hips up. I want to feel him moving inside me.

"Good to know." He kisses me tenderly...and then gets back to business.

He circles his hips and plunges inside me again and again and again. With each move of his hips, he inches me closer to a new edge, my panted breaths matching his.

I shift my legs to wrap around his waist, using his body to create more friction against my clit. "Oh, God. Oh, God, Oh, God," I say on a long moan.

"Come for me again," he grits out, and the sound of his voice strained with desire is all that it takes.

I'm steamrolling toward the abyss at neck-breaking speed, and nothing is holding me back.

My inner muscles tighten around his cock in a gratifying hug, and I cry out his name, louder this time.

No sooner have the words tumbled from my mouth, than Landon releases an equally loud groan, animalistic in sound. "*Fuuuuck.*"

I watch with blurry-eyed satisfaction as his orgasm powers through him. I did this to him. *Me.*

Once he's regained awareness and disposed of the condom, he climbs under the covers and pulls me to him. I rest my head against his chest. He runs his hand up and down my arm.

"That was nice," I say on a drowsy sigh.

"I'm glad you approve."

"Most definitely. I can't remember the last time I had sex like that. Correction, I can't remember if I've *ever* had sex like that. If I knew sex with a fake boyfriend was all it took, I would have found one a long time ago." I grin at him, expecting him to laugh.

But he's not laughing. He's frowning.

Okay, definitely not what I was expecting.

"You've *never* had sex like that?"

I brush my hand across his stomach. "Not everyone is great at it like you are, Landon."

He keeps frowning as if the idea of all the women in the world not experiencing orgasms like he gave me has greatly affronted him.

Maybe if he's really that concerned, he can create an online course to help men figure out how to please a woman. He'd probably make a fortune from it.

And then he wouldn't have to put his life at risk like he does now with his job.

My stomach does a not-so-impressive flip that ends in a belly flop at the thought. I have no idea why.

"How many boyfriends have you had?" he asks.

My hand moves up, and I absentmindedly draw circles and squiggles on his chest. It hadn't been on my agenda to admit to my romantic failures, but maybe the mind-blowing sex short-circuited my brain, because the next thing I know, I'm saying, "Just two. There was one in college, but he dumped me a week before graduation due to a job offer in another state.

"Two years later, I met my first and only serious boyfriend. But like my stepfather and biological father, he decided he didn't want to be part of my life. A few days after he told me he loved me, he sent me a text to recant all that and tell me he was through with me."

All right, not his exact words, but the sentiment was the same.

It certainly felt that way at the time.

Landon stiffens under me. "Was your relationship with your father and stepfather close prior to both men leaving your mother?"

"I thought so at the time, but I guess not. For all I know, they now have new families, with several kids and dogs and maybe a cat or two. All those things I wanted growing up, but never really got, other than Nikolai, who was the closest I ever came to having a sibling."

Landon's heartbeat picks up speed under my head. Not a whole lot, but enough for me to notice. "You and Nikolai were close?"

I nod. "Very much so. He used to have a brother and sister, but they were older and thought we were annoying little brats." I laugh softly. "They were probably right." I shift position, so I'm lying on my side, my head propped up with my bent arm. "We liked playing practical jokes on them. They didn't appreciate it."

"What kind of jokes?"

"Mostly silly, immature ones, but at the time, we thought we were geniuses. My aunt had a different opinion about the genius part. Especially after Nikolai and I glued his sister's science project shut so she couldn't open it."

Landon laughs. "You really did that?"

"Not our finest moment, I'll admit. She'd spent hours on the trifold display, so naturally, she wasn't too impressed with what we did." Understatement of the year. "Nikolai and I clearly hadn't thought things through. Because his sister wasn't above getting us back. We had to redo her project for her, which ended up looking better than anything she'd created. But that wasn't enough for her to not get her revenge."

"What did she do?"

"She took my favorite doll and soaked her in blue ink. The doll looked like a human Smurf after that. Nadia then painted Nikolai's favorite Star Wars spaceship bright pink."

That makes Landon laugh even harder.

"I believe that was the last time we pranked his sister." Nadia had proved she was the master, and we were mere amateurs.

"He sounds like a great cousin."

"He is. We haven't spoken for a while now. He's been busy." Running the family business will do that to a person.

"Do you miss him?" Landon caresses my arm again.

"Very much. Nikolai wasn't just like a brother to me. He was my best friend. He was there for me when my biological father left my mom and me. I was seven at the time and devastated. I knew my mom was hurting, so I had to be brave for her. But it was so hard. Nikolai was the one who was there for me, holding me when all I could do was cry. He was the one who did everything in his power to make me smile again.

"And then several years later, my best female friend died of leukemia. I didn't have many friends at the time, so like when my father left, I took it hard. Nikolai was there for me again. The same deal when my stepfather left my mom. Nikolai was the one who held me when all I could do was cry." He was also the one who told me I wasn't jinxed when it came to the people I loved. And no matter what, he would always be there for me.

"He sounds like a great man."

"He is. Life wasn't easy for him, either. Not later on anyway. When he was sixteen, his parents and siblings were killed when their vehicle blew up. Nikolai was supposed to be with them that day. We both were. But I got the flu and couldn't go. He was only going because I wanted to see the classical concert with him and his family. So he skipped out on the concert and went to see a hockey game with friends."

"I guess, in a way, you saved his life."

I smile at Landon. It's not a huge grin, but it's filled with sweet memories all the same. "That's what he used to say, too. He said if I hadn't gotten sick, we would've both died that day."

Landon threads his fingers through my hair. "I'm glad you got sick and weren't in the vehicle." His voice is little more than a whisper. He leans into me and brushes his lips against mine. "I'm glad you didn't die."

"Me too," I whisper back.

20

LANDON

My mouth moves on Chloe's soft lips, and a newfound respect for Nikolai Orlov burns in my veins.

But that still doesn't change anything.

He might have been there for her when her father and stepfather took on the role of douchebags, and when her best friend died of leukemia, but that doesn't alter who he is.

The boy who Chloe remembers and loves is nothing like the man he became. Somewhere along the way, he turned into a facsimile of their grandfather.

I pull away from Chloe just an inch. "What happened to your cousin after his parents died?"

A voice deep in the back of my head screams, *What the fuck are you doing? You're supposed to be kissing her.*

I ignore it.

Or try to ignore it.

Chloe makes a small sound, a barely-there *Do-you-want-to-discuss-this-now?* whimper. "My mother offered for him to stay with us. I was so excited because that meant I'd get to see him all the time. But then, my grandfather, her father, decided Nikolai would be better off staying with him."

That would explain things. Maybe if he had stayed with Chloe and her mother, he would have turned out differently.

Or not.

"I just wish he'd contact me and let me know how he's doing," she says, her voice a whisper, as I'm about to resume kissing her again.

Now that I have a better idea of why the two cousins are close—or were close—there are other things I'd rather be doing than discussing that asshole.

I mean, unless she can give me something to go on so the Feds can finally locate him. A family reunion with his grandfather would make our day.

Okay, maybe not Nikolai's day, but that's not my problem.

"Have you tried contacting him?" I ask.

She shakes her head. "I have no idea where he is." Her voice is like that of a kid who realizes Santa isn't real. "It seems to be a common theme when it comes to the men in my life. Everyone I love isn't interested in sticking around for the long haul.

"But I guess that's not entirely true when it comes to Nikolai. He might have vanished from my life, but he sent you to be my guardian angel. So at least I know he still loves me."

Fuck.

Her words slice through me like a hot knife through peanut brittle ice cream.

Because Nikolai Orlov is just one more man in her life who's let her down. One more man who cares more about himself than this sweet and giving woman beneath me.

"But now you understand why I'm not looking for love anymore," she says, smiling brighter this time. "Why I wasn't interested in dating you before I knew your job was the only reason you wanted to be with me. Now, enough of this discussion. I believe you were kissing me. How about we get back to that?"

Her eager eyes almost do me in. But despite what she might think, there's still a hollowness in them that cuts me to the marrow.

All I can do is hope that one day she finds a man who'll wipe it away and prove to her that not all men are like those who have done her wrong.

All I can do is hope someone can fix her broken heart with something stronger than Elmer's Glue.

All I can do is hope she finds someone who's the opposite of me.

21

CHLOE

The next few days after Thanksgiving break are a whirl of craziness at school. Landon and I spent much of the long weekend hanging out, talking about all kinds of things: hiking trips we've done (the places we've both been, places one of us have seen), humorous stories about when we were growing up (Nikolai and I weren't the only pranksters when it came to siblings and cousins), stories about our jobs (Landon's real job, as I already know about his misadventures in kindergartener-land).

Some things had us cracking up. Others resulted in a sympathetic ear.

All of it was nice—especially those times we shared while cozy together on the couch, with a new level of intimacy that hadn't existed before our first kiss.

I attended his hockey game with Isabelle and Jayden. Landon's team won, of course.

Landon and I also cooked together and shared about our families. Well, mostly I shared about my mom. I didn't have anything to say about the rest of my relatives.

And yes, there was also plenty of kissing and between-the-sheets hotness, much like we experienced after Josephine's party.

Even though Landon and I have only known each other for a short time, it feels like we've been friends and something more for years.

It feels both nice and unsettling—especially when what we have between us is only short-term. At the end of the day, this isn't a real relationship. I'm just enjoying that it feels like one while I can.

Enjoying feeling special, even though Landon and his team work for Nikolai, work for the boss of the Russian mafia.

At some point—hopefully sooner rather than later—our fake relationship and all the fun perks that come with it will end. Whatever favor Landon's team owed the mutual third party will be paid in full.

And my connection to the family I appreciate as much as I'd appreciate having my eyeballs coated with extra spicy hot sauce will be terminated for good.

Or is that last point too much to hope for?

But now the realization that we've got only three weeks before the Christmas concert is hitting hard. It's not a lot of time when you're dealing with kindergarteners.

We should've begun preparing months ago.

"That's really good, everyone," Josephine cheerfully says after Landon's class and my class finish singing "Jingle Bells."

Somewhat together.

Josephine shares a few pointers with the kids on how to project their voices, so the hard-of-hearing seniors can hear them.

The door opens, and Tabitha sails into the music room. She barely gives Josephine a glance. Josephine might be a famous former Hollywood and Broadway actress, but that doesn't seem to be of interest to Tabitha.

Andrew, who's sitting at the piano, watches her with great

interest. But that comes as no surprise. She has that effect on people with the way she enters a room, like a bristling wind bent on leaving a trail of broken twigs in her wake.

"I came to see how things are progressing." She says it in a tone that implies she has every right to be here. I'm not so sure about that, but I'm hardly arguing with her in front of everyone.

Or at all.

"Things are looking good so far," I tell her.

Josephine prompts the kids to sing the song for Tabitha.

From the corner of my eye, I catch her wincing at the sound. Fortunately, the seniors they're performing for are a lot more forgiving than she is. They're just happy to have the kids visit them.

"I've also made arrangements so the kids and residents can make Christmas decorations together," I tell her once the song's finished.

I bought the supplies myself with my own money, after seeing an ad online that melted my heart. The cute six-year-old girl in it was helping an elderly woman make an elf face out of a paper plate and bits of colored paper.

One of Tabitha's perfect eyebrows raises. "The school budget doesn't allow for frivolous spends like that."

"Someone donated the supplies."

Point. Match. Win.

I skip the part about how I'm the one who donated them. Witnessing the seniors having a good time—one that doesn't involve spiked eggnog and conga lines—will be an early Christmas present to me.

And considering I'm family-less, it's pretty much one of the few presents I'll get. So I plan to make the most of it.

"What about the costumes?" she asks.

"We've got someone working on them as we speak."

Translation: I'm looking at some late nights sewing the elf hats.

It means all that delicious sex I've been having with Landon will have to take a back seat for a while.

Or permanently, depending on how long it takes his team to locate the individuals who want this to be my last Christmas —if I'm even that lucky.

My gaze slides to him. He's watching the kids to make sure they pay attention to Josephine. But even then, I can tell he's listening to my conversation with Tabitha.

I bite my lip, my thoughts drifting to how he's not into Christmas decorations. That's more interesting than listening to her.

"So?" Tabitha says, glaring at me.

"So, what?" Why do I get the feeling she asked me a question, and I missed it because I was too busy thinking about Landon?

But at least I wasn't imagining him naked. In the shower. With beads of water trailing down his body.

Oops.

"Why do you have these strangers working with your students? You're the teacher."

Oh, right. Tabitha's still here.

My gaze darts to Josephine and Andrew to ensure they didn't hear her little outburst. "Do you even know who they are?"

She frowns. "Seniors from the home where the kids will be doing the show, I imagine." It's less a question than a statement of what she believes to be true.

"That's Josephine Ashworth and Andrew Stanton." I pause, waiting to see if the names ring a bell. Any bell.

She shakes her head, the frown still there.

So I spend the next several minutes highlighting each of their accomplishments, which makes for quite a lengthy and impressive list.

I finish the last of Andrew's with a *so-take-that* grin.

She gives me a brief nod that states: I'm impressed, but I won't admit that out loud.

My smile widens. "They were nice enough to help us out with the performance. And the kids are getting so much from their expertise."

From the other side of Tabitha, Landon smiles my favorite cocky grin, confirming what I already suspected. He's been listening in the entire time.

Tabitha doesn't see it. She's too busy glaring at me again.

She returns her attention to Landon. "I'm free for drinks tonight. I thought we could talk about the possibility of a full-time position with the school, once Zoe's maternity leave is over."

"Doesn't the principal typically make that decision?"

"I have connections that can ensure a position here."

I can almost hear a wink in her tone at the end of that sentence.

A laugh erupts from my lungs, and she swivels around to level another irritated look at me.

"Oops. Sorry. Hiccups." I flash her my most innocent smile.

"That's nice of you to offer," Landon says, drawing her attention back to him. "But I'm more of a free spirit when it comes to my job. That's why I prefer being a substitute teacher."

"Well, the offer's still on for the drinks."

"That's going to be a little tough. I have a girlfriend."

I guess Tabitha hasn't heard the latest rumor about us. She must be more out of the loop than she realizes.

Her eyes widen to the size of cymbals. "You do?"

He nods toward me in lieu of an answer.

Her head swivels between us like the girl in *The Exorcist* if she had OD'd on caffeine. "You two are dating? Since when?"

"Since last week," I say.

"Isn't that against the rules?"

I pretend to appear thoughtful "You mean the dating rules? Like no sex before the third date?"

Landon laughs a little louder this time. The kids continue singing behind him.

"No, I mean the rules about dating a colleague."

"Nope. There's no such rule. Which means we're free to date."

"Well, I guess congratulations are in order," she says, not sounding at all like she means it.

I bite my tongue to keep from saying, "We're dating, not getting married," and go with "Thank you" instead.

"Now that we've got that all straight," I say, "you really need to excuse us. We've got a show to prepare for and not a lot of time."

I gesture toward the door. She gets the hint and leaves.

Air rushes from my lungs in a relieved *whoosh*. "I thought she was going to cause trouble with the show after you told her I'm your girlfriend."

"She'd look rather petty if she did that after the rest of the parent-teacher association approved it," Landon says. "Even more so when they find out who's helping with the show." He nods at the two individuals leading the kids in a cheery rendition of "*Frosty the Snowman*."

AFTER JOSEPHINE CALLS IT A DAY WITH THE KIDS AND THANKS them for doing such an incredible job singing and playing their bells, Landon and I take our charges back to our classrooms.

The door between the two rooms is open a crack. Not because he needs my help with his class. He doesn't.

It's so he can do his real job, keeping an eye on me.

But with Adam doing his regular rounds of my classroom, and Jayden and Liam outside, there's nothing to worry about.

As long as I'm in the school, I'm safe.

As though I've just summoned him with my thoughts, Adam wheels his bucket and mop into my classroom and approaches my desk. I stand to talk to him.

"Miss R," Tommy says from his seat, "why do birds and bees make babies?"

He says it loud enough that everyone looks up from the Christmas craft they're making for the classroom walls.

The undeniable twitching of Adam's mouth gives away his thoughts.

Oh, boy.

Sex Ed isn't for a few more years.

I plant a desperate smile on my face and ask Adam, "Is there something I can help you with?"

The replying grin is anything but desperate. "I can wait." He nods for me to answer Tommy's question.

Of course.

"Well...um...it's just a saying. I mean, of course, birds have babies. They hatch from eggs. And baby bees hatch from eggs, too. Although in the case of bees, they don't look like baby bees when they hatch. And why do birds and bees make babies? Well, to increase their population. Otherwise, the world wouldn't have song and honey." I sound like a rambling fool, but my years of education haven't prepared me enough for this.

Tommy looks thoughtful for a moment, then nods. "Okay."

And I release a hard breath. "Hopefully, I haven't just screwed him up for life," I mutter so only Adam hears me.

Adam laughs. "If this is what it's like for Landon, I definitely got the easier job for this mission." He says it low enough so the kids don't overhear him.

"Mission" and "janitor" are two words you don't typically

associate together. Tom Cruise didn't drop from the ceiling in his spy gear to clean toilets.

"You might be right about that," I say. Although I don't doubt for a minute that the regular janitor doesn't have his hands full with the job.

"Is there something you need?" I ask Adam, glancing around the room to double-check that everything's in order.

"Landon won't be able to drive you to his place after school. He has to be somewhere else. So I'll be driving you instead."

TOP SECRET

AN HOUR AND HALF LATER, ADAM DROPS ME OFF AT LANDON'S town house. "Do you know how to reactivate the alarm?" he asks.

I nod.

"All right. Landon should be home in two hours. Don't answer the door while he's gone. I've been called in for the meeting, so I'm unable to keep an eye on the town house in the meantime."

"Okay." I jump down from his SUV, and he waits for me to enter the house before driving off.

I'm about to reactive the alarm, but my gaze lands on the living room. You wouldn't know it's the holiday season by looking at it.

It's kind of depressing.

I release Whiskey from his crate and take him outside to relieve himself. Conscious of the risk I'm taking, I keep an eye on my surroundings, ready to bolt inside if need be.

While he sniffs the ground, I contemplate the idea now swirling in my head, as well as the potential danger involved.

"How would you like to go on a trip to my apartment?" I ask

the furball. "I've got some Christmas decorations there." As well as protection that I didn't think to retrieve the last time I was there with Landon. "I could go get them and decorate your place. Then it would feel more Christmas-y. What do you think?"

He gives a happy bark...and takes a dump.

After I finish picking up after him, we return inside, and I grab my car keys. Since Landon won't be back for two hours, I don't bother to leave a note or text him.

I lift Whiskey into the front passenger car seat, and he makes himself comfortable.

"Don't go anywhere," I tell him. "You need to stay right there while I drive." Even though Landon is only Whiskey's temporary home, we've been working on training him. So far, it's still hit or miss if he listens to us.

Traffic isn't my friend today. It moves slower than a crawl. I'm sure even Frank, with his walker, could move faster than this. It takes over an hour to get to my apartment building.

I park my car and carry Whiskey inside. "Some of the stuff is in my apartment," I tell him. "The rest is in my storage locker in the basement."

I sneak him into my apartment first. The place looks exactly how I left it.

Just dustier.

But there's no time to worry about that now.

I find my penknife in the kitchen knickknack drawer and slip it into my jacket pocket. Next, I locate the box of my most prized decorations, the ones I didn't want to risk leaving in my storage locker. These are the ones from my childhood—the ones I made for my father and stepfather.

Deep down, I know I should throw them away, that I'm a glutton for punishment, but I haven't had the heart to do it. At one point, these simple decorations, which I've had to fix a few times over the years, were precious to the two men.

I take the box to the car and load it into the trunk. Whiskey and I return inside and head to the basement.

The light is already on when I step inside the eerie place.

I swear the basement's haunted, which is why I usually avoid it whenever possible. I hold Whiskey tighter to me even though I know I'm being irrational. I can thank Nikolai for my fear of all things paranormal. He used to tell some of the spookiest stories. If he ever decides to write horror novels instead of being the head of the mob, even Stephen King would concede that Nikolai is the king of all things creepy.

Usually, the basement light is turned off, unless someone is already in here or the last person forgot to turn it off. I strain to hear a sound to indicate that I'm not the only one in here. Nothing reaches my ears other than the typical old building noises, such as creaking pipes.

It's not a ghost. It's not a ghost. It's not a ghost.

At my locker, I lower Whiskey to the concrete floor and unlock the door with my key. "All right, let's find those Christmas decorations."

It doesn't take me long to locate the two large boxes filled with all kinds of holiday decorations, buried under everything else. "I really need to go through this place and get rid of some of this old junk," I mutter to myself.

Soft, hesitant footsteps approach from behind. The good news is that ghosts don't have footsteps. The bad news is that creepy clowns like Pennywise do.

Whiskey releases a puppy bark, and I spin around. A man I've never seen before is standing a short distance from us, a medium-sized moving box in his arms.

My heart rate speeds up, my palms grow slippery, and my breath slams on the brakes.

I toe the locker door shut and snap the lock together with one hand, all the while keeping my gaze glued on the man. One side of the box balances preciously on my hip.

Oh, fuckadoodle. Maybe coming here wasn't such a good idea after all.

A voice in the back of my head replies, *You think?* I ignore it.

The box slips on my hip, and I tighten my hold on it with my free arm.

The man lurches forward. "Let me help you."

I let out a small shriek, which riles up Whiskey. He runs between my legs...then changes his mind and runs around them, tangling me in his leash.

Not very helpful, I mentally chastise him, which is about as useful as eating peanut butter to ward off vampires.

The box resumes its disastrous slide down my body. I twist around, attempting to save it from making nice with the floor.

The man drops his box, and it lands with a muffled thump. No glass was broken in the making of this disaster.

He grabs my box before it can crash against the concrete and parks it by my feet.

Whiskey wags his tail and lunges toward the man, tugging on my calves.

I'm unable to untangle myself in enough time and go down like a felled tree.

Timber!

The next thing I know, strong arms wrap around me, keeping me upright. The crisp scent of a man's aftershave or cologne accompanies them.

"Are you okay?" he asks, releasing me once he's sure I'm stable on my feet—or fairly stable. He bends to scratch Whiskey behind the ear and unfastens his leash.

"Yes, thank you," I say, the tension in my muscles deflating like air escaping a hot air balloon.

I really need to work on my overactive imagination. This whole thing about having a contract on my head is making my paranoia work double time.

With his hand still on Whiskey's collar, the man passes me

the leash. "Here. You can free yourself now." He resumes fussing over Whiskey—who laps it up like a doubly absorbent paper towel.

I take his momentary distraction to untangle my legs and click the leash back on Whiskey's collar.

"He's a cute dog," the man says.

"Thanks. I take it you like dogs."

"I love them. I don't have one yet, but I'm looking at getting one soon."

Part of me points out that I should tell him that Whiskey's looking for a forever home. The other part screams out that Whiskey is Landon's dog, and one day soon, he'll realize that for himself.

I'm about to sheepishly point out that the apartment doesn't allow pets, but I don't get the chance.

"You're Chloe, right?" he asks, and instantly my Spider-Girl senses go on high alert. I take a step back.

Before I can say anything or hightail it out of here, he adds, "My grandmother lives in the building. She's told me all about you. I think she's hoping I might bump into you at some point and ask you out. I'm Eric, by the way."

Okay—that was unexpected.

I chew on my lip for a second, unsure what to say.

So I go with the partial truth. "I have a boyfriend."

"You do?"

I feel my eyebrows shoot up my forehead at his response.

"Sorry, that didn't come out right. Of course, you have a boyfriend. You're gorgeous."

A heat wave makes a beeline for my face, and he chuckles. "And now I sound like some loser using a pickup line."

Kinda. "Not at all."

"I'm sure your boyfriend tells you all the time that you're gorgeous. And if he doesn't, you need a new boyfriend."

I laugh. "I'll be sure to keep that in mind."

Eric bends down and picks up my box. "How about I at least make my grandmother proud and carry this up to your apartment for you?"

"Oh, that's not necessary."

"I insist. But if it makes you feel better, I can give it to you once we get there. You don't need to invite me inside if you don't want to."

"I'm not staying in my apartment right now. I'm staying with my boyfriend."

"My grandmother really is out of the loop. Not only was she unaware of you having a boyfriend, but she also had no idea that you're currently living with him. She needs to work on getting new informants." He winks at me.

"Most definitely," I say, laughing.

"Well, in that case, let me carry this to your vehicle."

"That's really okay." The last thing I need is a stranger walking me to my car when someone wants me dead—even if it would save me time. "But thanks for offering."

"Are you sure?"

"Positive."

"Well, it was nice meeting you, Chloe, and you, too." He pats Whiskey one more time on the head. "Maybe I'll see you around if things don't work out between you and your boyfriend." That part's directed at me.

"Maybe." But probably not.

Or you could give him a chance. Just because Mom made poor choices when it came to men doesn't mean you do, too. You made one mistake. One mistake doesn't make a pattern.

I ignore the voice in the back of my head. I'm not ready to test that theory out, especially while Landon is my fake boyfriend.

22

CHLOE

The drive to Landon's town house isn't any quicker than the one to my apartment. Christmas music pipes through the speakers, and I sing along, not caring that I look like an idiot.

Whiskey sits on the front seat, his paws on the armrest under the window, watching the world drive by.

It's dark by the time I park on the street outside Landon's home. The town house isn't much brighter, other than the faint light streaming through the gap in the closed living-room curtains from the lamp controlled by a timer. Which means Landon isn't home yet. But it's nice to know that I'm at least not entering a dark town house. Nor am I entering it alone.

Whiskey isn't much protection against someone with a contract on my head—Landon would need a full-grown Rottweiler for that. But at least I've got someone to keep me company.

And I have the penknife I retrieved from my apartment.

I open the front door and enter the security code. Whiskey happily enters the house and heads toward the kitchen. "I'll feed you in a minute," I tell him. "I just have to get the rest of the stuff."

I set the cardboard box on the floor and check my phone.

> Landon: Running a little late. Will be home in an hour.

It was sent twenty minutes ago. I send him a text in reply.

> Me: Okay. See you soon.

Forty-five minutes later—as I'm hanging up the imitation pine boughs on top of the kitchen cabinets—*Thank you, Pinterest, for that suggestion*—the front door clicks open.

And then...

"What the fuck?"

I peer over my shoulder, doing my best not to lose my balance on the stepladder. Landon is staring in disbelief at the decorations covering every available surface.

A few years ago, I fell in love with the Christmas farmhouse theme. Rustic wooden signs with sayings such as "Let It Snow," "Merry Christmas," and "Meet Me Under the Mistletoe" are scattered throughout the room, leaning against the wall and the corner of one bookshelf. Black-and-white checked cushions cover the couch, along with my favorite one with the close up of a reindeer's face, as if he's peeking into the camera lens.

The rest of the space is filled with pine boughs, small fake pine trees in tin containers, little red birds made from feathers, pillar candles with cinnamon sticks wrapped with pieces of twine and burlap sacks.

"Surprise." I climb down from the ladder. "I figured since you don't have any Christmas decorations, I'd put mine up."

His gaze jumps from the wreath on the table to me, and his eyebrows crunch together.

I swallow. Hard. "I'm sorry. I didn't realize you really don't like Christmas decorations. I thought it was because you don't have time for things like that. And because you're a guy." I shrug. "But if you don't like them, I can remove them."

When he doesn't say anything, I reach for the reindeer on the mantel, next to the wooden sign that proclaims "Believe."

"You drove to your apartment even though your life is in danger?" His voice comes out like high-grit sandpaper, and I wince.

"There's a good chance I did."

"Fuck, Chloe. I've been hired to protect you. That means keeping you from being killed. What part of that don't you understand?"

My body bristles and my tone comes out as chilled as the San Francisco Bay water in December. "I understand all of it. I'm not an idiot. And I'm sorry for trying to bring a little Christmas cheer into your otherwise non-cheerful existence."

Whiskey whimpers. At the heartbreaking sound, the memory of my father arguing with my mom flashes in my brain. Of him leaving the house.

That was the last time I saw him.

I turn away, so Landon can't see the tears clouding my vision. It was shortly after the holiday season when my father left Mom and me.

When I look at Landon, he's running his hand down his face. "None of that matters if something happens to you." Unlike before, the words come out worn, splinted—much like a block of wood that has been chopped into pieces.

My heart squeezes. What the hell happened for him to react that way?

I have a weird feeling it has nothing to do with me and everything to do with something that happened in his past.

I take a deep breath, fighting back the pain. The pain of my past. The pain inflicted by his reaction. "Look, I'm sorry you're upset. And yes, you have every right to be annoyed with me.

But nothing happened." Other than meeting a guy who wants to go out with me, but I decide to skip that little detail.

"Just because nothing happened doesn't mean it couldn't have. Just because I haven't screwed up my knees playing hockey doesn't mean that when I play my next game, it won't happen. You can't predict what's going to happen. All you can do is minimize the risk. And going to your apartment, on your own, doesn't do that. It increases it."

I pick up the twelve-inch, wooden Santa from the mantel. He's flat, other than the nose, mustache, and the arm holding a small Christmas tree against his body. His vintage, gnome-like appearance makes him look adorable, just like it did the day I found it.

My stepfather and I picked him up at a farmers market while looking for a Christmas present for my mom. I'd fallen in love with it, and my stepfather bought it for me.

I run a finger over the small chip in the paint on his round nose. "I'm sorry." I'm not really sure to whom I'm saying it: Landon...or my stepfather, since my mom and I weren't what he had wanted in the end.

Or maybe he'd discovered that my entire family was more than he had bargained for. For all I know, he discovered the truth about their links to the Russian mafia, and left to avoid being dragged in.

Can't say I blame him for that.

I sniff back the forming tears. "The last good memories I have of my father and stepfather are from the holiday seasons prior to them leaving. At least I'm lucky in that respect. They could've decided not to wait until after Christmas. I could have turned into someone who hates Christmas and the holiday season because I lost someone who meant the world to me. I didn't want that. I might go over the top with the holiday season, but that's due to having so many fond memories of that time of year. Memories I never want to lose."

A tear drips onto the Santa-gnome's face. I wipe it away with my thumb.

Warm, strong arms encase me and pull me into an equally warm, strong body. I stiffen for a second before the pain eases slightly, and I let myself melt into him. It's been a long time since I've admitted to myself why the holiday season is so important to me. Why it's so important for me to make it the best it can be for those around me.

And why I want to make sure the seniors in the retirement home have a wonderful Christmas, especially those individuals who aren't surrounded by their loved ones at this time of year.

With his arms still wrapped around me, Landon kisses my temple. I peer up at him to find him studying me, his face full of anguish that I know deep down isn't because of me.

"You're one of those people, aren't you?" My voice is hoarse from unshed tears. "Something happened to you around Christmas, and that's why you're the way you are. You don't hate Christmas, but you don't exactly embrace it the way so many other people and I do."

Landon doesn't say anything at first. He simply removes the Santa from my hands and studies it for a moment. Vulnerability shines in his eyes. A vulnerability that the tall, strong alpha man in front of me doesn't want to feel or reveal. To me. Or to anyone.

Something in my heart stirs—an emotion I've tried to hide from for so long, but Landon seems to be drawing it out from me.

And I don't know what to do about it.

Because falling in love isn't on the agenda.

Now or ever.

I cup his face in my hand, my thumb strokes his cheek. "You don't have to tell me."

My hand drops away, and I turn to leave.

I don't get far. Landon gently grabs my hand and hauls me

against him. His lips find mine, and he pours whatever he's thinking into that kiss, my heart speeding up in reply.

After a minute—or an hour, I really have no idea which—Landon pulls away slightly. He returns Santa to the mantel and leads me to the couch. Without a word, he sits and pulls me onto his lap. Whatever he's contemplating is hidden from his face. All I see is someone who wants to talk but doesn't know how.

Someone who feels vulnerable…and it's scaring him.

I straddle his legs. He threads his fingers in my hair, cupping my head with his powerful hands. His vulnerability shines back at me again, and this time it's me kissing him.

Doing what I can to drive the demons from him.

Doing what I can to say I'm sorry—sorry I indirectly caused him so much pain.

Sorry he had to go through whatever put the demons there to begin with.

His tongue slides along mine. I meet it stroke for stroke. I can't remember the last time it felt this way to kiss a man, with every nerve in my body a lit fuse.

I keep expecting his hands to start exploring my body, to rip off my clothes. But they don't. He just keeps kissing me. Driving my body insane with need.

I can't tell if he's waiting for me to make a move, allowing me to set the pace after everything I told him, or if he really isn't interested in going there. For now.

He's just following my lead as I try to fix the nicks in our armor before everything we've built up inside us—the thing that prevents further heartbreak—shatters.

We kiss for a while longer; then he rests his forehead on mine. "I told you I had a serious girlfriend after college. I loved her and figured she was the girl I would one day marry. She was a lot like you when it came to Christmas. She loved to decorate."

I stare at him for a heartbeat, surprise pulsating through me that he's telling me this much. But at the same time, icicles form in my veins, spreading throughout my body at his use of past tense, and I can't help but wonder what happened to her.

A deep sense of foreboding fills me, and I shift off his lap to sit next to him. I cover his hand with mine, wanting to know her story, but also willing to wait until he's ready to tell me.

If he ever tells me.

"So she was a decorator-holic like me?" I give him a soft smile.

"You could say that. She didn't even wait for Thanksgiving to be over. As soon as November first hit, the Christmas decorations would begin popping up everywhere."

His gaze moves around the room, and he releases a slow breath. "Six weeks before Christmas, she wanted to go to a house-warming party with her friends. I wasn't a huge fan of the women. To be honest, I thought they were stuck-up bitches. I told her that. Told her I didn't want her to go to the party." His eyes return to me. "As you can imagine, that didn't go down too well. She told me off, told me she was her own boss and didn't need me thinking I could control her life."

"Did she break up with you because of that?"

"No, she went to the party with her friends. I was playing in a competitive hockey league at the time, like I am now. My team had a game that night. I can't even remember who we were playing or if we won. I had no idea she'd gone to the party."

That deep sense of foreboding? It switches to dread—I have a feeling I know what he's going to say next.

But I'm wrong.

"Her friends quickly grew bored of the party, but Sarah was still talking to a colleague of hers. So they ditched my girlfriend and went out for drinks elsewhere.

"Sarah had driven with them. Instead of calling me to pick

her up—even though she knew my game would be over by then—she decided to walk the short distance home.

"Some guys at a local frat party saw her leave and followed her. They were drunk and being idiots. The best the police could figure out was that she got scared and tried to cross the street without checking for oncoming traffic first."

Landon's voice tightens, and his hands fist on his lap. "Two weeks before Christmas, her family finally removed her from life-support. She'd been on it for a month."

The chill inside me from a moment ago turns into an arctic freeze. "Oh, God, Landon. I'm so sorry."

"I was working for an engineering firm," he says, without acknowledging my reaction. "I couldn't get my head in the game after Sarah died. So I joined the military, figuring I was supposed to do something bigger."

"That you were supposed to protect those weaker than you?"

He nods. "My mom tried to convince me to become a cop—not that she and Dad were thrilled with me walking away from my job. It was safer, she said. But I didn't want safer. I didn't want to be a coward like those guys who harassed my girlfriend."

At what is no doubt a confused expression on my face, he clarifies. "They didn't stick around to help her after the car hit her. They ran off. Witnesses reported what they'd seen, and the cops pieced together what had happened."

"You're definitely not a coward. I might've only known you for a few weeks, but even I can see that. Never mind facing down the enemy while you were a SEAL, you've braved being a kindergarten teacher without any formal training or experience with kids."

He laughs, the tightness in his body visibly lessening. "You might have a point there."

I lift my chin and give him a smug grin. "I know I do." The

grin fades. "I really am sorry I took the risk when I knew better. And I'm sorry I did this"—I gesture at the Christmas decorations with the sweep of my hand—"without asking you first."

"That's all right. Sarah died seven years ago. For the most part, I'd thought I had moved on. I guess I haven't."

"You have nothing to feel guilty about, Landon. She chose not to listen to you. That's not your fault." I give his hand a light squeeze.

He nods. "You're right." Now, if only he sounded more convinced.

Eager to change the topic, I ask, "How was your meeting?"

"Long," is all he says, clearly eager to avoid that topic, too.

I push myself off the couch. "I was going to make hot chocolate and popcorn and watch a Christmas movie. Did you want to join me? Or we could watch something else."

"A movie sounds good."

While the hot chocolate heats, I make the popcorn.

"Did you find anything?" I ask Landon, who's searching Netflix while I'm getting everything ready.

"You really want a Christmas movie?"

"Yep. It's tradition." My tradition.

"They're mostly romances."

"Watching a Christmas romance isn't gonna kill you. You might even learn something from it."

He mutters something that sounds suspiciously like, "I highly doubt it."

I take the remote from his hand. "Always a skeptic, huh?"

"You know how many Christmas romances my mom and sisters made me watch growing up?"

I shake my head, lips pressed together to keep from laughing at his perturbed expression.

"Way too many. And they were never educational like my sisters claimed they would be."

I had no chance of holding back the laugh after that. I

might have not met Kathy and Evie—and probably never will —but I was already in love with them based on everything Landon had told me about them.

"Didn't they make your father watch them, too?"

"My father was a lot smarter than I was. Or maybe it was my mother who was the smarter one. She had a list of things that needed fixing around the house, which Dad never got around to doing. But he always suddenly found time to do them whenever my mother and sisters decided it was time to watch a romance."

That makes me laugh even harder.

Still laughing, I scroll through the selection and pick one that I'm sure Landon will hate, just because. I've seen it before, so I know it won't be super cheesy. No point giving him any ammunition.

He groans.

"Part of your cover," I tell him, "is that you have to watch the movies I want to see. And that includes Christmas romances." I fuel my tone with the right amount of smugness and wink at him.

"But that's only when we're in public." He reaches for the remote in my hand.

I bat it away. "Usually a cover means you have to live it twenty-four seven. There are no halfway in-betweens on this."

He rolls his eyes and lunges for the remote. I reach behind me, preventing him from getting hold of it. All I accomplish is that I make it too easy for him to knock me backward onto the couch.

With my arm still stretched above my head, I squirm under his weight, trying to get into a position that will make it easier to roll him off me.

He rocks his hips, his hard cock pressing against my core. I gasp.

This is not how I initially saw things playing out.

"How about we have a contest to determine who gets to pick the movie?" he asks.

"Yeah, okay. That sounds fair." Because I plan to win.

Right, maybe I should find out what the contest is before I so enthusiastically agree.

He rocks once more. "Whoever gives the other person an orgasm first gets to pick the movie."

I contemplate it for a second. "You've got yourself a deal."

23

LANDON

I rock my hard cock along her pussy, hidden under the fabric of her jeans.

It strains against the zipper of *my* jeans.

Fuck.

What the hell was I thinking?

Clearly, I wasn't. I'm only two steps from blowing my load, and my manhood is facing great peril thanks to the Christmas romance I'll be forced to watch if I don't win.

But I'm hardly going to let Chloe know that.

"So how are we doing this?" she asks. "Time each other and see who lasts the longest before they have an orgasm?"

"No. I'll be giving you an orgasm at the same time you'll be aiming to give me one. The first one to give the other person an orgasm is the winner."

Her eyebrow lifts. "I hope that doesn't mean as soon as you come, that's the end of the contest, and I don't get to experience an orgasm."

"That won't be an issue, because you'll be coming first. But yes, if I come first, I guarantee I'll finish what I started. No one goes unsatisfied."

"All right, may the best woman win, because I really want to see *The Christmas Prince*." She straddles my legs again and reaches for the hem of my T-shirt, a determined look in her eyes.

Dream on, sweetheart.

I pull the hem of her top up her body, exposing her white cotton bra. "No sexy underwear on a weeknight?" I tug the top over her head and drop it to the floor.

"Woof."

I peer over the edge of the couch, almost sending Chloe flying.

Her light purple top shuffles along the floor like a colored apparition.

Chloe laughs and reaches to yank the fabric off Whiskey. He jumps his paws onto the couch and glances between us.

"We might want to continue this contest upstairs," I tell her. "I'm not exactly looking to have an audience." This isn't a game show.

"Good idea." She moves off my lap. "Stay here," she tells Whiskey, even though doing what he's told isn't one of his superpowers.

He starts to follow after her.

"No, Whiskey," she says. "Stay." She takes another step forward...and so does Whiskey.

"Whiskey, bed." I point to his bed by the couch.

He tilts his head to the side, my command lost on him.

Like it is every time we try this.

"Dude, I don't think you understand. I'm about to get the orgasm of a lifetime, and you're staying here until we get back."

"Woof."

Chloe laughs and covers her mouth with her hand. "Sounds like he understands just fine."

"I guess I'll have to put him in his crate." The last thing I want is for him to scratch on my bedroom door at a crucial moment.

He lets out a little whimper, looks between Chloe and me, then walks to his bed and plonks down on it.

I grab hold of Chloe's hand and pull her along behind me. "The decorations look great," is the only thing I say before leading her upstairs.

They do look great. Sarah would've loved them.

The moment we're in my room—the door shut behind us—we're tearing each other's clothes off. But what starts out impatient quickly turns into something else.

Slow.

Languid.

A teasing seduction.

Another unexpected emotion hovers in the fringes. What I'm starting to feel for Chloe goes deeper than wanting to get her off and win the bet.

It's an emotion I don't want to examine too closely, especially not now.

Especially not when there's a movie at stake.

We continue removing each other's clothes until we're standing by the bed, naked. I don't even remember walking the short distance to it. Each exploring touch of her fingers short-circuits my brain. Each press of her lips against my body isn't helping it either.

I lower her to the bed, my intent of winning the contest for remote-control domination quickly forgotten. I want to worship her body, to show her she deserves so much more than her fathers and ex-boyfriends ever felt for her.

She deserves to be loved and wanted.

Yes, but you're not the man to do that. This is only temporary until the Feds find Nikolai Orlov and learn who has the contract out on her.

You aren't her real boyfriend.

Hell, she doesn't even know I work for the Feds. She still thinks I'm employed by her cousin. A cousin who hasn't done anything to protect her. If it weren't for Liam's team, she'd already be dead.

My stomach clenches. I push the thought away and focus on the beautiful nymph beneath my hands.

The one who has just wrapped her hand around my hard cock.

All I care about right now is showing her what she means to me, even if I can never say the words to her.

While she pumps her fist along my length, eliciting groans from deep in my chest, my thumb spreads the slick wetness around her clit.

My mouth finds a hard nipple, and I suck on it, tease it with my tongue and teeth. She moans and writhes, her body getting closer and closer to losing control.

That makes two of us.

Her hands are as busy as mine. One strokes my length. The other one plays with my balls, squeezing them, gently tugging on them. I'm so close to coming. Any more of this and I'll be too far gone, and that's something I'm not ready for just yet—and it has nothing to do with the contest.

I grab a condom from my bedside drawer, open the foil square, and roll it down my length. There's no doubt Chloe is ready for me. Her soft moans of my name, combined with her "Oh, Gods," are all I need to hear.

Neither of us will last much longer.

I position myself against her entrance. My cock begs to thrust inside her, to feel her soft, tight heat wrapped around it. But this, what we're about to do, has nothing to do with me and everything to do with her.

I slowly push myself in, torturing myself in the process, but it's worth it. Her unsuppressed cries are worth the near pain of taking things excruciatingly slow.

"Come for me, Chloe, and you'll get to watch whatever movie you want," I say between panted breaths. "I don't care what it is. I just need you to come first." So I can watch her explode around me.

That surpasses any movie.

Her gaze locks on mine, and whatever she finds there is all she needs to see. With a cry that Whiskey no doubt hears, her body shudders, and her heat tightens around me with a gratifying hug.

The pressure building in my lower region peaks to the point of no return, and a dizzying hot light engulfs me. I grunt out my release with a long animalistic noise...and collapse next to her on the bed.

I was right when I told Whiskey I was about to experience an orgasm of a lifetime. I can't remember the last time it was this intense.

This mind-numbing.

It takes me a minute to regain awareness.

I pull Chloe against me and kiss her temple. My hands caress her body, needing confirmation she's still here with me.

She runs her fingers across the expanse of my chest, clearly lost in thought.

"What are you thinking?" I ask because I really want to know.

She shifts to look down at me and gently kisses my lips. "It's nothing." Her skin is flushed from our lovemaking, and it practically steals my breath away.

"Are you sure?"

She smiles, and my heart squeezes in my chest at the sight of it. I love her smiles. They have a way of brightening even the dreariest day. But this one is so much more than that.

I cup the back of her head and bring it to mine for another soul-baring kiss.

And the popcorn, hot chocolate, and movie are quickly forgotten.

EVENTUALLY, WE DO DRAG OURSELVES OUT OF BED. WHISKEY needs to be taken outside. Plus, all the activity between the covers is making us hungry.

I grab my clean hockey jersey from the chair and toss it to her. "Here, put this on, and we'll go get something to eat and watch the movie."

She quickly slips it over her head. The heavy fabric drops into place, reaching the tops of her thighs.

My cock, exhausted as it is, stirs to life once more. It takes all my willpower, and then some, not to toss her onto the bed and make love to her again.

Downstairs, Chloe heats the hot chocolate and curls up against me on the couch as we start watching the movie. The bowl of popcorn sits perched on my lap.

The movie really is as sappy as I was expecting. But since it makes Chloe happy, I don't complain.

Or at least I assume she's happy. She rubs her fingers under her eyes.

"Are you okay?" I ask, looking between her and the TV screen.

"I always cry at this part."

That has me even more confused. It's not like anyone died or anything. Just the opposite.

Seeing the confusion stamped on my face, she clarifies, "I'm a sucker for happy endings."

I've never really understood why women cry at sappy endings. My mother and sisters were the same. They always had a box of tissues on hand whenever they watched what they called tearjerkers.

The corner of my mouth twitches up. "That seriously made you cry?"

"Sure, he finally got the girl. She realized she couldn't live without him."

"I'm betting the prince is just relieved he's finally getting laid."

Chloe smirks at me through a tear-stained face. "I'm sure that's exactly what he was thinking when he got down on one knee to propose." She snatches up the reindeer pillow next to her and hits me on the arm.

I grab my biceps, pretending to be gravely wounded. Cautiously, she lowers the cushion, and I pull her onto my lap, taking advantage of the movement.

Her eyes shine at me, and for a moment, we just stare at each other. The only sounds in the room are the faint snores from the direction of Whiskey's bed and the closing credits.

Her gaze drops to my lips.

I stroke my thumb against her cheek. There's no doubt about it, I'm falling for Chloe.

And I'm falling hard.

24

CHLOE

The final bell rings. "Don't forget to take your hats and gloves with you," I remind the kids. It never fails that someone forgets something in their rush to go home. As it is, they've been bouncing off the walls for the past hour, ready for the weekend to begin.

Once the last of the kids trails out the door to the hallway, Landon strolls through the one connecting our classrooms. It's been four days since I decorated his town house.

Four days since I felt something shift inside me during the contest to make each other climax first.

He flashes me a wicked smile and gives me a very thorough kiss.

My heart and breath respond, picking up speed. The same way they always behave every time he kisses me after the final bell. The kisses are now a daily occurrence, ever since we opened up about his old girlfriend and about my father, stepfather, and Mark.

Things have also shifted between us, but I can't put my finger on why exactly that is. I'm nothing more than a mission to him, a notch in the old proverbial belt.

My heart does a little flutter kick as if that's the only answer I need. But it might also be because he's still kissing me.

It's not a naughty, let's-get-down-and-dirty kiss. This kiss stirs something deep in my soul.

And I suddenly know why.

I'm falling for him. Even though I know better due to my past, my heart apparently isn't all that wise.

That, or it's just a glutton for punishment.

Yep, definitely the latter.

He pulls away. "You know what we still need?"

I glance around the classroom, trying to puzzle it out. "No, what?"

"To get a Christmas tree. We decorated the one at the seniors' home last night, but I don't have one in my town house."

"I thought you didn't do Christmas decorating."

"I didn't. But since you've already turned my living room and kitchen into a Hallmark Christmas card, we might as well go all-out and get a tree."

I grin, one step from clapping my hands like a little kid and doing a happy dance.

"Do you have any decorations for it?" I ask, instead. I didn't bring many tree ornaments with me when I raided my storage unit.

"We can get some after we get the tree."

Still grinning, I remove my coat from the hook on the wall. "Let's go get that tree."

AT THE TREE LOT, WE WANDER THE AISLES, HOLDING HANDS. THE place is quaint, with crafts set up to entertain the kids, a booth selling hot chocolate, upbeat Christmas music piped through the speakers, and employees dressed as elves.

Just add snow, and the setting would be a scene right out of a romantic Christmas movie.

I sip on my hot chocolate. "Wow, this is good."

"It's their secret family recipe," Adam tells me.

That's right, Landon and I aren't the only ones here. The reason Landon even knew about this location is because of Adam.

"Uncle Adam," Emily says, beaming up at the tall man. "Can we see Santa?" The five-year-old tugs on his hand, not giving him a chance to say no.

Landon and I follow the pair.

Santa has a short line, so the four of us stand in it, waiting for Emily's turn.

"I'm going to be a big sister," she tells Landon and me. She holds her hands out as if describing the size of a fish she just caught.

I crouch to her level. "You're so lucky. I've always wanted to be a big sister. I bet you'll be a super cool one."

Emily rapidly nods. "Are you Uncle Landon's girlfriend?"

"Yes, I am."

"Momma says Uncle Adam needs a girlfriend. She told me to ask Santa to bring him one for Christmas."

I look at the man in question in time to catch him rolling his eyes. "Your mother knows Santa doesn't have room in his sleigh to bring me a girlfriend. So you don't have to worry about asking him for that."

"Could you get Uncle Adam a girlfriend?" she asks me.

"Your Uncle Adam can get his own girlfriend," he responds.

She peers up at him. "That's what Daddy told Momma. She told him that he was wrong. And that she'd never get to be an aunt unless someone does something about it soon." Emily gives a hard nod, her face a mask of determination, and returns her gaze to me. "Will you get Uncle Adam a girlfriend for Christmas?"

"Unfortunately, I don't know anyone looking for a boyfriend. Everyone I know is married or is engaged or has a boyfriend."

The only exception is Kiera, and she's made it quite clear she's not ready for the dating scene yet.

Emily releases a disappointed breath. "I'm sorry, Uncle Adam. I tried."

"Maybe you should go with your original plan of asking Santa to bring him one for Christmas," Landon says on a chuckle.

I stand and elbow him in the ribs. "Oh, I'm sorry. Did I accidentally hit you?" I flash him a teasing grin.

He pulls me against his body and presses his lips against mine.

They eagerly return the sentiment.

I'm vaguely aware of a murmur of voices and then...

"Ewww. Don't kiss."

We separate, and I look at the little girl. "Did your uncle tell you to say that?"

She nods, her head moving in a jerky exaggeration.

The kid who's on Santa's lap scrambles off. Adam escorts Emily over to the man and lowers her onto his lap.

She stares at Santa, eyes wide.

Santa says something to her...and she keeps on staring.

Adam prompts her to say something. She nods, eyes still round with awe.

"I guess she won't be asking Santa to bring Adam a girlfriend after all," I say, laughing.

Landon wraps his arms around me from behind. "Looks like you might be right."

If whoever has a contract out on me sees us now, there'd be no doubt in their mind that he's my boyfriend. It might not be true as far as Landon's concerned, but no one would know that. He really is a good actor.

Landon's phone pings that he's got a text. He pulls it out of his pocket and checks the screen. A frown wrinkles between his eyes.

"Is everything all right?"

He doesn't respond, too busy typing his reply.

The phone pings again a moment later.

He returns it to his pocket. "Everything's fine."

He might say that, but his voice tells me otherwise.

If he really were my boyfriend, I'd try to get him to talk about whatever's bothering him. Maybe not here, in public, but definitely back at his place.

But he's not, so I'm not sure what to do.

Emily and Adam return. Her shell shock has vanished, and she skips toward us. Adam is right behind her, checking his phone.

His gaze lands on Landon. Landon nods at some unspoken question between them.

Without saying anything to me, Landon walks to a pile of trees leaning against a wall, their branches tied together with nylon string.

He grabs one. "This looks good." He walks toward a table where a woman is collecting the money for the trees.

"Is something wrong?" I ask Adam.

Emily is busy poking the tree next to where Landon grabbed ours. "This one." She points to it.

"Good choice," Adam says, no longer paying attention to her. He's busy typing on his phone.

With his eyes on the screen, he reaches in the general direction she pointed and grabs at the air instead.

I hand him the correct tree. He nods and slips his phone into his jacket pocket. "Thanks."

Landon has finished paying for our tree by the time we

arrive at the table. "See you," he tells his colleague, giving him a meaningful look that's lost on me.

Next, we go to a store that specializes in Christmas decorations and leave with enough ornaments to cover the tree. Ornaments he gave me free rein to choose.

Back at the town house, Landon sets up the tree in the living room, much to Whiskey's delight. The puppy keeps inspecting it, no doubt wondering why a spruce is now growing in the room.

Landon arranges the lights on the branches. He might be smiling, but there's something still off about him. The smile seems forced and is missing from his eyes.

"Are you okay?" I ask, repeating my earlier question. It's possible that memories of his dead girlfriend, and memories associated with the holiday season before she died, are being dredged up, thanks to our tree.

"I'm fine." He doesn't look at me when he says it. He studies the ornament in his hand as if memorizing every tiny detail.

THE DOORBELL RINGS AS I'M HANGING UP A WOODEN MOUSE decoration in the tree. Landon goes to answer it and returns a minute later with Ava, Liam, and Adam. The man and woman with them, both wearing suits, are the same ones who showed up at the school with the police shortly after my attempted kidnapping.

All look as though someone kicked a litter of puppies several blocks.

I smile at Ava. "Landon didn't tell me you were coming over."

She opens her mouth to say something. Landon cuts her off.

"This is Agent Foden and Agent Ramsey with the FBI." He nods at the two other individuals. They flash their IDs at me.

I scan everyone's faces, searching for a hint of what's going on. I draw a blank. Other than Ava's pained expression, no one else is giving anything away.

"What's going on?" I ask.

Ava steps forward. "Maybe you should sit down."

"No, I'm good standing." I look at Landon, silently imploring him to explain why FBI agents are in his living room. Is he in trouble because of who he works for? That would make sense. I'm sure my cousin is on some FBI's most wanted list. "Would someone tell me what's going on?"

"As you're no doubt aware," the woman, Agent Foden, says, "Vadik Orlov, your grandfather, has been indicted for a long list of charges,"

I nod. "What does that have to do with me? He's my biological grandfather, but I cut ties with the family years ago. I have nothing to do with him or any of his criminal activities."

"We know. As part of the case, law officials have been combing through his various holdings, looking for evidence for the upcoming trial. As well as searching for evidence of additional wrongdoings."

I nod in understanding, although I'm not really sure why they're telling me this.

"Three bodies were discovered buried in a wooded area linked to one of your grandfather's properties," Agent Ramsey says.

"Bodies?"

"They were human remains."

"Remains?" Nice. I've become a parrot.

"Skeletons, to be exact. Three males. Recent autopsies identified that they all died of blunt-force trauma to the head."

I frown, not understanding what this has to do with me. "Okay. So you found three male skeletons on one of my grandfather's properties. I'm not sure why you're telling me this. As I've already explained, I have nothing to do with that family."

Panic gnaws inside me like a beaver attempting to fell a tree. They seriously can't believe I have something to do with this.

Can they?

The agents look at Landon.

He turns to me. "Chloe, the FBI was able to identify the bodies. They belonged to William Reinhart, Curtis Cartwright, and Mark Greenwood."

My biological father, my stepfather, and my ex-boyfriend.

At their names, it's like a tap has been turned on, the blood rapidly draining from my head. I sway, the ramification ping-ponging in my thoughts. *It can't be them. The FBI must be wrong.* Not as convinced by my words as my brain, my legs call it a day, and I slump to the floor.

Landon catches me before my body has a chance to hit the hardwood. I'm vaguely aware of him scooping me up and placing me on the couch.

Despite the warmth of the room, a chill sneaks into my body, and I shiver uncontrollably.

Landon wraps his arm around me and says something to Ava. I have no idea what. It's like he's talking to her through glycerine, his words garbled.

Ava grabs the red-and-white plaid blanket from the armchair and hands it to Landon. It's the Christmas blanket I'd bought from my apartment. For once, it doesn't bring me comfort. It doesn't warm me up.

I could stand on the beach in Hawaii during a heat wave, and I still wouldn't warm up.

Landon says something else. Again, I have no idea what he's saying.

I try to piece all the bits together to make sense of everything. I come up blank. The only thing I can comprehend is the question that keeps repeating in my brain again and again and again.

Why were they murdered? Was it because they'd left me with a broken heart?

Or had they simply become twisted up in my family's criminal activities?

But that doesn't make sense. While my father and stepfather might have gotten caught up in it, since there's no way they could have not known about my family's dark side, Mark had nothing to do with that world.

I started dating him after I left my family.

They would've left him alone.

Or I assumed they would've left him alone. Was I wrong to believe that? Had I condemned all future boyfriends to a life of crime due to my family making them an "offer" they couldn't refuse?

A voice in my head whispers another possibility. *Or had it never been their intention to leave me? Did someone make the choice for them?*

Adam passes me a glass of amber liquid. My arms refuse to obey the simple command to take it from him.

Landon accepts it from him and lifts the glass to my lips. I don't understand what he's saying, but I do understand what he wants me to do.

I sip the liquid and relish the slow burn as it slides down my throat. For the first time since Landon broke the news, the numbness recedes a little, enough for me to accept the glass from him, the liquid sloshing inside it.

I take another sip, aware of several people talking, but I have no idea if they're talking to each other or if the questions are directed at me.

Had they really intended to leave me? Or did someone make that choice for them?

Ava sits on the other side of me and hugs me. "I'm so sorry, Chloe," she hoarsely whispers.

Had they really intended to leave me? Or did someone make that choice for them?

If they had been involved with my family's criminal activities, why were they murdered? Did they know too much? Did they all try to walk away, only to discover that there's no escaping once you agree to help my grandfather with that first request?

The thought of them stolen from me all those years ago finally forms a crack in the numbness. Tears dampen my face and the blanket wrapped around me.

Landon pulls me to him, and I sob into his shoulder.

For all those years...

All those years I believed I was better off not giving my heart to another man because every man who was important to me had left me, never bothering to contact me again.

And now I know why.

They'd never been given a chance.

I pull away from Landon. "Why?" I croak to no one in particular. "Why were they murdered?"

"We have no motive at this point," Agent Foden says, "but based on the autopsy, it's highly probable the same individual was responsible for each of their deaths, even though they took place over two decades."

Whiskey sees my wet face and whimpers. He then tries to scramble onto the couch. I don't have the energy to pick him up. Ava does that for me.

The little bundle of fuzz licks my hand and climbs onto my lap. I absently stroke his fur, letting the action semi-ground me.

"Chloe," Landon says, his arm still holding me. "Agents Foden and Ramsey need to ask you some questions. They're hoping it might answer why the men were killed and who was responsible."

I nod. The same questions are burning in my head...along with a new one.

Is Nikolai involved with the FBI? Is that why the two agents are with Liam, Adam, and Landon, as though that's a regular occurrence?

Okay, that's two questions.

Instead of waiting for theirs, I voice one of my own.

"Where's Nikolai?"

Landon stiffens next to me, but it happens so quickly, I'm not sure if I imagined it.

"We don't know," Agent Foden says. "That's one of the things we're hoping you can help us with."

"I haven't seen or heard from him in years, after I left my family because of their..." *They already know, Chloe. They already know your grandfather was the head of the mafia crime family.* "Because of their criminal activities. I wanted none of that."

"And he hasn't tried to contact you since?"

"He used to send me birthday and Christmas cards, but that was about it. I didn't even know if he was still with the family or if he had stepped away from it. He wanted to be a cop when he was a kid. I thought maybe there was a chance he'd done exactly that but decided not to contact me because things were too complicated."

It was my favorite story I told myself whenever I'd missed Nikolai.

"I can guarantee he's not with any police forces," Agent Ramsey says. "Your grandfather was shaping him to be the new mafia boss. And that's exactly what we believe he's doing. He took over your grandfather's role after Vadik Orlov was arrested. But he went underground."

"We're hoping you know something that will help us locate him," Agent Foden says. "Or if he tries to contact you, we can attempt to flush him out."

We're hoping you know something that will help us locate him…

His words echo in my head like the bells of Notre Dame. They repeat themselves again and again and again until they fade away.

I look at Liam and Adam and Landon in turn and feel a frown forming on my brow. "But you've spoken with him recently."

I catch the slight wince on Landon's face.

The FBI has no idea Landon and his colleagues are helping Nikolai, that they're the ones in contact with my cousin, not me.

They never wanted the FBI involved, but that's precisely what happened.

Does this mean they could go to jail?

It's Landon who answers my unspoken questions. "We haven't spoken to him. We were hired to track him down through you."

"Hired? Who hired you?"

"The FBI. We work with them from time to time, helping with some of their cases."

When I was eight years old, I accidentally crashed my bike into my favorite climbing tree. My bike was totaled, and my arm landed in a cast. At the time, I'd felt like the tree had betrayed me.

The pain and sting of betrayal I'd felt is nothing compared to what I'm experiencing now.

I pull away from Landon. "You lied to me." The words scrape my throat like sandpaper on fire. "You lied to me about who you are. You were using me all this time."

I stand, sending Whiskey tumbling to the floor, and back away from Landon, almost tripping over Ava's feet.

"Let me guess, you staged the attempted kidnapping so I would agree to be your girlfriend. Then you could use me to get to my cousin?"

This entire time I'd been kept on a short leash, all for nothing.

I'd poured out my heart, all for nothing.

I'd been falling in love, all for nothing.

"I bet all that stuff you told me about your old girlfriend was a lie, too."

Landon shoots to his feet. "That's not true." His tone is hard. I don't understand why he's mad at me. He was the one who manipulated me, not the other way around. "Everything else was true. The only thing that wasn't was who hired us. But I never said Nikolai hired us. That was all on you."

"But you never corrected me when I assumed he was the reason for your sudden appearance in my life. You've had plenty of time to tell me the truth, but you didn't. You kept stringing me along, making me think my cousin still loved me enough to hire men to protect me." My voice cracks again, the fissure in my heart widening with each bitter word.

The only thing saving it from completely splitting in two is the knowledge that my father, stepfather, and Mark might not have stopped loving me like I'd initially believed. They were murdered.

But Nikolai...he was another matter.

I'd loved him like he was my brother, like he was my best friend, but in the end, he was the one who had walked away from me.

By choice.

25

LANDON

I'm not one for feeling helpless. I'm a doer. A person who has to be in control of the situation.

But right now, a foreign sense of helplessness is winding its way around my heart.

It wasn't supposed to go down like this. None of it was—including Chloe believing her cousin hired us to protect her.

The lie is all on me.

I thought it would be easier to get answers.

I fucked everything up.

The look of betrayal on her face guts me. All I can do for several seconds is stare idiotically at her, trying to figure out how to make things better.

For her.

For me.

For us.

She turns to the agents. "I'm sorry, but I can't help you. I have no idea where he is."

She doesn't give them a chance to respond. She walks past them, chin lifted, and rushes from the room.

I step forward to go after her, but I'm pulled up short by Ava's hand on my arm.

"Let me talk to her," she says.

I jerk away from her, intent on going upstairs. Liam steps in front of me. "Let Ava talk to her first."

I grunt. "Do you seriously believe that will make a difference? Ava lied to Chloe about how she knew me. Everyone dealing with the case has lied to her."

"Yes, but I know her better than anyone in this room," Ava says. "You've only known her a few weeks. I've known her for a few years."

She doesn't wait for my reply. She tells the agents she'll be back and hurries after her friend.

Fuck. Fuck. Fuck.

I begin pacing the length of the living room. Fortunately, everyone has the foresight to keep out of my way. They practically dive out of my path, as if I'm in Santa's sleigh filled with firecrackers, and it's spiraling toward them.

A wise move, I might add.

While I pace, Liam, Adam, and the two agents discuss what to do next. Chloe used to be close to her cousin, and at one point, she meant the world to him. But that was when he wanted to be a cop.

People change.

When it comes to tracking down Nikolai, we've been wasting our time. He clearly doesn't see my boyfriend status with Chloe as a threat.

"Do you think Nikolai Orlov is aware of the contract on Chloe?" I ask the four individuals in the room.

"If we knew about it, then I'm positive he does, too," Agent Ramsey says.

"Yet, he's done nothing to protect her." My gut tightens. Shrinks to the size of a puck. Like it wants nothing more than to hit her cousin in the head and knock him unconscious.

"There's always a chance he didn't want to waste manpower on that. We're doing the job for him."

"And he didn't have an issue with it?"

The two agents shrug—the move perfectly synchronized to the point of being almost comical. "It could be we misjudged his relationship with Chloe, and he had no intention of contacting her."

My gut tightens some more. If Liam's team hadn't stepped in, would Nikolai have reached out to her to protect her? Or would she have been disposable, like the men in her life her grandfather killed?

Ava returns five minutes later with Chloe following behind her. Chloe doesn't even look at me, a suitcase in one hand. Neither of them appears happy.

Chloe heads straight for the front door.

What the hell...?

I steamroll my way over to her. "Where do you think you're going?"

"Back to my apartment." She doesn't spare me a second glance. "Someone will pick up the rest of my stuff."

"I'll go with you."

She shakes her head. "No, you won't. Consider our fake relationship null and void. I'm officially dumping you." She finally looks at me, pain and resolution swirling in the depth of those beautiful brown eyes. "At least that's the version that will spread through the teacher's lounge on Monday like an infestation of head lice."

I wince and then remind her, "It's not safe. You have a contract on your head."

Without a word, she opens the front door. Whiskey barks at her. She smiles down at him. "I'm gonna miss you, little guy. Good luck with your forever home. Hopefully, you don't have to wait long for it." She doesn't even look in my direction when she says it.

She scratches him behind the ear and leaves.

Fuck.

"Adam, you're back on surveillance," Liam says as soon as the door clicks shut. Adam nods and follows after her.

"What did she say up there?" I ask Ava.

"I'm sorry, I can't tell you. It had nothing to do with the case, if that's what you're wondering."

"Are you telling me you were swapping lesson plans up there?" I highly doubt it.

Ignoring me, she turns to her husband. "I told you it would be a big mistake for Landon to pretend to be her boyfriend."

"No, you said it would be a mistake for me to pretend *to her* that she was my girlfriend," I point out. "But that's not what happened. She knew going into it that the relationship was fake. She was fine with it."

Ava shakes her head, and there's some serious eye-rolling in her tone when she says, "Was she? I don't know about you, but she didn't look *fine* to me."

"That's because I let her believe her cousin still cared enough about her to make sure she's safe. I thought it would be easier that way." For the case.

Yep, I'm like a sundae. Two scoops of idiot with an extra helping of dumbass sprinkled on top.

"She spent most of her life believing that she was better off not loving anyone who was male since the men she loved eventually left her," Ava says. "Now, she believes her love will eventually kill any man she falls for. And she's not exactly thrilled that I knew her cousin didn't actually hire you guys and let her continue to believe that." Ava crosses her arms and glares at me.

My gut tightens even though I know I deserve Ava's anger. I dragged her into the lie, and I have a feeling it's going to take me a long time to make things up to Liam's wife.

"The part where she believes her love is deadly is crazy," I say.

"Is it? From her point of view, that's exactly what happened. The only exception is her cousin. And from the sounds of it, she'd be better off if a troll threw him off a bridge."

As an author of middle-grade fantasy, Ava has quite an active imagination.

I wouldn't be surprised if I'm in her next book—in the killing-off-the-people-who've-pissed-her-off way.

"Well, I'd be more than happy to take on the role of the troll for her." I turn to the agents, who are watching Ava and I go at it, their expressions stoic.

But I've been around FBI agents and Navy SEALs long enough to speak fluent stoic. They'd also be more than happy to throw me off the bridge.

"Does this mean I'm no longer working undercover as a substitute teacher?" I ask Liam.

"For the time being, I think it's best you maintain the cover. Despite what she might believe, she's still in danger. And you never know, the FBI might come up with a much bigger fish to fry from all this."

By FBI, he means his team. But he's hardly going to admit that in front of Agents Foden and Ramsey.

Relief swims through me. It shouldn't, but it does anyhow.

"What about the boyfriend cover?" That's the one I really want to know.

Because despite what Chloe might believe, I'm not ready to walk away from the cover yet—or from her.

26

CHLOE

"I don't blame you if you're still mad at me."

I turn toward the classroom door to discover Ava standing in the doorway. It's Monday afternoon, and my students have left for the day.

"I'm not mad at you." Not anymore, anyway. "I get why you couldn't tell me the truth."

The words come out softly, with no trace of anger, but that doesn't stop her from flinching.

I meant it, though. It would've been a different story if Liam and his team had been working for the dark side. I should be doing cartwheels.

And I would be—if Landon had been honest with me from the beginning.

"Like I told you Friday night," Ava says, walking toward me. "I'm really sorry I lied to you. Liam didn't want me to be involved because he knew it would put me in an awkward position. That, and he knows I'm a crappy liar."

A laugh bubbles up inside me. "Well, if it makes you feel any better, I would make an equally crappy lie detector. I guess

that's just another gene I never inherited from my grandfather."
Can't say I'm too sorry about that.

Despite everything, it feels good to be able to talk to Ava.
She's the only friend I have who I can discuss my family with.
My real family, not the fictitious one I tend to mention when
asked.

"You're not by any chance here to tell me I should forgive
Landon for lying to me, are you?"

Ava snorts a laugh. "Definitely not. You have every right to
be pissed at him. He should have been honest with you to
begin with." Her face softens. "While Landon and I might not
have known each other in college like I told you we had, I have
known him for several years. And the Landon I know doesn't
generally lie, unless it has to do with his job. That's just the
nature of what my husband and his team do."

Ava and I hug and it feels like a billion pounds have been
knocked off my shoulders.

"So what's going on between you and that dreamy
boyfriend of yours?" Kiera asks, entering the classroom as Ava
and I step away from each other.

"What do you mean?"

Don't look at his classroom. Don't look at his…

Oops. So much for that plan. I did a much better job not
looking that way while I was talking to Ava about him.

Kiera tilts her head to the side as if trying to get a good read
on me. "Usually, you two are inseparable. Today you were
doing everything in your power to avoid him. Not to mention
you remind me of an ant who's been dropped in a bucket and
desperately wants to climb out."

Yep, that pretty much sums it up.

She looks at Ava for confirmation.

Ava shifts on her feet, suddenly looking like that ant too. "I
should probably get back to my class and double-check every-

thing's okay." She can't get out of the room fast enough, and I do my best not to laugh.

"I realized that we were rushing things and..." I say to Kiera, "and maybe dating a colleague isn't a good idea."

Sounds like a reasonable explanation.

Too bad Kiera doesn't buy it. "This doesn't have anything to do with your abandonment issues, does it?"

"I don't have abandonment issues." I pick up the picture book left on Anton's desk and leaf through it. I've always loved this illustrator's work. It's similar to my style, but also very different.

"So you're saying that after what happened with your fathers and ex-boyfriend, you're not scared that the next guy will do the same thing? That's why you've been avoiding dating until recently when you met Landon, isn't it?"

The brush strokes look so real, you would never guess it was done on the computer.

"Chloe?"

I let out a hard breath and walk to the bookshelf in the reading corner.

"Like I said, I don't have abandonment issues." Not anymore, at least.

Now I have the-boogeyman-will-kill-any-man-I-love issues.

You know, the same issues every red-blooded American woman has.

Or not.

"Right. And the next thing you're going to tell me is that your eyes are bloodshot due to allergies."

"You never know. I could be allergic to...um...Christmas trees."

Smooth, Chloe. I mentally roll my eyes.

"Well, that would really suck, given that you live for Christmas. But it's not that, so spill it."

Where's Landon when you need him...even if I don't actually want him around? Before Friday night's big revelation, he was in my classroom as soon as the final bell rang.

I guess he finally got my hint that I don't want to talk to him again. Ever.

But what did he expect would happen once the truth came out? If he lied about that, what else was he lying about?

"Chloe, you're my best friend, and I love you, dearly. You know that."

I smile at her. "I do know that."

"As your best friend, it's my duty to take you out tonight and stage an intervention."

I laugh. "Sounds great, but I'm volunteering tonight, and afterward, I have to sew an army of pint-sized elf hats." That's one advantage of moving back to my apartment. I spent the last two days attempting to forget everything while busying myself with the hats.

And watching every Christmas kid's show I could find on TV.

Because who needs Hallmark Christmas movies when you've got *The Grinch* and *Rudolph the Red-Nosed Reindeer*?

That's right—holiday romance movies have officially been banned from my apartment.

"You're not volunteering tomorrow night, right?" Kiera asks.

"Nope. But I'll still be making elf hats."

"Perfect. Then we have a date. You. Me. Lots of spiked eggnog. And Project Elf Hat."

I grin, remembering exactly why I love her. "All right, you have yourself a date."

After she leaves my classroom, I half expect Landon to enter, purely out of habit. He doesn't. Instead, it's Isabelle who walks in through the main doorway.

"Hi. Is there something you need? I'm about to leave." I smile at her even though she's just one more reminder of Landon.

She smiles back, sympathy in her eyes. Sympathy I can handle. Pity is another story.

And if I were to hazard a guess, I'd say she's aware that my codename is now Black Widow. Except instead of being the one who kills men, they die by association, with me being the common denominator.

"I'm here to make sure you get to your car safely," Isabelle says.

So, Landon's old job.

"It's not necessary," I tell her. "I know the truth. All that was just a ruse so Landon could use me to get to my cousin."

She shakes her head. "The part about your cousin hiring us was a lie—Landon should never have let you believe that—but the part about the contract out on you isn't."

"But why would anyone want to kill me? I'm not part of my grandfather's world. Hell, I'm not even part of the family anymore. He made sure of it when he forbid my relatives—including my own mother—to contact me."

And because his money and approval meant everything to them, they willingly obliged.

Except for my mother. She did it for love.

She did it for me.

"I'm only a useful pawn in the turf war if my grandfather gave a damn about me."

It's not like he has to stress about me turning over family secrets to the state. They know a lot more about the "family" business than I'll ever know.

More than I'll ever want to know.

"I think you might be wrong about that," she tells me.

"I'm definitely not wrong. My grandfather has never cared about me the way he did my cousins. It hurt me as a kid, but once I realized the monster he really is—and I don't mean the blue kind who eats cookies—it didn't bother me anymore." I slip my coat on and grab my purse from my desk chair.

"Maybe the contract has nothing to do with your grandfather and everything to do with Nikolai."

"I haven't spoken to him in years, so I highly doubt that. Killing me is as likely to flush Nikolai out of wherever he's hiding as Landon pretending to date me was."

I head for the classroom door. Isabelle walks alongside me.

A memory slips in of Landon's strong hand holding mine as we walked to his jeep, and my heart clenches.

It's only been three days since I was in his arms and since we last kissed, but I miss him the way you miss the sun after countless days of rain.

Which is exactly why I need to volunteer tonight. The seniors always know how to brighten my day—even when it's their days that I'm supposed to make cheery.

"See you tomorrow," I tell Isabelle before slipping into the driver's seat. Even though I doubt there's an actual contract out on me, Isabelle will still be here tomorrow, pretending to be the school's receptionist. Landon's colleagues are convinced Nikolai will eventually contact me.

Based on what I now know, probably not.

As I drive past the familiar black SUV, I wave at Adam, knowing that he'll be following me to the retirement residence...and then following me home afterward.

***

"WHERE'S YOUR HOT BOYFRIEND?" AGATHA ASKS, PEERING OVER my shoulder. "I do so love it when he joins you. He's a delightful piece of eye candy." She winks at me, and I laugh.

"I'll be sure to tell him that." I don't have the heart to admit Landon and I broke up.

Or whatever it is when you're no longer with your fake boyfriend.

Everyone here loves him. It didn't take long for him to charm his way into their hearts once he started volunteering with me.

"So, where is he?" Bethany asks, also surveying the room.

"He had something he needed to do tonight and was unable to join me."

"What did he have to do that was more important than hanging out with a bunch of delightful old ladies?"

I grin at her. "Believe me, it would have to be super important before he skipped on hanging out with you."

I mentally groan at how at some point, I'll have to come clean with everyone here and tell them he's never coming back. Agatha and Bethany will no longer have their favorite piece of eye candy to drool over.

And Samuel and the men will no longer have their favorite poker player—that's right, they finally convinced Mathilda to let them play poker again.

By favorite, I mean Landon sucks at poker and loses to them about ninety-nine percent of the time.

I spend the next two hours helping with the different recreational therapy sessions designed to keep the seniors active, both physically and mentally.

The "Where's Landon?" question pops up numerous times. And each time I'm asked it, I inwardly curse him for instilling himself into so much of my life in such a short span of time.

I have no idea how I'm going to break the news to them that he's no longer volunteering here.

Maybe I can concoct some super cool story to explain his absence. Something dramatic that will rival *The Titanic*.

Minus the iceberg.

"I didn't know you work here," a man says behind me. I turn

around to find Eric, the good-looking man who helped me the other day with the Christmas decorations in my storage locker.

He smiles at me. It's a friendly smile, but it doesn't have the same impact as Landon's sexy smiles. They really should be registered as lethal weapons—no woman can survive them.

I feel my mouth stretch into what I hope resembles a genuine smile. That's what I get for letting my thoughts drift to my ex-fake boyfriend. "I volunteer here. What about you? What are you doing here?"

"I heard great things about the place…and well, I thought I'd check it out for my grandmother. Ever since my grandfather died a few years ago, I've been worried about her living alone in her apartment."

"I'm sure she'll love it here. The residents and staff are friendly, and I haven't heard any complaints about the apartments."

"Do you volunteer here often?"

"Three days a week. Most of the residents are like grandparents to me."

"I'm not sure if I could handle more than one set. My grandmother fusses over me like I'm still six years old."

"I think that's sweet. I don't have any grandparents." Close enough. "So I love having so many here. But I must admit they're getting to the point where they want to marry me off, so I can give them all a great-grandchild."

I'm not joking. A few hinted earlier that maybe Landon would be the one to knock me up—because God knows their own grandchildren aren't in a rush to be in a family way.

Their words, not mine.

He laughs. "That sounds like my grandmother. I think that's why she was devastated when I broke up with my last girlfriend."

"She really liked her?"

"Not at all. She was that desperate to be a great-grandmother. I'm positive she's got a competition going with her friends as to who's going to be the first great-grandmother."

"Well, I hate to tell you this, but things won't be much better if she moves in here. The seniors here are just as competitive."

"Do they know you have a boyfriend?" Eric asks, reminding me I'd told him the other day that I had one.

My face must have given something away because he cringes. "I'm sorry. I didn't realize you guys broke up."

"You don't have to apologize. It just happened the other day."

"That would explain the ghost my grandmother was positive she'd heard in your apartment yesterday. It wasn't a ghost, was it?"

"Nope. Just me. Or I'm assuming it was me and not a ghost."

"Bad breakup?" He openly winces. "I'm sorry, that was rude of me."

"It's okay. It just wasn't meant to be." Between the lies and the fate of any man who loves me, Landon and I were destined to be only temporary.

"So how devastated are you?"

"Are we talking on a scale of one to ten?"

"Chloe," Samuel says, shuffling toward us. "We need an extra player for our poker game. And everyone at the table nominated you to join us."

My mouth tugs up at the corners to the point where my cheeks ache. "That's because you know I'll lose." I'm just as bad a poker player as Landon.

He winks at me and offers his arm so he can escort me into the recreation room.

"It was nice seeing you again," I tell Eric, relieved to get out of explaining that on a scale from one to ten, I'm a twelve when it comes to my fake relationship ending with Landon.

After I finish my volunteer shift, I return to my vehicle, saluting Adam as I walk past his SUV. He nods at me.

In my car, I adjust my playlist to an upbeat Christmas song. The asphalt sparkles in the streetlights, the ground wet due to the rain that fell while I was inside.

I turn over the engine and pull away from the parking lot. Traffic is lighter now than it was when I arrived. As I draw near the first set of traffic lights, it turns green, and I continue through the intersection, following the car ahead of me.

I glance at the rearview mirror. To my surprise, Adam isn't behind me. Either he decided to stop the charade that my life is in danger, or he's more stealth than he's been.

That's the last thought I have before the sound of metal-hitting-metal rips through the passenger side of my car, and my vehicle is sent rolling.

My temple hits the side window, and the world goes black.

27

LANDON

My phone rings from the coffee table. Even without looking, I know it's Liam.

I mute the TV and grab the phone. On the TV screen is the sappy holiday Hallmark movie I was watching, but Liam doesn't need to know about that.

Whiskey is snoozing next to me on the couch. He's not supposed to be there, but he doesn't seem to care.

And at this point, neither do I.

We both miss Chloe.

I accept the call. "What's up?"

"It's Chloe," Liam says by way of a greeting. His tone has me jumping to my feet. "Adam called. There's been an accident. The paramedics are transporting her to St. John's hospital."

My long legs eat up the distance between the couch and the foyer. "Is she okay?" I already know the answer. I can hear it in his tone.

I snatch up my jeep keys from the side table.

"I have no idea. Adam couldn't tell me anything beyond where they're taking her."

"I'm on my way." I end the call.

The drive to the hospital takes far too long. The urge to channel my inner race-car driver accelerates, and I have to fight not to press my foot on the gas and weave through the traffic.

I also have to fight the urge to drive in the opposite direction, thanks to the memories from the last time someone I loved was hospitalized after a run-in with a vehicle.

Things didn't end so well for Sarah.

What if the same thing happens with Chloe?

What if she's currently in a coma and on life-support?

A new memory, of Sarah's parents pulling the plug, slams into me from all angles. It takes everything in me to ease my foot off the gas, and not get into an accident.

Adam is just inside the waiting room doors when I arrive. "How's she doing?" are the first words out of my mouth. The smell of disinfectant and dying people assaults me. I take a deep breath, trying to ground myself.

Keep it together, man. This isn't the first time someone I care about has been injured or killed. I was in the goddamn SEALs after all.

But for some reason, this time it feels different. More personal.

"I have no idea," Adam says. "They haven't told me anything. I'm not family."

Damn. I didn't even think of that.

I doubt as her fake boyfriend, they're going to tell me much either.

I stride straight to the front desk. "My fiancée, Chloe Reinhart, was in a car accident and was brought here."

The woman taps away at her keyboard and checks the screen. "Unfortunately, I can't give you any information right now."

"Can I see her?"

She shakes her head. "Sorry, you'll need to wait in the

waiting room. The doctor will call you when he has something to tell you."

I attempt a different tactic. "What should I tell her family?"

Am I planning to contact them? Hell, no.

She needs that as much as she needs an elf shooting pucks at her head.

"Exactly the same thing I told you." She flashes me a look that's part pity and part "now move along, please."

"Can't you at least let me know if she's okay? Is she conscious?"

"I'm sorry, I really don't know anything more than I've told you."

It's clear from her expression that she's telling the truth. I nod and pivot to return to Adam.

But instead of joining him, I keep walking out the sliding doors.

The memories of Sarah's accident continue to pound on me. I loved her, but that had meant shit-all. I couldn't protect her, no more than I had been able to protect Chloe.

The difference was it hadn't been my job to protect Sarah—not in the same way it was for Chloe.

I'd let down both women. I'd let down so many people.

I begin pacing in front of the hospital doors. "Fuck, I can't do this," I mutter to myself.

Fuck. Fuck. Fuck.

"Is there any reason you're making a trench in the sidewalk?" Adam asks. I didn't even notice him leave the hospital.

"What the hell happened?" My pacing doesn't slow. *I can't do this.*

"I don't exactly know. She left the seniors' residence, and I followed her. But a delivery truck cut in front of me. By the time I caught up with Chloe, her car was upside down in the middle of the intersection. Witnesses said they saw a truck plow through the red light at an excessive speed. It didn't stop to check on her. It kept going."

I continue pacing the entire time he tells me this.

"Do you know if the light had just turned red, and the driver didn't have time to stop?"

"According to witnesses, the truck had plenty of time to stop. If anything, it accelerated when Chloe approached the intersection."

"So, it was deliberate."

The fact that the driver didn't bother to stop after ramming into her confirms that. The motherfucker wanted her harmed.

I run my hand down my face, the helplessness from all those years ago worming its way in. I want to punch my fist through the wall.

Or better yet, the man responsible for putting Chloe in the hospital.

And while we're at it, how about I just add her grandfather, cousin, and everyone else in her family who embraced that life of crime.

If it weren't for them, things would be so different for Chloe. For one, she wouldn't be struggling with the belief that any man she loved would eventually be murdered.

The chill in the air seeps through my long-sleeved T-shirt. But despite the cold and the bone-chilling dampness, I can't bring myself to step back inside the building.

"Still no word," Adam says, returning at one point after checking with the unit clerk if there's any update on Chloe's status.

"You'd think they'd at least tell me something. What with me being her fiancé and all."

"You might have gotten further if you'd been more creative. Couldn't you have come up with something not so clichéd?"

I throw him a look. "I'll keep that in mind for the next time someone I care about lands in the hospital."

I pause my pacing long enough to catch Adam's raised eyebrow.

"So you do care about her."

"Of course I do. She's my fake girlfriend?"

I can practically hear the eye roll in his tone when he replies, "Since when was caring for someone necessary for being in a fake relationship?"

I pretend it's a rhetorical question and go back to pacing, my strides picking up speed. Between that and the anger and frustration flaring up inside me, I'm hot enough to toast s'mores on my body.

Liam and Connor approach us from the parking lot, concern lining their faces.

"Any word on how she's doing?" Liam asks.

"No," I grumble. "Even being her fiancé isn't getting me anywhere."

I'm not looking at either of them, but I can feel their questioning gazes directed at me.

Adam fills them in. "He told them that because he hoped it would get him some answers."

"I take it that didn't work," Liam says, not without a touch of humor in his tone.

Neither Adam nor I respond, figuring he already knows the answer.

Liam pulls out his phone. "Let me see if our FBI contacts have been given an update."

I pull up short. "They know about the accident?"

"I called them as soon as I heard. Adam told me enough to make me believe it was a targeted hit."

"There's a chance it had nothing to do with the contract," Connor says. "It's possible Nikolai Orlov is responsible. He's got to be aware that we're working with the Feds."

"And he believes Chloe knows something that will expose

his location," Adam finishes for him, nodding like this is a likely scenario.

Liam steps away from us for a moment to talk on the phone. A minute later, Agent Foden exits through the sliding doors and approaches us.

She gives me a nod. "I can take you to see her."

"I'd appreciate that."

She doesn't say anything as she leads me to a private room at the back of the ER. Agent Ramsey is standing outside the closed door, talking to a cop.

"Any idea who did this to her?" I ask them.

"We're examining several feasible likelihoods," Ramsey says.

I mentally fill in what he isn't saying. "In other words, you don't have any real suspects."

Neither agent flinches at my comment—or reveals what they're thinking.

"We suggested witness protection to her," Foden says. "But she's not interested."

Suggested? They've been able to talk to her for God knows how long, while I've been creating a trench in the sidewalk to rival the Grand Canyon?

I frown. "What do you mean she's not interested?"

"Exactly that. She said something about seniors counting on her for the Christmas show, and she doesn't want to let them down."

We'll see about that.

Without waiting for either agent to grant me permission, I push open the door and enter Chloe's room. The haunting hospital smell and my memories of Christmas past continue to press in on me—and double up the moment I see her.

San Francisco isn't known for temperatures that drop low enough for snow. But at seeing Chloe, lying on the bed, head propped up, an avalanche of frozen crystals crashes through my veins.

It's not Sarah. It's not Sarah...

I attempt to suck in enough air to fill my lungs, but they appear to have forgotten how to do that. All I see is Sarah's crumpled body.

Chloe's eyelids flutter open. Or at least one of them attempts to open. The other one is swollen shut due to the bruising on her face.

Her good eye gazes blearily at me, as though she's trying to focus on my face, but it's not quite there yet.

She's not in a coma. She's not going to die.

"Hey," I say, willing my legs to walk over to her, trying to mentally defrost them.

"Hey," she whispers back, voice hoarse, like it's forgotten how it's supposed to sound.

I feel my lips stretch into a soft smile, still unable to propel my body forward. "How are you feeling?"

The corners of her mouth attempt to twitch up, an epic fail as a result of the swelling. "I've felt better."

The sound of her voice loosens something inside me, the same way driving over a deep pothole jars loose something vital—something that keeps the engine together, keeps it running smoothly.

"Agent Foden said you're not interested in going into witness protection." My voice comes out even, empty of the emotion churning inside me. Flat.

"I'm not throwing away everything I've accomplished so far because of one stupid accident."

"Even though the next stupid accident might cost you your life?"

Might leave her in the same position her father, stepfather, and former boyfriend found themselves.

I resume pacing back and forth between the window and the door, the ice crystals starting to thaw.

"I'm not giving up everything I've worked hard for just because I was born into the wrong family."

"Is this because of the Christmas concert?"

She doesn't say anything; her eyes give away the answer.

"You're risking it all for a stupid Christmas concert?"

She lifts her chin, an act of defiance and determination that normally I'd find sexy.

Not, so much now.

Now it makes me want to glare at her while frosty tumbleweeds roll across the room, a stare-down to rival all western showdowns.

"You know that the concert means everything to those seniors," she says. "They're looking forward to it. The kids are looking forward to it."

"Are you telling me the concert's more important than your life?"

She winces, but I can't be sure if that's due to my words or because she's in pain. "I'm saying it's important to me since it's part of who I am. You need to protect people and feel like you're in control. And I get that I'm not making your job any easier.

"I'm sorry, I really am. But I was born into a family that lives for money, no matter how they get it. I'll never be able to make up for the pain they've caused, but I can try to make a difference in some people's lives." She sags farther into her pillow like a balloon that's lost some of its air.

"It's not your job to make up for everything your family has done, Chloe. That's on them." And the legal system.

"I know, but at least it's a start. Besides, it makes me feel good to know that I'm making a difference, I'm making people smile. Do you really want to take that away from me?"

Yes—if it means keeping her alive.

She's not Sarah. She's not Sarah.

"In that case, I can't be your fake boyfriend anymore."

The corner of her mouth twitches to one side. "If memory serves me correct, I already dumped you. Unlike our fake relationship, that was real." She releases a heavy breath and winces again. "Besides, maybe the killing curse doesn't differentiate between real love and fake relationships. It might get the wires crossed and end your life like it did the others. It's a risk you can't afford."

I should be telling her that she's got it all wrong. She's not responsible for the deaths of those men. She's not cursed. Someone else ended their lives.

I should be saying all those things, but that's not what I blurt out. "Good luck, Chloe, with everything. Adam or Jayden will be taking over my role with this mission."

My heart aches that I won't be there to watch the kids perform in the concert. They're working so hard to prepare for it.

I don't give her a chance to say anything else.

I walk out the door.

Liam and Adam are talking to Agents Ramsey and Foden in the hallway.

"I quit the mission," I tell Liam and keep walking.

I can't be around if anything else happens to her.

I've already lost a woman whom I loved because of the actions of someone else. I won't go through that again.

28

CHLOE

Four days later, Adam unlocks my apartment room door after driving me home from school.

Thanks to the Christmas Grinch, I have a broken arm, my ribs and left ankle are sore, and my face doesn't feel like it belongs to me.

But I'm still alive, so I'm incredibly thankful for that.

The part where I live in an apartment with no elevators kind of sucks. But after everything I've been through, I'm really not interested in staying anywhere else.

This is my home.

Adam steps inside, and I wait while he checks to ensure there are no nasty surprises. I'm hoping that also includes spiders, should he happen upon one.

"What the hell happened to you?" Eric asks, coming down the hallway.

Ignoring the discomfort, I grin at his shocked expression. "Yes, I know, I look fabulous."

He chuckles. "Yep, that's exactly what I was going to say. Does this mean you're not up for our first date quite yet?"

It's not just my body that's currently a mess. My clothes

aren't much better. Despite Principal Woodnut's insistence that I take another few days off to recover, I returned to teaching today.

As the paint on my pants can attest.

"My evenings will be busy for the next while. My kindergarten class will be performing for the seniors at the Golden Sunshine Retirement Village next week, and we still don't have enough elf hats." And thanks to my arm being in a cast, it's taking me longer than planned to finish them. I was only able to start working on them again yesterday.

"I can always help. I'm pretty handy with a needle."

"This is more a job for a sewing machine."

"My grandmother has one I can use. I'm assuming it still works. She hasn't used it in a bit. Her hands and eyesight aren't what they used to be."

Adam steps out of my apartment, and his gaze scrapes down Eric, as if he has X-ray vision and is making sure he's clean.

It's the same expression Eric is wearing as he checks out Adam—but probably not for the same reason. "Are you the ex-boyfriend who hurt Chloe?"

His tone makes me think of a young buck getting ready to challenge the alpha for buck supremacy.

Next, they'll be circling each other, antlers loaded and ready.

"No, this is just a friend of mine," I say in an attempt to stall the battle before it gets started. "Adam, this is Eric, the grandson of one of my neighbors."

They nod at each other. The tension in Eric's shoulders subsides. Not so much for Adam. But that's because he's on duty. This isn't a social call for him.

"I offered to help Chloe with her elf hats," Eric says, assuming, it would seem, that Adam knows what he's talking about.

"For the Christmas show," I clarify.

Adam smirks at Eric. "Right. You don't look like the type who knows much about sewing."

"I didn't realize there was a certain look you needed to have to be considered a competent sewer," Eric replies.

And we're back to them metaphorically circling each other again.

I roll my eyes and limp into my apartment.

My vision blurs at the sight in front of me. Landon's and my fake relationship truly is over—which shouldn't come as a surprise, given I dumped him.

Sometime in the last eight hours, Landon entered my apartment and returned the Christmas decorations I'd left at his town house. But he didn't just shove them into the big cardboard boxes I store them in. He decorated my apartment like I'd done to his home.

Even the Christmas tree and decorations we bought for his place have been relocated to my living room.

But in the short time since I last saw them, they've lost their holiday season sparkle—their reason to be merry.

Behind me, Adam says something to Eric, but I'm not really listening to him, so I don't catch what he says.

I walk to the tree and inspect the wooden squirrel decoration hanging from a lower branch. The squirrel's leg has been partially chewed, dedication of Whiskey. It must have happened after I moved out. I can almost imagine Landon attempting to coax it away from the teething puppy, and a slight smile sneaks onto my face.

Followed by the sensation of an invisible hand squishing my heart like it's a chunk of Play-Doh.

God, I miss those two.

The apartment door clicks shut. I peer over my shoulder to discover that I'm alone. Looks like I'll be working on the elf hats on my own after all. Not that it's a bad thing. I'll be so busy working on them, I won't have time to miss Whiskey and Landon.

I glance around my apartment. I really need a pet. Something to keep me company.

Maybe a cute goldfish.

Or a pet toad.

I quickly grab some dinner and settle myself in front of my sewing machine. I'm almost finished the hat I'm working on when someone knocks on my apartment door. I get up to open it.

Eric is standing on the other side of the doorway, holding a sewing machine.

He salutes me. "Royal elf-hat maker to the stars. Reporting for duty."

I laugh, my ribs protesting slightly. "I thought you were joking about helping me."

"I never joke about anything as serious as this." He winks at me, and I grin.

"How can I say no to that?" I open the door wider to let him in.

"Let me move my sewing machine over so you can set up yours," I say. "You do know how to use it, right?"

"My grandmother gave me a quick rundown, but I might need some help. I'm a financial analyst by day. Calculating option-adjusted spread I can do. Figuring out sewing machines is a little out of my league."

Twenty minutes later and a few rough starts, the elf-hat assembly line is in business. I'm responsible for cutting the pieces from the red velvet. We're both responsible for sewing the pieces together.

Eric is slow because sewing is a new skill for him. I'm slow because of my cast. We talk the entire time, which is another reason why we aren't working at supersonic speed.

He's entertaining, sweet, and funny. I'm not interested in

him romantically, but maybe I could introduce him to Kiera. You never know. They might hit it off and eventually became a cute couple—once she's ready to date.

Eric's phone pings a text, and he checks the screen. He responds to whoever sent it. "I'm sorry, Chloe, I have to leave. But I'm free tomorrow night to help you make more hats."

"That would be great. Thanks." Between the two of us, we've finished ten hats. Nothing to create new world records, but given the handicaps we're both dealing with—my arm, his lack of sewing background—we didn't do half bad.

My phone vibrates from the table. I peer at the screen.

Adam: You okay up there?

I grab the phone and reply.

Me: I'm doing great. Thanks. Going to bed now.

Adam: Let me know if you need anything.

Me: Will do. Good night Adam.

A sudden urge to text Landon races through me.

I stomp it down.

I refuse to be the fake girlfriend who misses her fake ex-boyfriend.

Now, I just need someone to tell my heart that.

29

LANDON

I'm watching a hockey game on TV when the doorbell rings.

This is the moment I've been waiting for. Whiskey's going to his forever home.

The vet clinic called two days ago to let me know they found a home for the puppy. A home that will give him all the love he deserves.

Whiskey peers up at me from his dog bed in the living room that is now devoid of all reminders of Christmas. It now resembles the room it once was before Chloe stepped into my life. The only things remaining are Whiskey and his supplies, and they, too, will be gone shortly.

And then my life can return to normal.

I packed up the decorations the night of the accident when I realized I couldn't be in Chloe's life any longer. Not when the risk of her dying was too great.

I've already gone through the pain of losing a woman I loved. I'm not interested in making that two out of two.

And yes, I love her. I don't believe in love at first sight. That's for fools and romantics. But even though we've only been together for a few weeks, what I feel for her is real.

Doesn't that just fuck all?

I turn the TV off and stand. "Your new family is here," I tell him. The enthusiasm in my voice has flatlined, and I can't find the will to resuscitate it.

But that doesn't matter. As soon as he meets his new family, he'll be excited for the two of us.

I open the front door. The father and mother are standing on the stoop, along with two kids, both under the age of ten.

"Hi. Landon?" the man says. "I'm Robert. And this is my wife, Mary, and our kids Chris and Lizzie."

Two eager faces grin at me. "Is it true you have a puppy?" Lizzie asks.

"That's right. Do you want to come inside and meet him?"

"Yes, please," they say in near-perfect chorus.

I move aside to let them in.

"Remove your shoes first," their mother reminds them before they can take a step into the house.

They practically charge inside, stopping long enough to fling their shoes across the floor.

"Sorry about that," she says. "They're really excited to meet Whiskey. But we haven't told them yet that we're adopting him. We wanted them to meet him first."

I try smiling, but my lips don't feel like cooperating. I nod instead.

Great. Now I'm a mute.

"Where is he?" Lizzie asks, reminding me of my students. She's the same age.

"In the living room." I point toward it.

We follow them and find the pair sitting on the floor next to Whiskey's bed. With a little bark, he unfolds himself and steps over the side to the awaiting kids. They hold out their hands for him to sniff.

"Oh, he's so adorable." Mary crouches between her two kids and lets Whiskey sniff her hand. She then strokes him behind the ear, just like Chloe used to do.

As expected, he laps up the attention.

And my heart breaks.

In the short time I've been his foster daddy, his puppy teeth have dug into my heart the same way they do with his chew toys. And my cushions. And shoes.

Well, just about everything he can find.

I've fallen for him in the same way I've fallen for Chloe.

Okay, not quite the same way, but the sentiment's the same.

The kids fuss over him, and he wags his tail at rapid speed. But then he wanders to me and parks his paws on my legs, tail still wagging. It's his sign for "Daddy, I want up."

I scoop him up and cradle him next to me. He cocks his head to the side, his eyes wide and hopeful.

He reaches up and licks my face.

This sets the kids off giggling.

I stroke his soft copper-colored fur, the shade slightly lighter than Chloe's hair.

A string of memories decides this is a good time for a memory-lane montage. Of Chloe, when we collected Whiskey from the vet. Of her coming up with his name. Of her loving him unconditionally like he deserves. Of him loving her the same way.

Of the way he made her laugh—how he made us both laugh.

The idea of giving him away is a punch to the gut.

There's an old saying that claims if you love someone, set them free. If they come back, they're yours. If they don't, they never were.

That might be true when it comes to humans, but I'm not sure how much it applies to a puppy. It's not like he can dig under a fence and come bounding here if he wants.

"You've changed your mind, haven't you?" Mary says, voice soft.

I stroke Whiskey's fur again and nod. "I'm sorry. I didn't realize he would grow on me the way he has."

"That's perfectly okay. Sometimes it takes the nudge of nearly losing someone to realize how much they mean to you."

"You're right. It does."

In Chloe's case, I walked away because it was easier than to risk losing her in the worst possible way.

But that's not true for Whiskey. No one's trying to kill him. He doesn't have a contract on his head.

And despite his rough start, he isn't attempting to push me away out of fear of loving someone.

I ignore the voice in my head, pointing out the irony of the last part. Pointing out that I'm as guilty of doing that to Chloe as she is of doing it to me.

30

LANDON

"Whiskey," I call out. "Walk?"

The bundle of energy comes barreling around the corner, his claws slipping on the hardwood floor.

Guess that answers my question.

He barks and jumps his paws on my legs. I bend down and attach the leash to his collar. His leg is fully healed now, which means we can go for a longer walk.

Which I desperately need.

And once I've done that. I'll go for a hard run.

Emphasis on hard.

I open the front door and am brought up short. Jayden is standing on the stoop, his hand raised toward the doorbell. Sitting next to him, with his tongue lolling to the side, is Mojo, his goofy Mountain Bernese dog.

"Mojo wanted to visit Whiskey." Jayden lifts his shoulders in a what-can-you-do shrug.

"Oh, he did, did he?" My gaze returns to his dog. "Is this true, Mojo? You begged Jayden to bring you over to visit Whiskey?"

"Woof."

Whiskey barks excitedly in reply.

Okay, still not buying it.

"We're just heading out for a walk."

"Perfect. We'll come with you."

Not exactly what I'd planned, but that's okay. I'm sure he's dying to get back home to Isabelle, so he can screw her brains out. Which means he won't be here long.

That doesn't mean I'm not happy to see Jayden.

But it does mean I have a feeling I'll want to go for that run even more once he leaves. I've known him too long to believe he just came over so the dogs can hang out together.

"What's really going on?" I ask after we've walked a block. "And don't give me that crap about the dogs spending quality time together."

"You're right. Liam told me what happened. That Chloe's accident freaked you out."

A squirrel darts up a tree ahead of us. Whiskey goes chasing after it, only to be brought up short, thanks to the leash. Mojo isn't the most energetic of dogs, so he keeps to our current pace.

"I screwed up. She was pissed when she found out I'd been lying about the real reason I was pretending to be her boyfriend, and it had nothing to do with Nikolai asking us to protect her. I let her push me away, and look what happened."

"The accident wasn't your fault. It would've happened anyway. Just on your watch instead of on Adam's."

"But at least then she wouldn't have been driving. She would have been in my jeep. She would've been a helluva lot safer than she was in her car." Especially since it looks like at some point someone had fucked with the airbags, which is why they didn't deploy during the accident.

"You really think that would've made a difference? Whoever has the contract out on her wants her out of the picture. Permanently. As it is, I bet they've got steam whistling from their ears because the hit man fucked up, and she walked away from the accident."

I open my mouth to argue.

He doesn't give me a chance. "I stand corrected. She got to be driven away in an ambulance. But she still survived."

"So that she can be a human target for another day."

"We won't let that happen."

A gush of wind sends several dry leaves tumbling across the sidewalk.

Whiskey pounces on one of them and barks proudly at me.

I bend down and pet him. "I know, you're a big scary boy. No leaf stands a chance with you around."

"But I think we both know this isn't what's got your knickers in a twist," Jayden says. "It's not only about the accident, am I right?"

I don't say anything.

"Look, I get it. I went through the same thing with Isabelle. I was paranoid of her dying due to the job. So I was an asshole, demanding she abandon her goal of being an operative because I couldn't handle it."

"Not the same thing, man. Isabelle is trained to look after herself." Thanks to Adam and me. Adam had taught her to be kickass when it came to handling a gun. Only Jayden wasn't aware of it at the time. "Chloe isn't. She's a kindergarten teacher who has no desire to do our job."

"So what? You can't handle the idea of losing her, so you'll give up everything instead?"

"What the hell are you talking about?"

"C'mon, everyone knows you're in love with Chloe." His gaze takes in my expression. "Okay, let me rephrase that. Everyone but *you* and Chloe knows you're in love with her."

"It's complicated."

He laughs, startling a bird in a nearby tree. It squawks in protest. I know how it feels.

"Complicated is the code word for coward. Everyone who is scared of love plays the 'complicated' "—he air-quotes the word —"card. But it's just bullshit."

"Wow, tell me what you're really thinking."

"I couldn't handle the thought of her dying. So I figured it was better to not love than to risk losing her. I was wrong."

"Yes, but I'm not. I lost someone I loved. I wasn't there for her when she needed me. She died. End of story."

Clearly, Jayden doesn't agree with me on the last part. "It's not the end of the story. What happened in the past is exactly that...in the past. You can't be chickenshit when it comes to love just because you're afraid of losing the person. It means living each day as though it might be her last, making sure each one counts and isn't wasted."

"Shit, what Hallmark card did you steal that from?"

He slaps me on the shoulder, grinning. "What can I say? Love makes you profound."

31

CHLOE

Some people hate Christmas shopping. They hate the crowds, and they hate trying to find the perfect gift.

They prefer shopping online and getting it all done with a click of the mouse.

Not me.

I love Christmas shopping. I love the sounds and the smells and the sights of the holiday season.

Online shopping can never beat that.

"Oh, this is cute," I say to Kiera, picking up a onesie with a cartoon reindeer on the front. We're currently looking for a present for her new niece.

"They're all freaking cute." She takes it from me and searches through the neat stacks for more. "Did I tell you, my sister bought tickets to a charity event for while I'm visiting her in Lake Tahoe?"

"What kind of charity event?"

"It's some fancy masquerade ball she's been helping organize. Which means I need to buy a dress for it."

"You don't sound too thrilled."

She grabs a onesie with a smiling snowman on it. "I don't

know. I think I'd be happier just wearing PJs and hanging out with my niece. Getting a dress seems like too much effort."

"You could always hope your fairy godmother pays you a visit and turns your ratty old pajamas into a beautiful ball gown." I grin at her impishly.

She laughs. "I like that idea better."

"But don't they usually come with pumpkin coaches and kisses at midnight with a stranger?"

"Given there are no royal princes in Lake Tahoe at this time of year—or any time of the year—I don't have to worry about that part of the fairy tale coming true."

"I don't know, being kissed by a good-looking stranger, royal or otherwise, sounds pretty wonderful to me," I say on a dramatic sigh that has her laughing.

"You miss him, don't you?"

Her out-of-the-blue question surprises me. "Miss who?"

"You know very well who I'm talking about."

"Who, Landon?" At her nod, I continue, "In case you've forgotten, he hasn't gone anywhere. He's still substituting for Zoe's class."

Kiera doesn't know the real reason Landon's and my whirlwind romance came to an abrupt end. But she also doesn't know the truth about my family, and why Mark, my stepfather, and my father disappeared from my life.

Nor has the news mentioned the discovery of their bodies. The FBI seems to be keeping it under wraps for now.

"Are you having second thoughts about spending Christmas with your sister and brother-in-law?" I ask, needing to change the subject.

She shakes her head, then shrugs. "Maybe. But I know I need to go. I've avoided visiting them there since..." She leaves the words hanging and shrugs again. Her husband died on a ski hill in Lake Tahoe. "It's time I finally say good-bye to him."

I smile softly at her. "I think you're right."

"Will you help me find a dress?"

"And get to be your fairy godmother? Absolutely."

We continue with our Christmas shopping. One of the sad parts about not having a family to share the holidays with is that it means I don't have many people to shop for. Which is another reason I love shopping with Kiera.

She does have a family.

I do, though, buy my mom a present like I always do. And like what has become tradition, I'll send it to her without saying who it's from.

And she'll do the same.

For a second, I wonder if the FBI has told her the truth about her two husbands. Was she aware that her first husband was dead when she married my stepfather?

My phone rings. I remove it from my purse and answer it.

"Chloe," Principal Woodnut says. "Have you spoken with Tabitha Windhouse yet, to get her approval for the costumes?"

"I left a message, but she never got back to me." I have no idea why I need Tabitha's approval. I've already told Principal Woodnut I paid for the material myself.

"Can you try her again? I just want to ensure there are no hitches when it comes to the concert."

In other words, she doesn't want me to give Tabitha a reason to be a pain in the butt when it comes to other school events.

"I'll call her again now."

"Thank you, Chloe."

I end the call and speed-dial Tabitha's number. It goes to voice mail again. God, I really hope she's not avoiding my calls on purpose.

I leave her the same message as before and ask her to call me as soon as possible.

"Trouble with Tabitha again?" Kiera asks.

I tell her about the issue.

"I wouldn't be surprised if one of her kids has an activity tonight," Kiera says, "and Tabitha had to drive them to it."

"Good point. I'll try her again later."

Once we've finished buying presents, we head to a store that has fancy dresses.

"Wow, these are gorgeous," I say as we search through the racks of ball gowns in rich jewel colors. "Your fairy godmother couldn't do much better."

Kiera pulls out a burgundy ball gown. The top is made from velvet and has a sweetheart neckline held up with spaghetti straps. The floor-length skirt is layers upon layers of gauze fabric with a slight shimmer to it.

"It's gorgeous. Try it on."

"Isn't it a little too much?"

"For a ball? No, I'd say it's perfect. You'll look like a princess."

She returns it to the rack. "Maybe I don't want to be a princess."

"Everyone wants to be a princess, to feel special for just one day. And you more than anyone deserves that. Besides, what does it hurt to try it on?"

She removes it again. "Okay, I'll do it. Are you trying one on, too?"

"I'll pass. I'm not the one attending a ball." I'm not even doing anything for New Year's Eve, other than watching the countdown on TV and watching a movie.

I won't even get to kiss anyone at midnight.

So basically, my typical New Year's Eve celebration.

Kiera disappears into the dressing room. I glance at my phone, checking to see if anyone has texted me, even though I know no one has.

"Merry Christmas," a deep voice says behind me. "Ho ho ho." The crisp ringing of a bell cuts through the air.

I turn to find Santa walking toward me. But this isn't an old man who was made up to look like him. This man is a lot younger…and there's something oddly familiar about his eyes.

"Merry Christmas, young lady." He says it loud enough for everyone to hear and rings his bell again. "Do you have a holiday wish you want to tell Santa?"

Instead of giving me a candy cane, he hands me a Christmas tree ornament shaped like a shooting star. The silver threads—woven like a dream catcher—sparkle in the store lights.

Why does it look so familiar?

"If you wish on a shooting star," I ask Nikolai, "does the wish really come true?" Our families were staying in a large cabin in a forest—like in a fairy tale—the summer after my father left. Nikolai and I had snuck out of the house, and were studying the stars twinkling in the late-night sky. I'd never seen so many before then.

Nikolai enthusiastically nods. "I'm positive it's true."

"Have any of your shooting-star wishes come true?"

He thinks about it for a moment. "Not exactly, but maybe I didn't do it right."

"There's a right way to make a wish?"

The memory fades, replaced with a new one. Now I remember why the star is so familiar. It belonged to Nikolai's family. I bought it for their Christmas tree after the shooting-star conversation.

"Nikolai?" I whisper, my voice too stunned to come out louder than that. "What are you doing here?"

"I came to check on you. Heard there's a contract on your head. Sorry about that." He flashes me the angelic smile I remember from when we were kids.

It usually meant he'd been far from angelic.

"Thanks," I say with a small smile I don't mean. "How long have you known about it?"

"I also heard you've got a bodyguard."

Still do. Somewhere.

I resist the urge to glance around and track down Adam.

"What are you doing here?" I ask again.

"I wanted to check that you're okay. The Feds are obviously doing a crappy job of protecting you."

"And you're doing a better job?"

He snorts a quiet laugh. "*Touché.*" The smile vanishes from his face. "The only reason they're trying to protect you is because they want something from you."

"And what's that exactly?"

"What have you told them about our family?"

I finger the ornament. If I hurl it across the room while making a wish, does that count? "That's not an answer."

"And neither is that."

Now, that's the Nikolai I remember and loved.

"What does it matter what I've told them?" I ask. "It's not like I'm aware of any big secrets they don't already know." And for that, I'm grateful.

I'd hate to consider what kinds of skeletons are lurking in my family's closet.

Nikolai's face relaxes for a moment, and I'm reminded of the boy I used to know. The boy who used to be my best friend.

"Do you know anything about the murder of my last boyfriend, Mark Greenwood, or about the murder of my father and stepfather?" Maybe Nikolai can give me the answers the FBI and I seek. "Do you know why they were all killed?"

His expression gives nothing away. "You can't trust anyone, Chloe. Please promise me you'll—"

"What do you think?" Kiera asks behind me, interrupting whatever Nikolai was about to say.

I turn to find her walking toward me in the gown. And for a second, Nikolai is forgotten.

I grin at her. "You look gorgeous. You have to get that dress. It'll be perfect for the ball."

And it will be. With her blonde hair cascading over her shoulders in light waves, she looks breathtaking.

"In that dress, I'm positive you'll have a magical night."

"I could definitely use magic to get through it." Her gaze flicks to Nikolai. "What do you say, Santa? Can you spare me some magic for the night of the ball?"

"I'll see what I can do." He places his hand on his belly, which has obviously been augmented with pillows. "Ho ho ho."

"You're getting the dress, right?" I ask Kiera, ignoring him.

"You don't think it'll be too much? I mean, it is only for one night. And it's not like I have a date to impress."

Her gaze returns to Nikolai, and a puzzled frown forms between her eyes. "You look familiar. Have we met before?"

He shakes his head. "You're probably confusing me for someone else."

"Maybe." The word is drawn-out, uncertain. "All right, I'll buy this dress," she says to me and returns to the change rooms.

I turn to Nikolai.

The boyish look is back on his white-bearded face. Only it's the sad smile I remember from when his father told him he couldn't be a cop when he grew up. "I've missed you, Chloe. I miss how we used to talk about our dreams for the future. I guess neither of us pursued them in the end."

"Well, given eight-year-old me dreamed of being a princess, that's not too surprising. I haven't exactly had too many princes cross my path."

"Have you tried kissing a frog? I've heard that's the best way to land yourself a prince these days."

"Darn it," I say, snapping my fingers. "The last frog that crossed my path was stretched out on a dissection tray. And I don't think kissing a dead frog works quite the same way."

Something moves in the corner of my eye. I don't have to turn my head to know it's Adam. The question is, why did

Nikolai take the risk of being discovered when he knows damn well I'm not here on my own?

Did he really believe the Santa costume would make a difference?

"I really am sorry, Chloe," he says. "About everything. Just remember the star. It has the answer to everything."

Before I can respond, and ask what the heck he's talking about, he pulls a gun from his sack and whirls around. This is followed by a series of gunshots from every angle.

Screams fill the air, muffled by the loud pounding of my pulse in my ears.

On instinct, I dive to the ground, praying Kiera does the same in the change room. Praying that stray bullets don't hit her or anyone else.

Nikolai steps forward, still shooting at the unseen target.

And then he's no longer walking.

His body sags to the floor.

I scream...because despite the man he's become, he once meant the world to me.

Even though deep down I know it's a dumb move, I wiggle over to him, still clutching the shooting star. I'm vaguely aware of tears staining my face and dripping on the gray carpet.

"Nikolai? Oh, God, Nikolai, say something." I check his pulse. Even before the confirmation, I know he's dead.

A sob escapes me, and I look up, only to spot something even more chilling through the racks of clothes. It propels me to my feet.

My ears are ringing from the shooting. Muffled sounds of someone yelling reaches out to me, but I don't stop to see who it is. With my wish slipping softly from my lips, I half stumble, half lunge at the two injured men on the floor: Landon and Adam.

Landon is gripping his shoulder. Blood seeps between his

fingers. Adam looks dazed, blood dripping along the side of his face.

"We need an ambulance," I scream to anyone who can hear me.

Adrenaline courses through me. It's the only thing pasting me together.

I drop beside Landon, mentally going through what I learned in the first aid course I took last year. They didn't cover gunshot wounds, but the instructor taught enough for me to know that I have to stop the bleeding. Now.

"Hold this." I tuck the star in his free hand—hoping it'll bring us both luck—and yank at a bright-pink ski jacket on the nearby rack. It tumbles free of the hanger.

"You know, pink isn't really my color." Somehow, he manages to chuckle.

Ignoring his smartass comment, I lay it on the floor behind him and cradle the back his head with my hand. "I've got you, Landon," I say gently. "Lie down so I can check your shoulder."

Groaning, he shakes his head. "I need to check on Adam."

"I'll help him next. But I need you to lie down first. Okay?"

He nods, and with my help, does as I asked. I push myself to my feet and grab a bunch of cotton tops from nearby hangers. I fold them into makeshift pads and gently pry his hand away from his shoulder.

Blood gushes from the wound.

Fuck.

It's not a big hole, but that doesn't mean anything if the bullet hit a major blood vessel.

I carefully place a pad of clothing on it. "I need to move you a bit so I can check for an exit wound."

He nods. The pain on his face clenches my heart like it's one of Whiskey's chew toys—minus the high-pitched squeak.

With my help, he moves his upper body enough for me to

peer under his shoulder. His shirt is covered in blood, but there doesn't seem to be an exit wound.

I ease him down again.

"I'm going to check on Adam. Promise me you won't go anywhere." The last words feel like they have to push past the squeaky-toy-sized lump in my throat. "And promise me you'll hold on to the star. Rumor has it, it's luckier than a shooting star."

To the casual onlooker, it sounds like I just mean for Landon to stay where he is. But it's more than that. I've already lost three men that I loved, I can't lose him, too.

Not this way.

When he doesn't answer, I repeat it. "Promise me, okay?"

"I promise," he mumbles and tries to move. "Adam."

I lean down and kiss his forehead. "I love you," I whisper softly enough so he can't hear me.

A man crouches next to Landon, his breath fast, as if he'd sprinted here. "I'm an off-duty paramedic. What happened?"

Relief almost knocks me on my butt at his words. "He was shot in the shoulder." I could kiss the man on the forehead like I did Landon, but he's got more important things to do—like saving Landon's life.

The paramedic gaze shifts to Adam. "What about the other man?"

"I was about to check on him." I crawl over to where Adam's slumped on the floor. "Hey, Adam." I shake his shoulders slightly, not enough to really move him. But enough to check if he's conscious.

He moans in response.

The paramedic is asking Landon questions, and he tells Landon his name. Rob.

Kiera, back in her regular clothes, joins us, pale and shaking, and stands by Adam's feet.

Her gaze shifts from Adam to Landon and then to the guns

next to them. Her eyes widen in fear. "Shouldn't we get those guns away from them before they hurt anyone else?"

"They're the good guys," I say, examining Adam's body for additional signs of injury. "Where the hell is the ambulance?"

"It's on its way," a man in a uniform says, approaching. Mall security. "The cops, too." He hands me a first aid kit, gun drawn. "Is the other man alive?" He nods in Nikolai's direction.

Rob looks up at me, and then at where the security guard had gestured.

I shake my head. "No, he's dead." My voice cracks into a hundred pieces, but I'm not sure for who, exactly. The man who I haven't seen in many years, or for the boy who was at one time my world.

"Why were they shooting at Santa?" Kiera asks, voice trembling. "Since when did the good guys try to kill Santa?"

Since Santa tried to kill them first.

I have no idea if Landon and Adam realized Santa was Nikolai in disguise, or they shot at him simply because he fired at them first.

"Hey, Adam," I say. "Can you hear me?"

"Where's Landon?" His voice is barely loud enough to be heard over the chatter of freaked out customers. I can hear a man tell everyone to stay back, to give us space.

"He's right here. He's okay. You're both going to be okay." I glance over at Rob, but he's too busy dealing with Landon to confirm that I'm right.

God, please tell me I'm right.

"I need you to call Ava and tell her Landon and Adam have been shot," I tell Kiera. "She'll know what to do."

Kiera moves away to make the call.

Adam pushes himself to sit.

I put my hands on his shoulders. "Hey, you need to lie down until the paramedics arrive."

"I'm fine, Chloe." He looks over at Landon. "He's in way worse shape than me."

"Speak for yourself," Landon mutters. "I'm ready to run a couple of laps. Maybe enter the Ironman Triathlon."

"I somehow doubt that," Rob says.

"What are you doing here?" I ask Landon. "The last I heard, Adam was the one who was keeping an eye on me."

"Is there any particular reason your cousin showed up here while you happen to be in the store? And don't tell me he happened to be in the neighborhood, playing the role of a mall Santa." His tone isn't pissed, just weary.

I squeeze my eyes shut, willing the last few minutes with Nikolai to be permanently erased from my memory.

I open my eyes, and my gaze catches sight of the star still in Landon's hand. Fresh tears spill from my eyes again. "I have no idea."

32

CHLOE

Several hours later, I'm sitting in the waiting area outside the surgical suites at the hospital where Landon and Adam were taken.

I'm not alone.

Liam, Connor, Adam, Jayden, and Isabelle are with me, waiting to find out how Landon's surgery went.

They're not the only ones. Ava and Kiera are also here.

"You love him, don't you?" Ava asks quietly next to me. I've just finished getting Kiera up to speed on everything that's been going on for the past few weeks.

"I do. I shouldn't. We haven't known each other for long, and I promised myself after Mark that I wouldn't make the mistake of loving another man again."

I'm as skilled at ignoring my own advice as Pooh is at ignoring his rumbly tummy at the sight of honey.

Ava flashes me a small smile—a smile filled with wisdom and smugness. "I've long since learned that, for better or for worse, the heart and brain often have opposite opinions. Your job is to figure out which one is right, but it's not always the one you hope it will be."

"But at least now you know the men you loved didn't leave you because they stopped caring," Kiera adds. She still looks taken aback at the news that the three men she's referring to were killed over the last two decades.

"No, they were murdered," I say, my heart as heavy as cupid's statue with pigeon poop on it. "And now I've unwittingly cursed Landon to the same fate."

Ava wraps her arm around my shoulder. "Life isn't a fairy tale. There are no curses and things like that—just don't tell that to my readers."

"She's right," Isabelle says. "Don't let fear prevent you from loving someone because you're afraid something bad will happen to them." She glances at her fiancé before turning back to us. "You'll miss out on so much if you let that guide your heart."

"Does Landon know you love him?" Kiera asks.

I shake my head and shrug. "It hasn't really come up. Besides, he was nothing more than my temporary fake boyfriend. What we shared was all part of his cover. And then there's the part where he lied to me."

"He truly believed that was the only way he could get close enough to you to protect you," Isabelle says.

I give her a pointed look. "And to discover where my cousin was hiding."

She cringes. "Yeah, that too. But you understand why he needed to locate Nikolai, right? Why we were all hired to ensure he didn't follow in your grandfather's footsteps?"

I nod because that part I do understand. As much as it hurts that Nikolai died—and I'm sure it will hurt even more later on, once I know Landon will be okay—at the end of the day, he was still the new crime boss. And as a crime boss, it meant doing illegal activities that could lead to more loss of life.

Kiera rubs her hands together and grins. "Does this mean you're going to tell him you love him?"

"I don't know if—"

"He'll be okay, Chloe. You have to have faith in that. You're not cursed. And once he's in recovery, you'll kiss him on the lips—"

My mouth curls to one side. "You mean true love's first kiss?"

She laughs. "Something tells me you've already kissed him. So it's a little late for that magical kiss. But you *will* tell him how you feel."

"And what if he doesn't feel the same way about me?" Although telling him while he's still under the effects of the anesthesia might make things a little easier. It'll be like a truth serum...but he won't remember later what I told him.

So maybe she's on to something—even if that's not what she meant.

"Then we'll all come over to your apartment with ice cream and help you get over him," Isabelle says. "We won't let you go through this alone."

I smile at the three of them, and for the first time since leaving my family, I don't feel so alone anymore.

Their optimism is heartwarming, though a little misguided. I suspect Isabelle and Ava are in the dark as much as Kiera is about his girlfriend who was in a coma. It changed how open he is to allowing another woman into his heart—much like I've been.

"You do realize they might not even let me see him," I point out. "I'm not family."

"So you'll tell him once he's home from the hospital."

What none of them say—but which is a real possibility—is that we still don't know if he's going to live.

I do an impressive mental roundhouse kick to that thought. He'll be okay. A little worse for wear for a while. But if he wants me in his life after this ordeal is over, I'll be more than willing to give him all the blowjobs he wants if it helps him heal.

He's going to be fine. He's going to be fine. He's going to be fine….

TOP SECRET

AFTER WHAT FEELS LIKE SEVERAL LIFETIMES, A WOMAN IN SCRUBS enters the waiting area.

Every pair of eyes in the room shifts in her direction.

Please let it be Landon, I silently beg. I mean, unless she's come to share bad news…

"Landon Reed?" Her expression gives nothing away.

We stand, and I grip Kiera's upper arm. I'd be surprised if she has any circulation left in it.

"We were able to remove the bullet," the surgeon explains. "He sustained damage to his shoulder, but it could've been a lot worse. He'll need rehab over the next few months to help it heal."

"But he'll be okay?" The words leave my lungs in a big rush of air.

"He'll be stiff for the next few weeks. And he'll need a lot of help in the beginning."

"I hope he does a better job following doctor's orders than you did when you were shot," Liam says to Jayden with a smirk.

Isabelle laughs and pats her fiancé's arm. "I suspect he won't be any better than Jayden was. We might have to duct-tape him to his couch."

"Duct tape might not be a bad idea," Adam says. "Landon isn't the most gracious when it comes to accepting help."

"Wait until he gets to the part where he needs help showering for the first few days." Chuckling, Jayden throws his arm around Isabelle's shoulder. She turns bright red and slaps his hand.

He laughs harder and pulls her in front of him. His arms wrap around her waist.

"I can do it," I blurt before my inner filter realizes what I've just volunteered to do. "I...I mean, I can help him while he's recovering. If he wants me to."

Liam nods, looking slightly relieved. "Can we see him?" He asks the surgeon.

"He's still coming out of general anesthesia, and it's late. You can see him tomorrow during visiting hours."

Kiera, Ava, and Isabelle give me a he's-going-to-be-okay hug.

Now, I just have to hope he'll want to see me after everything that's happened.

33

LANDON

I can't say I've ever wondered what it feels like to be hit by a train, but with the way my body aches, as I slowly open my eyes, I have a pretty good idea.

It takes a moment for my eyes to adjust to the light in the room.

The hospital room.

Vague memories of what happened scroll through my mind. Following Chloe to the store because we'd received a tip that Nikolai would be there. Spotting him dressed as Santa. Having Santa pull out a gun and shoot at Adam and me.

I went down, but that didn't stop me from getting in a few shots first.

I don't remember too much after that—other than Chloe kissing my forehead and whispering something I didn't catch.

Everything else is a colorful blur.

The copper-colored hair of the sleeping woman curled up on the chair catches my attention. Chloe's good arm is resting on the back of the seat, her head on it like it's a pillow.

Her hair shimmers in the light spilling from the window. If

it weren't for the ache in my shoulder, I'd assume I'm dead, and she's an angel.

Christ, she's fucking beautiful.

I watch her for a few minutes, my mind growing less cloudy with each passing moment.

The door slowly opens, announced by the creak of the hinge. Chloe stirs awake and blinks, her expression adorably confused.

"Hey, you're awake." Her voice is heavy with sleep.

"Perfect timing, too," the nurse—who I met earlier when she checked on me—says. She smiles at me. "How're you doing?"

"I've been better." I've also been a lot worse. So there's always that.

"I need to check your wound." She turns to Chloe, who's stretching her arms above her head, and flashing me a view of her stomach.

A stomach I've licked and nibbled, all the while making Chloe moan her sweet sounds.

Fuck, I've missed that.

"You might want to step out while I do that," the nurse tells Chloe.

"I'm fine." Chloe's eyes widen, and her gaze shifts to me. "I mean if you're okay with that. I figured since I'll be looking after you once you've been released—at least until you're feeling better—that I should get used to how it looks." She stumbles over her words and points to my shoulder.

"Sweetheart, I don't need someone looking after me. I can take care of myself."

"I see someone has alpha-male issues," the nurse says, amusement in her tone and in the gleam of her eyes. She pulls the hospital gown down from my shoulder, exposing a shitload of gauze taped to my skin.

She peels it away and checks the wound. "Looking good so

far." She presses the tape back against my skin. "I'll change it when I bathe you in a bit." She turns to Chloe. "Unless you want to do the honors. Although from where I'm standing, you're not doing much better than he is. You two look like a matching set with your arm in a cast and his in the sling."

Chatting merrily, she checks my vitals and unhooks me from the heart-rate monitor, then leaves.

"I'm so sorry about your shoulder," Chloe says once we're alone. "I don't know why Nikolai shot at you. I didn't even know he had a gun on him until it was too late."

She sits. Jumps to her feet. Sits. Jumps to her feet.

"I'm beginning to think someone's turned you into a yo-yo since the last time I saw you."

"I know. I mean, I don't know about the yo-yo part, but I mean I...well, I don't know what to say. I can only imagine how it looked to you and Adam. That I'd lied to you all this time and knew where Nikolai was when I didn't. He just showed up at the store when Kiera and I were there. In that costume. I guess he was tailing me, or someone reporting to him was tailing me."

I've hopped onto the Chloe Express. Next stop? The land of confusion.

I raise my hand, hoping to put the brakes on her words. "We were counting on him coming out of hiding when I became your boyfriend," I say when she pauses long enough for me to get a word in. "He knew that Liam's team does contract work from time to time with the FBI."

I don't exactly want to talk about any of this right now. I'm just amazed she's in my hospital room.

Or maybe she isn't.

Maybe I'm hallucinating that she's here.

To be certain, I pinch myself on my injured arm.

"Did you just pinch yourself?"

"I wanted to make sure I wasn't dreaming."

"Dreaming? Which part do you think you're dreaming? The part about being shot, because I don't know about you, but I'd call that a nightmare."

"I'm referring to the part where you're standing in my room. The last time we were together, before your accident, you were pissed at me for letting you believe Nikolai hired me to protect you."

She winces and chews her lower lip for a heartbeat. "I was wrong about my cousin. He would've done anything for me when we were kids. But that's not the man he became.

"And I also understand that I had nothing to do with my father's, stepfather's, or Mark's deaths. I wasn't the one who murdered them." She steps forward. Uncertainty buzzes around her like static electricity.

She opens her mouth to say something but seems to change her mind.

I reach out to her.

She takes hold of my hand, being careful of the IV needle inserted in it, and closes the gap between us. "Soooo? How's Whiskey doing with his new family? Ava told me they have two kids. I bet he loves that."

"They didn't adopt him." I fight to keep the corners of my mouth from twitching up.

"Oh, no. Are they crazy? He's absolutely adorable. How could they not want him?"

"I didn't say they didn't want him."

"What happened? Why did they change their minds?"

"They didn't change their minds. I did."

She gasps, the sound so soft only the slight jerk of her chest gives it away. "You're keeping him?"

I nod, then wince as a brief pain rips through my shoulder.

Sympathy and something else shines in her eyes. She releases my hand and cups my cheek.

I turn my head slightly and kiss her palm. "I couldn't imagine *not* having him in my life."

"You're his forever home?"

"That's right. I'm his forever home."

She strokes my cheek with her thumb. "Even if something bad might happen to him?"

"Even then."

Something in the way she smiles tells me she understands the full impact of my words. She leans down and brushes her lips against mine. They linger for a moment. "I love you."

The words are so soft, I'm not sure I heard them correctly.

My heart beats loud and fast in my chest. If I were still hooked up to a heart rate machine, the nurse would be running in here to check that I'm okay.

Tell her how you feel, my heart implores. *Tell her that you love her, too.*

My brain has a different view of things. It's one thing to love an animal and lose them. That's hard enough. But to lose a person you love, that would be devastating.

Been there. Done that.

And yet here I am, very much alive—bullet hole in my shoulder notwithstanding.

"You can't be chickenshit when it comes to love just because you're afraid of losing the person. It means living each day as though it might be her last, making sure each one counts and isn't wasted." Jayden's words rattle around in my head. Like they have for the past forty-eight hours.

"I love you, too." My voice is low, but there's no doubt what I said. The words ring loud and clear from deep in my soul. Words that have been there for the past few weeks, waiting for my idiot brain to get with the program.

Chloe and I have both lost people we've loved, and yet here we are, still standing.

All right, technically, I'm not standing. I'm lying in a

hospital bed thanks to her asshole cousin. But the sentiment remains the same.

Chloe stares at me for a heartbeat, her eyes shiny with hope. Her gaze shifts to the clear bag hanging from the IV pole next to my bed.

I know what she's thinking, but she couldn't be any further from the truth. "When it comes to how I feel about you, I'm more than lucid. The drugs pumping in my veins have nothing to do with that."

"No regrets tomorrow?"

With my free hand, I bring her head to mine. "Definitely no regrets."

And then we're kissing.

The best drug around.

I run the tip of my tongue along her lower lip. And it's like the parting of the red sea. Her mouth opens to my mine, and her tongue meets mine, stroke for stroke.

I have no idea how long we've been kissing—maybe a few minutes, maybe a lot longer—when the sound of a creaking hinge penetrates my brain.

I ignore it. Kissing Chloe is much more important than checking who just entered my room. If they know what's good for them, they'll turn around and leave.

"Well, I'd say he's as good as new," Jayden says, not bothering to keep the amusement from his voice. This is met with a soft laugh that I'm guessing belongs to Isabelle.

"Leave him alone." If her voice is anything to go by, she's smiling.

"Yes, leave us alone," I say as Chloe starts to pull away. "We're busy."

"We can see that." This time the words come from Liam. I look past Chloe to find the entire team, along with Ava, standing in my room.

"You're definitely looking more with it than you were earlier," Liam says.

"That must've been some magical kiss. She woke up her grumpy Prince Charming." Isabelle laughs and glances at the ceiling. "And she didn't even need mistletoe for the magic to happen."

"Earlier?" I ask.

"I came to check on you this morning," Liam says. "You were still groggy. I'm not surprised you don't remember."

Shit, I hope I didn't say anything I'll later regret.

"Are you all here to spring me out of this place?"

The expression on Liam's face smothers all hope of that. "Hate to be the bearer of bad news, but you're going to be here for a few days."

Yeah, I don't think so. I grab the cover. "I'm good to go now."

Chloe parks her hand on mine, preventing me from ripping the cover off my lower body. "You were shot in the shoulder and had surgery. You're not going anywhere for now." Her thumb strokes against my knuckles. "But once we spring you out of here, I'm staying with you for a bit to play nurse. And to help you with Whiskey."

Dirty thoughts pop into my head of her in a sexy nurse's uniform, though I doubt that's what she meant.

I flash her a lopsided grin. "You've got yourself a deal."

We've got a lot of lost time to make up for.

And I plan to make the most of it.

34

CHLOE

The day I've been waiting for is finally here.

I step off the school bus and watch the kindergarteners file out and line up in front of me. Josephine and Andrew are also with us. Excited chatter vibrates through the group.

Once the last kid is accounted for, I direct everyone into the building through the door Landon is holding open.

It's been a week since he was shot and one day since he was released from the hospital and into my care. I don't know who was more thrilled: Landon, for finally being freed from his own private hell—his words, not mine—or Whiskey, for finally having his daddy home.

The puppy ran circles around Landon the moment he walked through the door.

Amy, the substitute teacher who's covering Zoe's maternity leave, walks the kids into the building. Josephine and Andrew follow.

I smile at Landon. "Thank you."

He leans in and gives me a brief kiss. "You're welcome."

"Do you two ever stop kissing?" Adam says, approaching us.

"Nope," we say in near unison.

"We have to make up for while he was in the hospital," I remind Adam.

None of the kids, so far, have questioned why the assistant janitor is joining us for the concert. They're just happy to get to see Landon again. They even made him a Get-Well card while he was recovering.

It's a picture of a snowman with a broken arm.

At least I think his arm is broken.

"I didn't think it would be possible, but you two are worse than Jayden and Isabelle. "

"Just wait until you fall in love," I tell him, "you'll be just as bad as us."

"I doubt it."

"You want to make a wager on it?" Landon asks.

Adam holds out his hand. "A hundred dollars that by the end of next year, I'll still be happily single."

"You're on."

They shake on it, with Landon using his nondominant hand.

Amy and I pass out the elf hats while Josephine guides the kids through a quick warm-up.

"You ready, everyone?" she asks.

Forty-eight kindergarteners call out "Yes" in a loud chorus, which causes the adults in the foyer to laugh.

"I think they're ready," I say, grinning.

Landon rests his hand on my lower back, and we all enter the recreation room. Folding chairs are lined up in tidy rows, and the piano is now located to the side of the makeshift stage.

Landon goes to join Samuel and his cohorts. Amy and I get the kids in position.

They won't be entertaining only the seniors who live in the building. Some of the seniors' family members are also here. It's a full house.

Andrew takes his seat at the piano.

"Hello, everyone," I say into the microphone. "Thank you for having us here today. First, I'd like to introduce you to the two people who helped make today possible. Josephine Ashworth helped to get our little singers' performance ready."

She curtsies. Loud applause fills the room. Everyone knows who she is. She doesn't need much of an introduction.

"Tony-Award-winning Andrew Stanton will be accompanying our delightful choir on the piano. We're so honored to have these two wonderful and talented people with us today."

Again, the audience breaks out in loud applause.

As do the kids—mostly because they love jumping up and down while clapping and shaking their bells.

"And on stage, we have the kindergarteners from Dalhousie Elementary." Loud cheers, whistles, and applause spread through the room like a rising tide. I step aside to let Josephine take her position in front of the kids.

That's when I spot Eric, wearing a suit, sitting next to an elderly woman who's been a resident here for the past several months. So, she's definitely not his grandmother.

He notices me looking at him, gives a small wave, and returns his attention to the stage.

The first notes of "Jingle Bells" play, and the kids begin singing and ringing their bells. By the time the final song draws to a close, every face in the audience glows with a smile.

Applause fills the room again, louder than before. Those who can get to their feet give a standing ovation.

The kids eat it up, smiling and waving and jingling on the spot.

Mathilda, the director of the residence, walks to the front, and the loud applause slowly peters out. "Thank you so much for the delightful performance," she tells the kids. "We're truly blessed that you agreed to join us for our Christmas party. We now have snacks and crafts set up in the cafeteria, if you'd all like to join me there."

As far as the kids are concerned, she said the magic word. They bounce around, cheering.

"HOW ARE WE DOING HERE?" I ASK SAMUEL'S TABLE. AMY, Landon, and Adam, as well as the resident staff, are helping the kids and seniors at the other tables scattered throughout the room.

He flashes his shiny white dentures at me and nods at Anton. The little boy's craft project appears to have met a blizzard of glue. It oozes over the toilet paper rolls, red construction paper, and pipe cleaners. "I think we might be out of glue."

"You might be right." I smile at Anton. "I'll get you some more."

I pick up the paper plate that had the glue and walk to the table at the front of the room. I awkwardly unscrew the large white container with my good hand and attempt to pour glue onto the plate. Nothing comes out.

Not a problem. The rest of the supplies are in the other room.

I walk through the open doorway to where I'd stashed everything when I last volunteered here. I crouch next to an open cardboard box and locate the glue.

"Great concert," a deep male voice says, practically startling me out of my underwear. Eric. "Sorry, didn't mean to scare you."

"That's okay. I didn't hear you enter." I lift the container and stand. "And thank you."

His gaze flicks to something over my shoulder. Out of instinct, I start to turn to check what he's looking at.

Before I can turn fully around, something pokes me in the back. The container of glue is yanked from my hand from behind.

"Don't even think about screaming," a harsh voice says as a strong whiff of bad breath, laced with garlic, assaults my nose. "Or else I'll shoot a few rug rats to teach you a lesson. Do we have an understanding?"

A shiver runs through me, turning my body ice cold. Frosty the Snowman has nothing on me.

I nod my head, the movement barely perceptible.

"You can't trust anyone, Chloe." I guess Nikolai was right about that.

Oh, God, what do I do now?

My grandfather never taught me self-defense, but that doesn't mean I didn't sign up for a class with Kiera a few years ago—just in case.

But there's a huge difference between a classroom setting and real life. For one, the worst that can happen in the gym is that you end up on the mat, your pride slightly bruised.

If I screw up here, a bruised ego will be the least of my problems.

Plus, the instructor never went over a scenario like this, or any scenario involving more than one person.

Eric—if that's even his name—stands casually in front of me as if none of this is going down. "How 'bout we go for a little ride?"

How about I knee you in the nuts and make your voice climb a few octaves?

Sounds like a plan to me—if he were close enough for my knee to be acquainted with his man parts. And if his evil sidekick wasn't poking me in the back with the deadly weapon.

"I'd rather not, if that's all right with you." I barely manage to squeeze the words out of my suddenly dry throat.

"I wasn't actually giving you a choice."

I swallow and channel the inner ass-kicking girl that I'm positive is buried beneath the surface—a thousand leagues beneath the surface, but it's still there. *Be brave. Stall him.* Give Landon a chance to realize I'm missing before I really *am* missing.

"I know, but a girl can always hope she's wrong. You do realize my boyfriend's here, and he's the jealous type?" A boyfriend who has hopefully noticed I'm no longer in the cafeteria and is looking for me.

Okay, not exactly the ideal plan, given Landon's shooting arm is currently in a sling. There's not much he can do about my predicament.

But Eric and his baboon don't know that.

My gaze darts to my purse, sitting in the corner—too far away to be of any good, my penknife tucked safely inside.

"You mean Landon Reed, the man your cousin put a hole in? Although if he'd done what he was supposed to, the hole would've been in Landon's heart. Same deal with Adam Hathaway."

I feel a frown form between my eyes. "What do you mean if my cousin had done what he was supposed to?"

In books and movies, the good guy always gets the bad guy to get caught up in a running monologue, spilling his motives for breaking the law because he likes to hear himself speak.

Unfortunately, this is one of those areas where fiction doesn't meet fact.

I know that—but there's nothing wrong with hoping *he* doesn't realize it.

Eric pulls a gun out of a holster hidden under his jacket.

So much for Plan A.

Too bad I didn't have time to concoct a Plan B.

He waves the gun, gesturing for his evil sidekick and me to take the door opposite the one I entered through. The one that doesn't lead directly into the cafeteria.

I have no choice but to do as he demands. The sooner we leave, the less likely someone else will get hurt. My false bravery can only get me so far.

As it is, Tabitha will never let me live this down…if I survive. She was against me doing the Christmas show, and now I've inadvertently given her a reason to say "I told you so," even if she couldn't have predicted this.

Reluctantly, I head out the door. They hasten me toward the main entrance. Behind us, the happy sounds of kids and laughter wave good-bye.

Once we're outside, Eric and his sidekick direct me to a black sedan waiting in the handicap parking spot.

"Seriously? You parked in handicap parking? You don't even have a permit for it." I mentally smack my hand over my mouth. I know I shouldn't speak to him that way, but I can't help it. Blame it on my nerves. I have a tendency of talking like this whenever I get super nervous.

As in, I-could-possibly-die, super nervous.

He huffs a laugh. "So, sue me."

I inwardly will that if there's a God, he'll ensure the duo get slapped with a hefty fine. That's the least he can do.

Eric opens the rear passenger door, and Evil Sidekick gives me a shove to get in.

For a second, I deliberate telling them where to shove their preconceived notion that I'll go willingly.

What are they going to do if I don't do as I'm told—kill me?

I have no doubt that's already on their agenda.

Go figure. I finally decide to risk love, and now I'm the one who's going to die.

But as long as there's even the teensy tiniest possibility I can escape, I need to embrace it. "If I get into the car, will you tell me what you meant by 'If Nikolai had done what he was supposed to, the hole would've been in Landon's and Adam's hearts'?"

"Sure. Whatever. It's not like it'll make a difference if you know or not."

Evil Sidekick gives me another unfriendly nudge in the direction of the open door.

"Didn't your mother ever teach you manners?" I grumble as I climb in. He snickers behind me and slams the door shut.

Eric walks to the other side of the vehicle and climbs into the back seat to sit next to me. Evil Sidekick turns over the engine and screeches out of the parking lot like a bat about to be boiled in a cauldron of scalding water.

With each passing second, reality sinks in. No one knows I've left the building. No one knows where I'm going.

"All right, you got what you wanted," I say to Eric, doing my darnedest to sound polite. "Now, you can explain what you meant."

I'd ask him why I have a contract on my head, but to be honest, it doesn't really matter. That knowledge won't change anything.

And you don't have to be Einstein's offspring to understand why someone wants me dead. It can be summed up in two words: my grandfather.

Revenge runs rampant in his industry.

I guess no one told whoever wants me dead that they're wasting their time. I'm not exactly up there on his list of favorite relatives.

"Your cousin made a deal with my boss. If Nikolai killed Landon and Adam, the contract on you would be called off. He was quite adamant you'd be left alone after that."

Unexpected warmth fills my chest at his words. Okay, not entirely appropriate since Nikolai had intended to kill the two men just to spare my life.

"I really am sorry, Chloe. About everything."

I turn away from Eric, so he can't see the tears in my eyes.

Nikolai knew that once he fired at Landon and Adam, his life would be forfeit. He had purposely died to protect me.

"Where are we going?" I ask a few minutes later, after somewhat recovering from the realization of what had actually gone down the day my cousin died.

Eric doesn't bother to answer. He must have missed the part in the movies where the bad guy does the longwinded monologue.

Instead, he removes his phone from his suit pocket and talks to someone in Russian.

Damn, why did I have be so inept at learning languages? If I had been fluent like my cousins, I'd be able listen to Eric's side of the conversation.

Although from the terse way he's speaking, maybe it's just as well I can't understand him. I doubt he's talking to his lover about their great sex life.

For a while, I deliberate my escape plans. But it's hard to plot your escape if you don't know where you're going.

I can't even text Landon on the sly about my predicament. My phone's in my purse at the seniors' residence.

My only hope is that he and Adam have noticed I'm missing. But again, that won't be of much help if they have no idea where I'm headed.

Yep. I'm screwed.

That thought echoes loudly in my head once we leave the city limits.

I go back to contemplating all the possible methods of escape I've seen in movies and TV shows over the years.

Which doesn't amount to much. It's not often the heroine of a romantic comedy finds herself in a similar situation.

I mentally curse myself for not recently marathoning on 007, *Mission Impossible*, and the Bourne movies. And any other movie that would've trained me to make my daring escape.

After two hours of driving, I'm beginning to wonder if we're going to Canada. I've always wanted to go there—Vancouver sounds nice—but I've never had the opportunity.

But visiting the country as a hostage isn't exactly how I envisioned finally getting there.

My hopes of Eric and Evil Sidekick being caught at the Canadian border come to a screeching halt, as the signposts along the highway indicate we're heading toward Lake Tahoe.

Snowflakes swirl in the air and splat against the windshield. Pine trees add to the wintery wonderland. And all hope of escape gets buried under an avalanche of snow.

Even Frosty the Snowman and Olaf can't help rescue it.

The car eventually pulls to a stop in front of a secluded house built of logs and stones. As far as I can tell, there's nothing else within several miles.

Any other time, I'd consider it romantic, a great setting for a couple to escape to for a few days. The house is large, with picturesque windows and a wraparound porch.

"Wow," I say, forgetting myself for a moment. "The place is gorgeous."

Gorgeous and very familiar.

I've been here before.

Several times when I was a kid. This is where Nikolai and I had talked about making wishes and shooting stars.

The image of the shooting-star ornament he gave me flickers in my memory. *"Remember the star. It has the answer to everything."*

What were you trying to tell me? I silently ask him.

"It belonged to your cousin." Eric doesn't sound as impressed with the location as I am. "It's where he's been hiding since your grandfather's arrest, causing all kinds of havoc on my boss's business."

Which means the FBI is clueless about this property—not exactly good news for me.

"According to Nikolai's lawyer," Eric continues, "Nikolai bequeathed it to you."

"His lawyer told you that?" So much for attorney-client privilege.

"His lawyer's been working on our side for the past year."

"And now that Nikolai's dead, you're taking over his cabin for your evil clubhouse?"

"More or less. For now, anyway. Until the Feds discover its existence." He climbs out of the car while Evil Sidekick opens the door for me.

"You, out," Evil Sidekick barks, waving his gun at me. I'm seriously thinking of renaming him Evil Asshole.

I slowly slide out of the car, glancing around the area that still reminds me of an Enchanted Forest. Nikolai and I used to pretend that magical creatures resided here. Some wondrous, like unicorns and hippogriffs. Others scary and devious.

My gaze shifts toward Evil Asshole. Well, I guess I know what category he falls under.

The cold air grips its icy tendrils around me, penetrating the light-knit fabric of my dress. I attempt wrapping my arms around myself to ward off the chill—not easy when your forearm is in a cast.

"Inside," he-of-so-few-words grunts.

Not wanting to give him a reason to shoot me now, I walk up the wooden steps, pull open the door, and cross the threshold.

I'm rewarded with an interior that is as gorgeous as the exterior. The small foyer opens into a spacious living room. Against one wall is a grand brick fireplace, which Santa would never have to worry about getting stuck in. A huge wreath hangs on the wall above the mantel.

Nikolai loved Christmas as much as I did as a kid. From the looks of things, that never changed for either of us.

A giant Christmas tree stands in the corner, and the entire room has been decorated. Some of the ornaments I recognize. They once belonged to Nikolai's family. The room has a cozy, rustic look I could easily imagine being showcased on the cover of an interior design magazine.

The house looks exactly as I remembered—beautiful and timeless.

"You go that way." Evil Asshole shoves me toward a door with a deadbolt.

A deadbolt I don't remember from the last time I was here.

I stumble forward.

He slides the deadbolt to the side, opens the door, and pushes me inside. The door closes before I can retort.

Not that I had a brilliant retort sitting on the tip of my tongue...or anywhere else on my body.

I look up to check the windows in case they aren't locked—which is highly doubtful.

Instead, I find something I wasn't expecting.

35

CHLOE

"Tabitha? What are you doing here?"

I stare at the woman tied to the wooden chair between the two twin beds. The two beds that Nikolai and I slept on when our families stayed in the house.

"Not much. Just hanging around. And let me guess—you're not here to rescue me?"

I stalk the short distance to the window and attempt to push it open. It doesn't budge.

"Damn it." I examine the frame, searching for a way to unlock it. Nikolai and I never had an issue with it before. It was how we would sneak out of the house to watch the stars after our bedtime.

I quickly come to the depressing conclusion that we won't be escaping through it. It's like the window's been glued shut.

"I take it that's your way of saying we won't be leaving that way," Tabitha says.

I don't answer. There's something I need to find out first.

I stride the short distance to her chair and work at loosening the knots in the rope. "How long have you been here?"

"I don't know. A few days."

That gets me to stop what I'm doing, and my gaze flicks to her face. "How come this is the first I'm learning you're missing?"

"Maybe because no one knows it. My kids are with my ex-husband for the week. I'd planned to do all my Christmas shopping and baking while they were gone, so I had no appointments for anyone to realize something was wrong when I didn't show up for them."

"But why are you here?" If Eric and his sidekick were hoping to lure me here with Tabitha, they picked the wrong person.

"Because I knew info they didn't want you to find out."

The knot I was working on finally gives up its battle, and I free her arm from the chair.

I start working on the other knot. "What's that?"

"I should probably explain something first. I started dating Eric a few weeks ago. He seemed like a great guy at the time."

I can see how she initially thought that. At first glance, he comes off as sweet and funny. Any sane, single woman would easily fall for his boyish charms.

"But then he became awfully interested in you," she says. "He lives in the same building as you, which is how he knew who you were."

"No, he doesn't. His grandmother lives in my building. He was just visiting her there." As the words fall from my lips, I realize how wrong I am. The odds of the grandmother of one of my grandfather's enemies living in my building is pretty much zero.

"If that's true, I have no idea where he hid her. I never saw her when I was in his apartment. And the place doesn't look like an elderly woman lives there. There were no photos or anything else that you would associate with a woman who's lived a lifetime."

I remove the rope from Tabitha's other wrist and drop it to the floor.

"At first, I was pissed at you because of what happened with my husband," she continues. "I was sure the same thing was happening again, only this time with my new boyfriend. I must've had too much to drink one night and said some not-so-great stuff about you. He took that the wrong way and figured I was a vindictive bitch, which he thought worked in his favor.

"He confided in me, convinced me to help him out. But then I realized there was something seriously wrong with him, and I was planning to warn you. Oh, by the way, it's never a good idea to let a man know about your intentions. Lesson learned."

For a second, I digest everything she just told me. "Well, now I know why you weren't returning my calls." I straighten to stand and survey the room. "I've been here before. When I was a kid. My family stayed here a few times."

Hopefully, Eric and the Evil Asshole haven't explored this room like Nikolai and I did one day when we were supposed to be sleeping. We'd been positive we would find hidden treasure in the bedroom or at least a map to tell us where to find it in the forest.

I move the chest of drawers to the side, sliding it and the rug it's sitting on across the floor. It's not overly difficult—beyond the part where I'm wearing a cast. My forearm aches at the slight exertion. Tabitha helps as best as she can, her body sore from being tied up.

The movement of the rug slowly reveals the hidden trapdoor beneath it. The trapdoor I'm sure even Mom and Nikolai's parents didn't know about.

Please still work.

We position the drawers in front of the doorway. The corner of them accidentally hits the door with a soft thud, warning Eric and Evil Asshole we're up to no good.

Tabitha and I freeze, the air in my lungs too scared to leave.

We wait for several rapid heartbeats, listening for any sign we weren't the only ones who heard it.

Silence greets us beyond the muffled sound of the two men talking nowhere near the door. I have no idea what they're saying, nor do I care. As long as they're too preoccupied to check on us, we're gold.

Releasing the air from my lungs, I give Tabitha a thumbs-up, and what I hope is a reassuring smile.

I point to the trapdoor. She turns to it, and a soft gasp escapes her. She slaps her hand against her mouth.

The sound was barely more than a wisp. Nothing to worry about.

It's the next part I'm more nervous for.

I grab the metal ring on the trapdoor and cautiously pull it open, willing the hinges not to squeak. They don't listen. I pause, eyes wide, heart galloping. *Shit, shit, shit.*

Tabitha glances around the room, yanks the duvet from one bed, and covers the trapdoor with it. "On the count of three, I'll make a loud distraction," she whispers, "and you quickly open the trapdoor. Hopefully, between the blanket and me, they won't hear the hinge."

I nod. She raises three fingers. "Oh, and try not to take this too personally."

Before I can puzzle out what she means, she has counted to one.

"You fucking bitch!" she screams as I yank open the trap-door. "You stole my husband from me!"

I have no clue if her plan worked, but I do know I'll be forever deaf. Her mouth was right next to my ear.

I carefully lower the door to the floor. Cold air rushes into the room from our new escape route. Tabitha peers in horror at the dirt ground, which is only about two feet below.

I mime that we'll have to crawl to safety.

She mimes, *What if there's a bear down there?*

I think that's what she's miming.

I shake my head and mime, *There's not enough room for a bear.*

She mouths something else. I have no idea what. I shrug.

Which isn't the answer she was looking for.

She mimes, *There are spiders down there*, and shudders.

I'm about to mouth "Fine, then stay here," when the floorboards outside the bedroom door creak.

That's the only motivation Tabitha needs. She swings her legs into the opening and drops with a soft thud to the ground. There's barely enough room for her to lower herself to her belly.

She half crawls, half drags her body forward.

"Do you think they're wrestling in there?" Evil Asshole says from the other side of the door, sounding a little too turned-on, if you ask me.

I don't wait around to hear what Eric thinks. I jump into the hole and follow after Tabitha.

Neither of us is dressed for escaping kidnappers. Dresses and heels aren't exactly the ideal survival gear. Dirt and debris that has blown under the cabin, scraps at my hands and legs and finds its way into my cast.

Goose bumps crowd my skin, and I curse Eric for not being considerate enough to kidnap us during the summer.

Or better yet—not at all.

I strain to hear any sounds to warn me our escape has been discovered. A scraping of the drawers in front of the bedroom door. The clatter of footsteps. Angry voices.

But the only noises I can hear are the pounding of my pulse in my ears and my rapid breaths. If we're lucky, we'll be long gone before they notice we're missing.

Tabitha is pressed against the wall when I emerge from under the tight crawl space. A couple of her blouse buttons have come undone, and a few are now missing. There's a small tear in one sleeve. Streaks of dirt are smudged on her face, and her pencil skirt is covered with mud and pieces of dried leaves.

I can't imagine I look any better. But I'd be more than happy to put up with a lot worse if it means being far away from here...preferably in Landon's arms (or at least his good arm).

I focus on the memory of how it feels to be wrapped in them. How it feels to cuddle with him on his couch while watching Christmas movies. It's the memory of those two things that keeps me moving, that gives me a reason not to give up.

Love and hope, that's all I've got keeping me going at this point.

It's enough for now.

But if winter coats and boots should magically materialize, I wouldn't complain.

"What now?" Tabitha asks.

Good question.

"The last house I saw when they drove me here was at least a mile away." I point in that direction. "I have no idea if there's anything closer the other way."

Her face pales. "I can't walk that far, not in these shoes." She gestures at her cute red stilettos with white bows—like some sort of candy cane.

She's right, though, especially with the amount of snow we have to walk through. If she doesn't lose her shoes in the snow, there's still the risk of a heel breaking.

Plus, our feet will freeze off long before we find help.

I shiver uncontrollably and attempt to warm myself up with my hands. That's about as useful as opening a locked door with an ice cream cone. "Their car is parked out front. Maybe Big, Bad, and Ugly left his keys in the ignition."

She takes a step forward. "Great, let's go find out."

I grab hold of her arm. "If they're in the living room, they'll see us. We have to be stealthy about it."

Fortunately, I chose my dark-green knit dress for the concert and not my burgundy one. Tabitha's neutral-colored outfit does a better job blending into the background.

Channel your inner pine tree.

In first grade, I was cast in the role of a tree in our school play. I was a fantastic tree, if you ask me. So, all I have to do is relive that moment...minus the song I had to sing.

We inch our way closer to the front of the house, listening for any sound to indicate our escape has been noticed.

Part of me—a tiny part—is curious why Eric and Evil Asshole haven't already killed me. The FBI discovered there's a contract on me. In my grandfather's world, that generally means murder.

So why am I still standing?

Both great questions—that I can deliberate *after* we're far, far, far away from here.

The car isn't completely out in the open, but close enough. It also doesn't help that the deciduous trees are naked. Foliage would've at least provided some shelter from watchful eyes.

We sneak toward the car, using whatever we can find to provide further cover. Every part of me screams to run the rest of the way. I ignore it.

The world around us is silent, as if nature is watching us with bated breath. I'm surprised the loud and rapid *thub thub thub* of my heart doesn't spook an equally loud bird in a nearby tree—and send it squawking in alarm.

We finally make it to the front passenger door, and I slowly open it. It's not locked, which I take as a positive sign.

Too bad it's the only positive thing about this escape attempt. The key isn't dangling in the ignition.

At the realization we're screwed, it feels like someone hurled a boulder at my stomach, knocking me on my butt.

Double damn.

Okay, Plan A didn't work. Now I just need a Plan B.

I glance up at the sky, in case Plan B is written there. If it is, the thick clouds and falling snow are obscuring it.

Keeping my head down, I search the passenger side of the car for anything that might help us. But there's not much I can look through without drawing attention to myself.

Tabitha's shivering uncontrollably. We both are. We need to go somewhere warm, or else we'll be popsicles before we have a chance to get the hell out of here.

Once Tabitha and I have finished hunting through the car, I glance at the house, mentally inventorying everything I noticed in the living room during the short time I was in there.

"There's a phone in the living room," I tell her, keeping my voice low. "But I don't know if the landline actually works."

"Are we talking about the same place where those two men are currently holed up?" She flashes me an irritated, you've-got-to-be-kidding-me scowl.

"That'd be the one. All we need to do is take them out of commission. Even for a short time. And tie them up."

Right—that sounds easy enough.

The execution? That might be a whole different hockey game.

For the next few minutes, we brainstorm ideas until we narrow it to one strong possibility.

All right, it's the only possibility we come up with. It's getting too damn cold to think. And if we don't act now, we might never have another chance. Our hands are turning into icicles.

Great, if we were Elsa from *Frozen*.

This situation is made worse because part of our plan involves making snowballs. We work as quickly as possible, doing our best to ignore the cold.

I imagine I'm in Hawaii, building a sandcastle with the hot sand.

I'm sorry to say that visualization exercise is a bust.

"How's your throwing arm?" I ask Tabitha once we're finished.

"Pretty good. I used to be a pitcher on my high school softball team. I wasn't the star pitcher, but I could hold my own."

That's good enough for me.

I can't throw a baseball to save my life, and right now, that's precisely *not* what we need.

She sets up in position, and I pick up a large branch from the ground. It's thick with smaller branches and twigs poking in all directions.

I let out a hard breath. "Okay, you ready?"

"Ready."

Cautiously, I creep through the deep snow to the porch, praying the men don't spot me. I slowly mount the steps, hoping they don't creak.

I listen for a brief moment to the sounds from inside, then channel my inner-Ninja-slash-world-series-winning-baseball-player self.

I nod at Tabitha, who gathers a snowball and hurls it at the living room window.

Splat!

I listen to see if that got the evil duo's attention. Nothing. I nod at Tabitha to throw another one.

Splat! Splat!

"What the fuck?" a muffled voice grumbles from inside the house. The sounds of heavy boots clunking across the hardwood floor follow it. Both are barely heard over the rushing of the pulse in my ears.

I adjust my grip on the branch and take a slow, steadying breath.

You can do this.

The door opens, and Evil Asshole steps through the doorway, his gun in his hand.

Before he has a chance to spot me, I swing the branch with all my might. Like our lives depend on it.

Which they do.

Twigs and sharp branches hit his face, rendering him off-balance.

A loud bang splits the air, but I don't have time to check where the bullet went. The follow-through of the branch causes him to fall backward, and his head hits the stone part of the wall, hard.

Hard enough to knock him out cold.

I don't have time to appreciate my handiwork, though. Eric comes out to see what the heck is going on.

And gets a snowball in the face.

There's an old saying that warns never to poke a grumpy bear with a stick.

I ignore it and jab at Eric in his side.

This buys Tabitha enough time to dive for evil sidekick's gun.

With shaky hands, she aims it at Eric. "Drop your weapon." She says it with the same authority I've seen her wield during a PTA meeting.

But alas, it doesn't have the same impact on him that it does with everyone else.

"Hmm. What do you think, Chloe," she says, "if I turn him into an eunuch?"

Eric makes a scoffing noise and steps forward.

Tabitha's innocent expression twists into a smug smile, and she lowers the gun, aiming it at his groin. "My ex-husband was a louse. We can all agree on that. But do you know the one thing that he did right?"

Eric doesn't answer.

"He used to take me to the shooting range. He thought it was romantic. I figured it might come in handy one day. Looks like one of us was right.

"Now, unless you want to spend the rest of your days without a functional set of balls, I suggest you put the gun on the ground and lie on your stomach.

"And just so we've got it straight, my hands are shaking because it's fucking cold out here. So you might want to take that into consideration. Chloe and I won't be straining ourselves to drag your bleeding bodies inside the nice, warm house. We don't want to ruin the beautiful hardwood floors with your blood."

I don't know if he believes her or not, but in the end, he doesn't want to take a chance and is clearly attached to his man parts. He lowers the gun on the floor and does what she says.

Ten minutes later, both men are tied up with the rope from the bedroom. I found more in the shed behind the house. It seems that Nikolai really liked rope.

And Tabitha and I made good use of it.

By the time we finished tying them to the dining room chairs, they can't move—other than their necks, feet, and fingers. I won't be surprised if it takes the authorities well over an hour to untie them.

"I had no idea you were an excellent markswoman," I say to Tabitha as I walk to the phone by the wall.

She grins at me. "I'm not. My ex took me to the shooting range only the one time, and I didn't come close to hitting the target. I made it clear I never wanted to go back."

She turns her grin to the two immobilized men, who are staring dumbfoundedly at her. "But they didn't know that."

36

LANDON

I enter the cabin and almost fall to my knees at the sight of Chloe.

Standing there.

Alive and looking maybe a little badass.

When Adam realized Chloe had gone missing at the retirement home, we contacted the team and the FBI to alert them that we had a situation. The home's director showed us footage from the security cameras.

We couldn't see what happened when they disappeared into the supply closet, but it was clear who'd taken her.

One man was known by the FBI, a henchman for one of Vadik's rivals.

That was all they needed to piece together who had a contract out on Chloe.

The only problem was, the FBI had no idea where the two men had taken her.

It wasn't until three hours ago that we finally got our answer when Chloe called me.

With my healthy arm, I pull her to me. "Thank God you're okay," I say against her hair.

Eric and his goon are lucky the FBI got to them first.

I mean, sure, the hand-to-hand combat would have been a little lopsided, considering I'm currently shorthanded. But that doesn't mean I wouldn't have tried.

My gaze lands on the two men tied to the chairs. Agents Foden and Ramsey don't appear to be in a particular rush to undo them—and I can see why.

"Did you tie them up?" I ask Chloe, unable to keep the grin off my face. Pride rushes through me at how she managed to take down the two men on her own.

She nods toward the hallway as Tabitha enters the living room. "We both did."

Tabitha is smiling, an equal amount of pride on her face.

It seems that Chloe failed to mention a few details when she called me. Okay, a lot of details, from the looks of things.

I glance around the living room. "Nice place." The interior reminds me of a rustic ski lodge, not your typical location for hiding individuals who've been kidnapped.

"Thanks," Chloe says.

I must've been looking at her funny because she clarifies what she meant. "It appears that I now own this house. It was Nikolai's. This is where he'd been hiding while the FBI was searching for him. Eric told me Nikolai bequeathed it to me."

The corners of her mouth turn down. "Those two are the reason Nikolai shot you and Adam." She points to the two in question. "Their boss made some sort of twisted deal with Nikolai. If he killed you two, the contract on my head would be dropped."

"But he didn't kill us. He only injured us."

"Which is why they kidnapped me. He died trying to protect me, but in the end, it didn't change anything."

I can feel my eyebrows draw together. "Something doesn't seem right. The FBI had reason to believe someone had a contract out on you, but other than the hit and run, no one has made any other attempts on your life. They've just been attempted kidnappings."

"I've been wondering about that, too. Maybe the contract wasn't to kill me."

"It's possible. But they might have planned to kill you after kidnapping you, only they needed something from you first. Something that Nicholai obtained after the hit and run. It could also be that the contract was a way to flush your cousin out, and when he died, they needed you because he had something they wanted." All those possibilities seem likely. "And there's still a good chance this is tied directly to your grandfather. We can't ignore the likelihood that the reason you were kidnapped was to get something out of him."

The two men watch on in interest, as if I'm Bruce Wayne, and they're hoping I'm going to reveal Batman's true identity.

I nod at the two cops assigned to keep an eye on the two men. "Pass me that blanket."

One of them tosses it at me. "Is it okay if I talk to her in Adam's SUV?" I ask the two agents. "I'd rather those two don't overhear the conversation."

Agent Foden nods her consent. One-handedly, I place the blanket over Chloe's shoulders and lead her to the vehicle. Once inside it, I start the engine and crank up the heat.

"I'm sorry for what happened," Chloe says, gaze fixed on the windshield.

Huh? "What do you mean?"

She turns her gorgeous brown eyes to me. "For making you worry about my safety. For making you wonder where I'd gone. I understand if this is too difficult for you. If you want to end things with me."

"Why would I want to end things with you?" I stroke her cheek with my thumb. It's velvety to the touch. Like I knew it would be. "I'm in love with you, Chloe. Nothing's going to change that. Yes, it killed me that I hadn't realized you were missing until after you were gone. I'm supposed to protect you, but I did a crappy job."

Her eyes search mine, and she presses her index finger against my mouth, stopping what I was going to say next. "You're not supposed to protect me, Landon. You're on medical leave until you've been cleared to work. And according to Liam, you're on medical leave for at least two months, probably longer. So, no, you're not supposed to be protecting me. You're my boyfriend, not my bodyguard."

I grunt, the sound which is best described as caveman. "I know that, but protecting you is in my job description as your boyfriend. It's in the fine print."

She laughs. "I must have missed that part."

"I have no intention of ending things with you," I say, making sure there are no doubts about that. "And what happened to you isn't your fault. No more than it was Sarah's fault she was killed or my fault. I understand that now."

My hand shifts from her cheek and knots in her hair. I bring her close to my mouth. She doesn't resist.

And then we're kissing like I promised myself I would do once Adam and I arrived here.

Our tongues tangle, treasuring every moment we still get to enjoy as a couple. I do have questions I need to ask her, but they can wait for a few more minutes.

For now, I want to kiss the woman I love.

Eventually, we come up for air—mostly because I don't exactly want the FBI to come looking for her and find me making out with their star witness.

"You wanted to ask me some questions?" Chloe prompts, reminding me that was one of the reasons we're in Adam's SUV.

"The FBI has been hunting for Nikolai ever since your grandfather's arrest. How come they weren't aware of this cabin, but those two men tied to the chairs were? And did they know about it before Adam and I killed him, or did they only learn about it after Nikolai's death?"

"Eric said it was Nikolai's lawyer who told them about the house. The lawyer is on Eric's boss's payroll. Nikolai didn't realize that."

"Which brings us back to the possibility that Eric believes you have something his boss wants." I look at the house, where another mystery is currently hanging out with the Feds. "Tabitha—what does she have to do with any of this? Did she know your cousin and where he was hiding? Is that why she's here?"

"I don't think she knew Nikolai." Chloe explains how Tabitha ended up here.

All I can say is the woman might want to quit dating for a while. She's definitely a magnet for losers if her ex-husband and Eric are anything to go by.

"Do you have any idea what it is Eric believes you have that's important enough to kidnap and kill you?" I ask.

Shrugging, she shakes her head. "No idea at all. Like I told you before, I stepped away from my family a long time ago."

"Did Nikolai send you anything? A letter or something as simple as a birthday card?"

"Nothing. Not in a while anyway." Her brow scrunches. "The day you were shot, he gave me the shooting-star decoration. But it's nothing more than a Christmas tree ornament."

I know the one she's talking about. It's on our tree at my town house. Jayden and the guys moved the tree and Chloe's decorations back there while I was in the hospital.

"I didn't realize it was from Nikolai."

"He gave it to me in the store. He approached me and asked me if I had a holiday wish I wanted to tell Santa. Then he handed me the ornament."

"Did he say anything else about it? Perhaps give you a clue about what it means?"

She shakes her head again. "He told me to remember the star. That it has the answer to everything. I knew what the star symbolized. Or at least I thought I did. But other than that, I have no idea what he meant." A frown briefly drifts onto her face. "But maybe I'm wrong. Maybe I do know what he was trying to tell me."

"What do you mean?"

"My mom and I, along with Nikolai and his family, came here a few times when he and I were kids. The two of us would sneak out of the house and watch the stars. We had a discussion at one point about making wishes on a shooting star. Maybe the ornament was his indirect way of telling me he now owned this house. He must have known he was going to die that day, that taking you and Adam out was nothing more than a suicide mission."

Her chin dips, and she sniffs. I kiss her temple, wanting to do anything to soften her pain.

Adam and Agent Ramsey exit the cabin and head our way. Adam is carrying what appears to be a journal.

"Stay here," I tell her. "I'll be right back."

I open the SUV door and climb out before they reach the vehicle. "I haven't finished talking to her. Is there something you need?"

Adam shows me the brown, leather-bound journal. "Chloe needs to see this."

I nod for him to give it to her, and the three of us join her on the other side of the SUV. She has already hopped down by the time we get there, the blanket still wrapped around her shoulders.

Adam hands her the book. "Read the page marked with the ribbon."

"What is this?" she asks, frowning lightly.

"One of our agents found it in Nikolai's desk," Agent Ramsey says. "He wrote it for you, or at least that's what the introduction suggests. Our guess is that he wanted you to find it, but the men who kidnapped you found it instead...and that's why they were so interested in you. Read what it says." He points at the journal.

Still frowning, Chloe opens it and reads the page, allowing me to read it alongside her.

...I'm so sorry I let you down, Chloe. You were the world to me, and nothing about that ever changed. I never wanted to be part of our grandfather's legacy, but the man is crafty and found a way to drag me into it. I didn't want you to suffer the same fate. I convinced him to allow you to go free. That came with consequences, some you know about, others you don't.

If you're reading this, it's most likely because I'm dead, and you've learned about the cabin. This is my legacy to you...and what I'm hoping will be the end of our grandfather's reign over the family. I'm hoping this means you and your mother will finally be reunited. She misses you very much.

She misses you and will need you when she finds out what really happened to her husbands. Both of them were murdered by her father. Not by his hands exactly, but by the hands of Victor Hedmead. This was also the case with your boyfriend, Mark Greenwood. He never dumped you like you were led to believe. I was the one who sent you the text after he disappeared. I wanted you to be able to move on and not waste years waiting for him to return. I'm sorry for the role I played in that deception. I never wanted you to get hurt.

You're probably wondering why they were killed. There was no one reason. With your father, our grandfather erroneously believed that he would eventually want to be involved in the family's criminal activities. He couldn't have been more wrong. Your father had no idea about the true nature of Granddad's business when he married your mom, and she did everything she could to keep him from finding out the truth. He didn't say anything to your mom about Granddad's proposition, but he confronted Granddad and made the mistake of threatening to expose him. Your father greatly underestimated the old man.

I'm guessing your mom never told you, but your father supposedly left a letter for her, telling her that he was concerned for his safety and was disappearing before anything could happen to him. The letter was forged by one of Granddad's associates. Our grandfather lied to her and told her that as long as your father didn't say anything about the true nature of the family's business dealings, your father was quite safe. He also ensured that your father paid child support, even after he was long dead. Your mother never suspected the truth.

As for your stepfather, Granddad learned his lesson and didn't try to recruit him into the family business. I don't know all the details, but your stepfather stumbled across something that would have incriminated dear old Granddad and could have brought down the house of cards. Like with your father, Granddad managed to hide his tracks so no one grew suspicious about your stepfather's sudden disappearance.

Chloe sniffs but keeps reading, tears streaming down her face. I want to take the journal away from her, to stop her pain, but I also know she needs closure. She needs to know why the three men were murdered.

If Mark Greenwood hadn't had aspirations of becoming a prosecutor, he might still be alive. I don't know if he ever told you that, or if he continued to let you believe he was studying to become a corporate lawyer. He stumbled across something linked to you and your estranged family and started to investigate a suspicion he had. He got too close to the truth, and Granddad had him removed from the picture. And like with everyone else, the old man planted enough evidence to make it look like Mark had quit law school due to not being able to handle the stress, and that he moved away to start a new life. Since he had grown up in the foster care system, it was a lot easier to make him disappear.

The FBI probably doesn't have enough information to figure out who was responsible for the deaths of all three men. I do. I have the evidence for that, maps to show where their bodies were buried, and evidence for so many other crimes that our grandfather was responsible for. Evidence that will ensure the Orlov crime family is forever destroyed. The family has resulted in so much loss over the years, including the death of my parents, Dimetric, and Nadia. It's time for it all to end so that you can truly start anew.

Just remember this: X marks the spot.

I am so proud of you, Chloe. No matter where I wind up after my time on earth ends, I want you to always remember that.

Nikolai

Chloe wipes the heel of her hand against her wet cheek. I wrap my arm around her waist, providing her with my good shoulder to lean on for now. And later, once we're home, to cry on.

And I'm positive Whiskey will be delighted to lick away her tears.

"X marks the spot." With tears still running down her cheeks, she turns around, scanning our surroundings. "Aye, aye, Captain." Her tone is that of a pirate—a pirate muttering to herself.

As if in a trance, she pulls away from me and walks away from the cabin. Adam, Agent Ramsey, and I exchange looks and follow after her.

We end up at a large tree with an X carved in the bark. The letter isn't even an inch tall—easily missed if you don't know what you're looking for. At the bottom of the tree is a hollow opening.

"The night Nikolai and I talked about wishing on a shooting star, I'd asked him if he could wish for anything, what would it be. He said to be a pirate. The next day, we searched for the best location to hide treasure should his wish ever come true." Chloe kneels and inspects the hollow opening for a moment.

She reaches inside, drags out a large metal box, and looks up at Agent Ramsey. "I think this is what you're looking for."

Ramsey tries to open it. "It's locked."

"I possibly know where the key is." Chloe groans. "It's on my keychain...back at the seniors' residence. In my purse. My mom gave it to me last Christmas...or at least I assumed it was from her. We send each other presents every year but never sign them, so my grandfather had no idea what we were up to."

"I grabbed your purse after we realized you were missing," I tell her. "It's in Adam's vehicle."

After retrieving her purse from the SUV, we all return to the warm cabin, and Ramsey unlocks the box. The key had been cleverly disguised to look like part of a key chain, decorated so no one would clue in that it was more than just an ornament. Inside the box are a memory stick and a stack of documents.

Only the FBI agents get to peruse them, but from what they can tell us, Nikolai had been storing evidence for a while that paints Chloe's grandfather in a terrible light.

All right, a worse light than he's already in.

There's also a note from Nikolai, asking Chloe to hand over everything to the FBI. And there's evidence that the two men who kidnapped her are actually on her grandfather's payroll, and not on his rival's. Like the FBI, they were searching for Nikolai. His grandfather knew Nikolai had damaging evidence against him.

And Nikolai wasn't afraid to use it.

Once the two agents are finished talking to Chloe and Tabitha, we're allowed to leave.

"You're driving, right?" I ask Adam as the four of us return to his vehicle.

"It's my vehicle." His tone rings with a no-duh attitude.

"Good. Tabitha, you're riding up front with him. I'll be busy making out with my hot girlfriend in the back seat." Who was hot before, but even more so after she took down those two assholes who kidnapped her.

Adam groans. "Christ, don't tell me I'll be forced to watch you two going at it every time I check my rearview mirror."

"So, don't check the mirror." I wink at Chloe.

She laughs.

I might not get to work for the next few months—the idea of which isn't sitting well with me—but at least I'll get to spend it with the woman I love.

And there's nothing I want more than that.

EPILOGUE
CHLOE

Three Months Later

I place the vase of white roses in front of the headstone. From a nearby tree, a bird chirps a cheerful tune. Even the rays of sunlight pushing past the breaks in the clouds seem joyful.

It's almost as if Nikolai is watching me from heaven, smiling his approval of the life I'm now living. A life he could have lived if not for the family business.

A business he played a role in taking down.

At the neighboring grave, Mom replaces my stepfather's red roses that she'd left the last time we were at the cemetery. They sit contently next to the flowers I set there a few minutes ago. My father's and Mark's graves are also here—far, far, *far* away from the Orlov family plot.

All four men were important to me. All four men deserve to be remembered in a way that had nothing to do with my grandfather.

Like me, Mom hadn't known her two husbands were dead. She thought they had divorced her. She'd had no idea when she signed the divorce papers that both men were dead. My grandfather's reach had gone further than we realized. His crooked lawyers made sure of it.

Landon rests his hand on my lower back, and I smile at the man who helped return my mother to me.

I kiss him. "Thank you."

"You're welcome," he murmurs before brushing his mouth against mine.

This isn't the first time we've come to the cemetery since the four men were buried here. And each time we've come, Mom has joined us. Despite everything that happened, she never stopped loving either husband.

She just assumed her father had scared them off, which was why she never remarried after my stepfather disappeared.

But I suspect that might be changing soon—especially now that her father no longer has a role in her life.

I grin at the handsome man with her, who I've gotten to know over the past two months. Nigel's wife passed away from ovarian cancer over a year ago, and Mom was the one who helped superglue his broken heart back together—first as his friend, and then as something more. He's been doing the same for her after she found out the truth about her husbands.

Somehow, the news of their deaths hasn't scared him away.

And for that, I'm thankful.

He kisses her temple, and I swear my face will split in two if my grin gets any wider. They're freaking adorable together.

"You ready for your surprise now?" Landon asks me.

I nod. The four of us climb into Adam's SUV, which Landon borrowed because there isn't enough room for all of us in his jeep.

"You're not going to give us a hint where you're taking us?" Mom asks. "Not even a tiny one?"

Nigel laughs. "You remind me of my three-year-old granddaughter."

That has Mom pouting, but the gleam in her eyes says the opposite.

"Did Landon tell you where we're headed?" she asks him.

"He might have hinted, but I swore an oath that I wouldn't tell either of you."

Landon pulls out of the cemetery parking lot.

"Does the surprise have anything to do with Liam reinstating your status?" I ask. Until Landon finally received his medical clearance two days ago, he hadn't been allowed to join his team on missions. And for the past two months, he'd been stuck behind his desk.

He was about as thrilled at that as a guppy coming face-to-face with Jaws.

Landon flashes me a cocky grin. "Nope."

"You're really not planning to tell me, are you?"

"Not until we get there."

The only thing he *has* told me is that we're going to Wine Country. And to pack for the weekend.

It's late morning by the time we pull into the driveway leading to Enchanted Springs Winery. Ahead of us are two buildings, Mediterranean in design. A fountain sits in front of the smaller one. The other building is long, like a barn.

"Wow, it's gorgeous," I say.

"Glad you like it."

Landon's mysterious grin only piques my curiosity more.

"Are we here for a wine tasting?" I ask as the four of us walk toward the building, Landon holding my hand.

We drove past a few wineries on the way, but he didn't so much as slow down at any of them. In fact, it's like he's been here before. He knew exactly where he was going without turning on the GPS.

"Not in the typical sense," he says.

Mom and I share a confused glance.

We approach the smaller building, and Landon opens the

door for us to enter. The tingle of a small bell above the door announces us.

The only other person inside the store is a woman in her forties, examining a bottle of wine. She looks in our direction and a warm smile grows on her face. "Landon, it's nice to see you again."

My curiosity cranks up tenfold. Landon never mentioned he knew anyone here.

She shakes his hand. "And you must be Chloe Reinhart."

I nod. "That's right."

"I'm Regina Helm. It's nice to finally get to meet the owner of the winery." She spreads her arms wide, gesturing to the building and the vineyards beyond the walls.

But she's not looking at Landon when she says it. She's talking directly to me.

Huh?

"What do you mean?"

"Your grandfather bought the property several years ago and put it under your name," Landon explains.

"He did?" That's an odd thing to do after you boot your granddaughter from the family. "How come he never mentioned it to me?" An unwelcome thought hits me like a stick of salami to the head. I groan. "God, I'm going to be nailed with back taxes, aren't I? It's not like I declared this place to the IRS."

Was this the old man's final act of vengeance because I wanted nothing to do with the family business?

Nice.

"You don't have to worry about that. Your accountant was making sure the IRS was kept happy so no one inadvertently stumbled across your grandfather's connection to the place. He wasn't listed on the papers."

Well, that would explain a few things.

"So, this is mine?" My voice comes out sounding like a chipmunk who's been stepped on.

He nods.

"But I don't know anything about running a vineyard."

"Neither did your grandfather," Regina says. "That's why he hired my husband and me to manage the vineyard and the winery. And...well...we're hoping you'll still keep us on now that you're officially the owner." Her expression reminds me of when Whiskey's eager for a treat—a treat he loves with all his doggy being.

In the short time Landon and I have known each other, he has gained the ability to guess what I'm thinking. And this time is no exception. "One of Liam's contacts looked into the winery and the books. He was impressed at how well it's doing."

I smile at Regina, thankful no one is expecting me to suddenly take over the helm. "Well, in that case, I don't see any reason for things to be changed around here. Other than the owner needing to become educated about what's involved with running a winery. I hope you'll be willing to help me there."

She beams brighter than a firefly's glowing butt. "Absolutely. Thank you."

Landon threads his fingers with mine. "Now, if there are no objections, I'm stealing my girlfriend to show her around."

He doesn't wait for a reply. Not that it would've probably mattered if there were any. Either way, he plans to steal me.

And I'm more than thrilled to be stolen.

By him—and only him.

He leads me out the door we came through and escorts me to the side of the larger building, where no one can see us. He presses me against the wall, every part of his body making contact with mine.

My body hums with excitement, with happiness, with need.

"This is you showing me around?" I ask on a lusty laugh.

Landon's eyes darken. "Yes. I figured we'd start right here.

With me showing you how much I love you...while it's just the two of us."

And he does precisely that.

His kiss like no other kiss.

His touch like no other touch.

Because he loves me as I love him.

The moment between us grows heated, which comes as no surprise.

What does surprise me is the music that suddenly starts playing on Landon's phone.

"Hit Me with Your Best Shot" by Pat Benatar.

It's the song that plays whenever Liam calls him about work.

Landon curses under his breath, and I can't help but giggle even though I have a feeling I'm not going to like the call any more than he does. It's the curse a man makes when he's about to be cock-blocked.

Landon accepts the call. "What's up, Liam?" There's a pause while he listens to whatever his boss has to tell him. "No, I haven't...not since he left for Nevada to visit his grandmother.... He said it was a potential mission but didn't say much else.... Really?...Okay. See you Monday."

Frowning, he ends the call.

"What's wrong?" I ask.

"It's Adam. He's missing. The last time anyone saw him, he was entering a chapel in Vegas...to get married."

EXCERPT FROM DECIDEDLY WITH LUCK

KEIRA'S STORY…

December

For as long as I could remember, I'd always loved fairy tales. Even before becoming an elementary schoolteacher.

More specifically, I'd always loved Disney's versions of the classic fairy tales.

Have you ever read Hans Christian Andersen's original story of *The Little Mermaid*? There are no singing lobsters, no happy endings. The little mermaid doesn't sail away into the sunset with her handsome prince.

Nope, not at all.

Spoiler alert!

She sacrifices herself so the prince can live, and the sea witch transforms the little mermaid into sea foam.

Unlike the original fairy tales, Disney leaves you with hope for a happily ever after, hope for a new beginning.

This was all fine and wonderful, but as I stood at the entrance to the hotel ballroom—my glittering silver stilettos feeling as though they were glued to the floor—I questioned if that would be the case for me.

Of course, it will.

Embracing that flicker of hope, I resumed reciting in my head my goal for the evening: *Project Kissing Under the Mistletoe.* A kiss under the mistletoe from a handsome stranger. A happy-for-now ending to the night—and a baby step toward moving on after my husband's death a year ago.

I scanned the sea of ball gowns and tuxes and elaborate masks, searching for a particular blonde in a dress of black tulle. *That's right.* In addition to the Jingle Balls ball being a fundraiser for testicular cancer, it was a masquerade ball.

My sister waved at me from across the ballroom, next to the grand Christmas tree decorated with a flurry of gold and red ornaments.

Brittany and her husband were the reason I was here tonight instead of back home in San Francisco, knitting mittens for foster kids in Boston. They were the reason I was wearing the mask covering the upper portion of my face and the stunning burgundy gown.

Don't worry. This wasn't the anniversary of my husband's death. That had passed a week ago with me spending the day reading the love notes he used to leave all over our house.

Love notes I'd saved in a big floral box every time I found one.

On the day of the one-year anniversary, I'd sipped a glass of Enchanted Springs Chardonnay, the same wine we'd served at our wedding, and read the notes aloud.

Roses are red, violets are blue, I want to have hot sex with you.

A poet, he was not.

And then there was the note I had saved for last:

If I die before you, I want to be the star in the sky that grants all your wishes.

I inhaled a long, fortifying breath, channeling my inner Disney princess, and wove my way through the throng of merry partiers.

The conversation I'd had with Stephen after I'd found that note sashayed into my head. The conversation where he told me that if he did die before me—way, way, *way* down the line— he wanted me to fall in love again.

After this, he proceeded to list all the men he thought were viable options, in case they were available at the time.

"But definitely not Stinky Pete," he'd said.

"I don't think you have to worry about me ending up with the villain from *Toy Story Two*."

Stephen barked a laugh—the laugh he always made when he thought I was being cute and adorable. "I was talking about my teammate. Pete Mundy. His hockey skates smell like he melted Limburger cheese in them."

I grinned at him and kissed him sweetly on the cheek. "Okay, no, Pete Mundy. Anyone else?"

"Logan Mathews."

"Is he a yah or a nah?"

"A definite yah."

"I'm sure his wife would have something to say about that." Logan had been Stephen's best friend and teammate in college, and his best man at our wedding. Now, he played in the NHL— with Chicago, last I'd heard.

"All right, I'll add him to the list," I'd said with a grin, even though my heart had been splitting into a billion fragments at the thought of Stephen possibly dying before me.

My sister's red lips curved into a wide smile under her black-feathered half mask as I approached.

"Kiera." She beamed at me like I was a baby who'd taken her first wobbly steps. "Let me introduce you to the charity's biggest supporter and my dear friend." The way she said it, you would've thought she was talking about royalty. "Lucinda, this is my little sister, Kiera. Kiera, this is Lucinda Mathews." The woman's surname came out in a hushed whisper.

I bit back the urge to curtsy to the much older woman

standing next to Brittany. Lucinda's gold-and-cream gown, diamond earrings and necklace, and spritz of floral perfume gave her a queenly air.

"Hello, my dear." Her voice was dry and brittle, like antique parchment paper, yet filled with warmth and a spark of something.

Amusement, perhaps?

Remember the part about me resisting the urge to curtsy?

It would seem my body failed to get that message. Luckily, I'd had spent years perfecting the skill as a kid, back when I believed in fairy godmothers and dreamed of one day marrying my own prince.

Lucinda chuckled, and I felt my face heat as I straightened.

"And this is my grandson, Grayson." She gestured with a wave of her hand to the tall, dark-haired man next to her. His half mask was simple and black. If the way his tuxedo embraced his body was any indication, the man made keeping in shape a top priority.

I held out my hand for him to shake—because heck if I was curtsying for him. But instead of shaking it, Grayson lifted my hand to his mouth and pressed a soft kiss to it.

At the feel of his mouth against my skin, my body shouldn't have reacted like hot lava swirled within its depths. My breath shouldn't have hitched with sudden longing. And my lips shouldn't have tingled, craving to taste his mouth on mine.

None of those things should have happened—with a stranger, no less. A stranger who might not even be single.

ACKNOWLEDGMENTS

The idea for the Love Undercover series came about in an unusual way. Two years ago, I took a Romance Writers of America (RWA) workshop about the CIA. I mentioned it to a friend, and she told me I should write a spy rom-com series. At the time, I was busy writing the By the Bay and Copper Creek books, so a new series wasn't in the works. But one of the topics covered during the workshop focused on female agents during the Second World War. I became fascinated by their stories, so much so that I started doing research for a historical novel.

It was Brenda St. John Brown, a fellow romantic comedy author, who suggested that maybe I *should* write a spy rom-com series. She knew about my research. I had so much fun writing the first book in the series (*While You Were Spying*), I couldn't wait to write Landon's story. Thank you to everyone who fell in love with Jayden and Isabelle's story and wanted more books in the series. And a special thank you to the members of my Facebook reader group (Stina's Sweethearts) for suggesting Whiskey's breed and name.

This story wouldn't be the same without my editor Bev Rosenbaum, as well as Hope and Jessica from Flat Earth Editing for the copyediting and proofreading. All three individuals helped make this book sparkle. The same is true of Brenda St. John Brown, who always shares her brilliant suggestions and wisdom when it comes to my romantic comedies.

And as always, hugs and kisses to my husband Ralph, my

three kids, and my cat Callie for your love and support over the past several years.

ABOUT THE AUTHOR

Born in Brighton England, Stina Lindenblatt has lived in a number of countries, including England, the U.S., Finland, and Canada. This would explain her mixed up accent. She has a kinesiology degree and a MSc in sports biological sciences.

In addition to writing fiction, she loves photography, and currently lives in Calgary, Canada, with her husband and three kids.

For news about her books and to sign up for her newsletter, check out her website at:

stinalindenblattauthor.com